HIDDEN LEGACY
Margaret Way

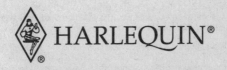

HARLEQUIN®

TORONTO • NEW YORK • LONDON
AMSTERDAM • PARIS • SYDNEY • HAMBURG
STOCKHOLM • ATHENS • TOKYO • MILAN • MADRID
PRAGUE • WARSAW • BUDAPEST • AUCKLAND

ISBN-13: 978-0-373-78238-3
ISBN-10:   0-373-78238-1

HIDDEN LEGACY

www.eHarlequin.com

Printed in U.S.A.

ABOUT THE AUTHOR

Margaret Way takes great pleasure in her work and works hard at her pleasure. She enjoys tearing off to the beach with her family at weekends, loves haunting galleries and auctions and is completely given over to French champagne "for every possible joyous occasion." She was born and educated in the river city of Brisbane, Australia, and now lives within sight and sound of beautiful Moreton Bay.

Books by Margaret Way

HARLEQUIN SUPERROMANCE

Don't miss any of our special offers. Write to us at the following address for information on our newest releases.

Harlequin Reader Service
U.S.: 3010 Walden Ave., P.O. Box 1325, Buffalo, NY 14269
Canadian: P.O. Box 609, Fort Erie, Ont. L2A 5X3

This is for Debbie Macomber,
a woman much to be admired.

CHAPTER ONE

SHAFTS OF LATE-AFTERNOON sunlight pierced the high arched windows of Alyssa Sutherland's studio, turning the huge panes of glass into sheets of liquid copper. Inside the studio, it was as if someone had switched on dozens of electric lights. Caught in the golden illuminance was a large open area with white painted walls, dark, rough-hewn ceiling beams and dark-stained timber columns that supported the soaring ceiling. Visitors to the studio often expressed the opinion that it was more like a country antique shop than a workplace, for the room was filled almost to overflowing with all manner of beautiful and valuable objects, often used as props in Alyssa's paintings. As a centerpiece stood an easel, with a half-finished canvas on it. The artist was at work, her blond head suffused by the sun's radiance.

It took a few moments for the dazzling incandescence to pass by the windows, leaving the delicate, dusky mauve that heralded the brief twilight of the subtropics. Alyssa broke off with a sigh, placing her paintbrush in an earthenware pot of solvent, then wiping her fingers on her paint-spattered smock. She had lost all notion of time but a glance at the wall clock told her she'd been working all afternoon without a break, stopping now and then to stare at the painting—a still life of bread, wine and fruit in a Ming dynasty bowl—to see how things were progressing.

No magic there today. She doubted a good night's sleep would help much, either—if she could even subdue her jangled feelings long enough to sink into oblivion. Despite the exquisite strains of Bach's A Minor violin concerto blossoming out of one corner of the studio, her head was seething with angry words.

A serious relationship had been brought to a bruising end. Brett had packed up his possessions and left the house they'd settled into barely a year before. Only a year—that was how long their relationship had survived the initial pleasures of being together before taking the downward slope into the stresses and strains of two very different people trying to live in harmony.

Alyssa saw it as Brett's relentless drive to back her into a corner. From the day he'd moved in, he had begun to assert an urge to dominate. That diminished her sense of guilt about the split-up. She believed in equality, but Brett had been more interested in exerting control. She'd finally had enough and found the courage to say so. What she'd often heard was painfully true—you had to live with someone to even *begin* to know that person…and maybe not even then.

Troubled in mind and spirit, Alyssa turned away to pour herself a cup of coffee. She knew she drank too much of it, but late at night when she was working, the caffeine kept her awake and her senses razor-sharp. Coffee in hand, she settled into a leather armchair, leaning her head against the plush upholstery, her mind returning to that final scene…

IT ALL BEGAN innocuously enough, as major upsets often do. One minute she and Brett were sitting on the deck finishing the steak and salad dinner she'd prepared for them, the next, something he said—something she found jarringly mean-spirited—triggered a powerful reaction in her. The straw that broke the camel's back, as she now thought of it. In the preceding months she'd usually shut up at such provocative moments. Anything for peace although she realized now, with a pang of self-disgust, they hadn't been her finest moments. But on that occasion she'd sprung up from her chair, distraught tears in her eyes.

Let it out, Alyssa! You can't stand it anymore!

Her intense response had nothing to do with the topic at hand; it had everything to do with her growing feelings of repression. "I can't be with you anymore, Brett! You…you damage my psyche." That was the way she'd come to think of it. How had Brett Harris turned from the man who claimed to love and admire her unreservedly, into a partner determined on controlling her? And in such a short time? It was a side of him she'd never seen, let alone imagined.

That evening he, too, had jumped up, apparently as ready to engage in a major confrontation as she was. His action had toppled a beautiful long-stemmed crystal wineglass that predictably broke, breaking up a valuable set of six. Strangely enough, when she'd decided to use those particular glasses she had a presentiment one of them might break.

Brett cursed his clumsiness, sucked at a tiny cut on his hand, but ignored the dark-crimson wine stain that spread over the white cloth. "Damage your *psyche?*" He had developed an irritating habit of repeating her words as though he found them incomprehensible. "What sort of mumbo jumbo is that?" He followed her into the house, a whipcord-lean young man just short of six feet, dark-haired, with hypnotic dark eyes and handsome if rather hawklike features. His hands, not as attractive as his face, clutched the back of the sofa. His dark eyes glittered with contained contempt. "You can't mean that, Ally?"

"I do!" Her voice sounded stricken. "These last six months have been awful. It's truly the end for us."

His response was to take her forcibly her by the shoulders. Alyssa considered any sort of violence, especially violence toward women and children, totally reprehensible. She had often had occasion to express her views, working pro bono for a women's refuge during her short career as a lawyer. He was well aware where she stood on domestic violence. "Every time you come back from visiting that bloody woman, you're different," he accused, his face tight. "Zizi egged you on to do this. Zizi's always overstepping her role—ridiculous bloody name. Okay, you might've called her that when you were a little kid but it sounds stupid now. She's never liked me, has she? I could *kill* her." The expression on his face carried real threat.

"That's appalling!" She shook him off angrily. "And you a man of the law!"

"I'm a *man* first," he reminded her, anger flashing in his eyes.

"So, does that mean you have the right to lash out?" she shouted at him, although shouting wasn't her style. "Zizi is not at fault here," she said, trying desperately to calm herself. "She had nothing to do with my decision, so keep her out of it. It's about the two of us. It's not working, Brett. You're becoming intolerable to live with."

He released a sharp whistling breath through his nose. "*I'm* becoming intolerable? You're the who's up until all hours of the night when I want you in bed with me. Goddamn that bloody woman!" he exclaimed, his handsome face ugly with hate. "She's had far too much influence on you. She works on you until she takes over your mind."

It was all so unfair! Zizi's influence had always been *good*. Zizi was her confidante and dearest friend.

"Oh, spare me!" he groaned at her defense of her great-aunt. "The facts contradict your judgment. Your great-aunt's never had the guts to live in the real world, floating around that old plantation house like some bloody witch. Hell, she's more than a touch mad. Your grandmother, her own sister, has said as much."

It was regrettably true. "Gran and Zizi are different kinds of people," Alyssa said quietly, putting more space between them. "Zizi's living the life she wants. Without her I wouldn't be what I am today. She taught me not only how to paint and see beauty in so many different places, but about life in general. I don't know what I'm going to do when she leaves me."

"The old bitch will live until she's ninety!" Brett scoffed."You have *me!* Aren't you supposed to love me? You have your parents, plenty of friends. You're supposed to be such a fine painter—"

Alyssa rounded on him, saying the words she'd long held back. "You're jealous of what I do, aren't you?"

He didn't even attempt to deny it. "I'm jealous of anything that takes you away from me. When you're working you don't even remember I exist. Couldn't you have stayed a lawyer? You know how upset your parents were when you left the firm."

"That was two years ago, Brett. Mom and Dad came to terms with it. I was always a dutiful daughter. I did what they wanted. I just never got any satisfaction out of practicing law. That's *your* world, their world. It's not mine. I'm an artist, but you don't want me to be one. My painting's only made you resentful. You'd be thrilled if I said I was going to stop painting altogether."

"You bet!" He spoke with frightening grimness. "It was Zizi who managed to convince you that you had *the gift!*" He couldn't resist the note of parody. "She even managed to pull a few strings to get you a showing. She chucked her own career—it didn't give *her* satisfaction or fulfillment—yet she pushed *you* into it."

"I'm making money, Brett." She was regaining a little of her composure.

"You're making money at *last,* you mean," he reminded her sharply, totally overlooking the fact that he was living in *her* house. "Your parents bought you this place." Obviously that devalued her standing in his eyes. "So you got some acclaim. You have more going for you, that's all. You're young. You're beautiful. You come from a distinguished legal family. Even dotty old Zizi was a name in her day. Elizabeth Jane Calvert! What happened to her? How come she burnt out overnight?"

Alyssa tried slow, deep breathing. "No one knows the answer to that one." Not family, friends, agents, dealers. While still in her twenties, Zizi's brilliant talent had earned her considerable renown. Those were her glory days, the ten-year period between 1960 and 1970. But Zizi had retired at the very early age of thirty to a reclusive life in an old sugar plantation house in tropical North Queensland. It had caused a sensation in the art world.

Alyssa's eyes rested on the middle distance. Other famous artists had fled to the North to escape the rat race and gather the beauty of the tropical environment into their souls. North of Capricorn was glorious. She and Zizi had often cruised around the dazzlingly beautiful coral cays and emerald islands of the Great Barrier Reef in Zizi's little sailing yacht, *Cherub*. It was Zizi who'd discovered that she had talent as a sailor. Indeed, by age sixteen she far outstripped her mentor much to Zizi's amusement and pride. She loved the sea. She loved sailing. It was in her blood.

From time to time, other prominent artists who'd belonged to the colony had emerged from their rain forest sanctuaries to travel south to the big cities to show the civilized art world what masterpieces they had created. Zizi, however, had stayed there.

Infuriated by Alyssa's inattention, Brett seized her by the arms. "Snap out of it, Ally! You can't think I'm going to let you walk away from me! Not after what we've been to each other. I love you. I can't possibly let you go. I hold your precious Zizi responsible for the change in you."

She stared into his dark eyes, seeing a tiny red glow in their depths. "All Zizi wants is for me to be happy. I *tried,* Brett."

"You shouldn't have to *try!*" He shook her as if she were a child and a good shake would bring her to her senses.

"Take your hands off me." Flinching, she broke away, rubbing her shoulder.

He came after her. "You're everything I want, Alyssa. I'd kill anyone who tried to take you from me."

Alyssa saw the violence in him, but she was driven by a risk-everything determination.

They stood a few feet apart, regarding each other like the warring couple they'd become. "You're very needy, Brett. You want my undivided attention and if you don't get it I have to tread my way through a minefield of scowling and sulking that goes on for days. It has to come to an end. I'm an artist. I'm going to remain an artist all my life."

"Like Zizi?" His voice was full of contempt.

"I hope I'll be like Zizi one day. I certainly haven't reached her level of excellence yet."

Brett threw up his hands in an impotent gesture of rage. "Who the hell even remembers the genius's name these days?"

She sighed wearily. "Everyone in the art world knows of Elizabeth Jane Calvert. The private collectors who have her early paintings treasure them. They won't part with them. That's why they never come on the market…something did go seriously wrong in her life."

"She hasn't told you all about her nervous breakdown, has she?" he sneered. "Your grandmother said she had one. The trouble with you is you're brainwashed!"

"And you're a coward, attacking a woman in her absence."

He stared back at her as though she'd drawn blood. "You go out of your way to provoke me. But I love you, Alyssa. I've loved you since I first laid eyes on you."

She shook her head. "You fell in love with the way I *looked*, Brett. And with who I was, the daughter of two senior partners in the firm."

"I fell in love with *you*. I fell in love with you before I even knew who you were. There's something missing, though. You let me make love to you, but I can't get close to you. Not your heart or your mind. One of these days you'll discover that painting isn't enough!"

"That's not going to happen, Brett." She spoke with finality.

His face contorted. "Well, I hate it! It's separated us." He lunged for her and she backed away swiftly, protecting herself from possible physical harm. "We can work this out," he insisted. "If we break up, it'll be a huge mistake. This is all that bloody woman's fault."

Distressed as she was, she was still desperate to show compassion. "I'm sorry, Brett. Truly sorry. But this is *my* life. I don't love you."

Brett sloughed off his civilized veneer as a snake sloughs off a skin. He surged toward her and struck her openhanded, but with such force she staggered back and fell to the floor, hitting her head against the foot of a teak cabinet.

For long moments he gazed down at her, rooted to the spot. Her long hair tumbled around her face in an ash-blond storm. In the fall, two buttons of her silk shirt had slipped their holes, so he could see the upward curves of her breasts.

Desire soared. He wondered what it would be like to take her right there, on the polished floor. He hunched down, wanting nothing more than to have her whether she wanted it or not. "Oh, God, Ally, I'm sorry. Forgive me." Common decency briefly exerted itself.

He tried to get his arm around her, but his sexual excitement was showing in his flushed skin and his glittering eyes. Alyssa resisted wildly. One side of her face was scarlet, her skin bearing the imprint of his hand. Somewhere deep inside her ear a phone was ringing stridently, yet the outer shell was deaf. "Get out!" she cried, swallowing down her shock. She wasn't going to grieve over their breakup anymore. This new Brett was a *monster.*

He just knelt there, staring at her. "You're so beautiful!" Lust was coming off him in waves.

It presented a clear threat. "Get out!" Alyssa repeated, beyond fear. "You're a brute and a coward. Violence is a sickness, an illness, a disease! You're *sick!*"

The cold outrage in her voice, the condemnation in her eyes, slammed the brakes on hard. Brett started to remember who *he* was; more importantly, who *she* was. He thrust a trembling hand through his hair. "How did this happen?" he asked in a wondering voice.

Alyssa scrambled unaided to her feet, although she felt ill and more than a little dizzy. "I can tell you this. It will *never* happen again. *Get out!*"

He did.

Of course there were innumerable phone calls, messages she didn't answer. Sheafs of her favorite flowers arrived, red roses galore. She refused to take delivery. It was over. Dreams had turned to ashes. She'd seen the *real* Brett, the dark side that had been hidden inside him. She could never ignore it now. She prayed he wouldn't be foolish enough to stalk her, or show up at her door. She knew he was capable of it; she'd glimpsed that disturbing glow in the depths of his eyes. She wanted to keep their breakup private. If the full facts got out, it could mean the end of Brett's promising legal career. She had no wish to harm him. She simply wanted out!

LOOKING BACK at her life over the weeks that followed, Alyssa felt deeply perturbed at how virulent Brett's attitude to Zizi had become. He'd actually spent very little time in Zizi's company, only two or three visits. She had so wanted them to like each other but as Brett had been at pains to tell her, he'd immediately perceived Zizi as a threat.

How could she have been so wrong about him? Her spirits sagged beneath the weight of her bad judgment. On her most recent visit to Zizi, she'd wisely gone on her own. They had a perfect, harmonious week together, sharing an empathy that went even deeper than the one she shared with her much-loved mother, Stephanie, and certainly her formidable grandmother, Mariel, Zizi's older sister.

Then there was Zizi's marvelous old plantation house, Flying Clouds. She'd adored it at first sight. As a child, it had seemed to her that there was no other house in the entire world like it. For one thing, it had a widow's walk. She'd never heard of such a thing, let alone seen one. She'd found it thrilling beyond words to pace the narrow walkway looking out to the turquoise Coral Sea.

The house, a profoundly exotic jungle mansion, had a history. Of course it did. A Captain Richard Langford, an English adventurer-entrepreneur, had built it in the late 1800s. At that time Australia had been announcing to the Old Country that it really was the land of opportunity. Captain Langford had answered the call. It was his beautiful schooner, *Medora,* hired out for trade or charter that had brought him a fortune before he'd eventually turned his attention to starting a small shipping line that serviced the eastern seaboard. His ancestors today ran the giant Langford Container Lines, which transported anything and everything all over the world—automobiles, antiques, fine arts, boats, industrial machinery, whole households of personal effects, you name it. There was no stopping progress, and the Langfords had prospered.

Was it any wonder that in her make-believe games she'd often played the role of wife—and sometimes daughter—of that heroic sea captain? She'd stand high up on the observation platform, waiting for a glimpse of his ship returning home. Other times she was the grief-stricken widow, shedding real tears. For a change she'd be Peter Pan or Wendy and even the infamous Captain Hook. *Treasure Island* was a favorite and so were all sorts of swashbuckling pirate games— anything to do with the sea. Sometimes she was the beautiful damsel in distress, held for ransom, other times the dashing pirate. Zizi had always given her just the right old clothes to turn into a costume. Those were unforgettable days for the kind of child she was. Zizi understood her imaginative nature far better than anyone else. She was a dreamer, a great reader, often devouring books way beyond her years. It was Zizi who'd understood and nurtured her compulsion to draw and finally, paint.

Zizi!

She'd been totally happy at Flying Clouds, with the bond between them deepening steadily through the years. They both loved the house, although Zizi made it clear from the outset that it was haunted by the benign Captain Langford. At any rate, both of them found they were remarkably easy in his company. Captain Langford had actually died in his bed, but one of his descendants—another Richard and a renowned yachtsman—had drowned off the Reef when his yacht, *Miranda,* had capsized and sunk without trace during rough monsoon weather. That was in the late 1960s.

Some time after that, Zizi had made her final escape to the tropical North where, in her youth, she'd painted some of her most ravishing canvases. Back then she'd stayed on and off in the artists' colony long since disbanded. With her intimate knowledge of the area, she'd had the great good fortune to acquire Flying Clouds cheaply, as most people, certainly the locals, believed it to be haunted.

The setting alone captured the imagination. The

entrance fronted on to a private road lined by the white flowering evergreen species of frangipani that in the lush tropical climate had grown into very big trees. The rear faced the glorious Coral Sea, with a long, sea-weathered boardwalk that led to a zigzag flight of steps and on to the beach.

The house was of fine proportions and remarkably grand for the area. According to local folklore, Captain Langford's mother was an American shipping heiress who'd lived in such a house when she was a girl. Whether that was true or not no one knew, but all agreed it was a good story.

The two-story—three if one counted the widow's walk—was constructed of brilliant white stuccoed sandstone with deep verandas decorated and embellished with distinctive white cast-iron lace railings that appeared again on the upper walkway. The verandas shaded the house from the tropical sun while still allowing every available sea breeze to pass through. The shutters for the French doors, three to either side of the solid cedar front door, and the door itself were painted so dark a green that in certain lights they appeared a glossy black. The huge roof was a harmonious terra-cotta red.

At some stage before the turn of the twentieth century, Flying Clouds became a working sugar plantation using native labor brought in from the

Melanesian and Polynesian islands. This scheme, at first a fairly innocent importation of cheap labor, quickly degenerated into the cruel practice known as "blackbirding," when Pacific Islanders were more often kidnapped from their island homes than offered paying jobs. The Queensland government had finally outlawed the practice in the early 1900s.

These days the house was almost lost in a luminous green jungle that was forever breaking out in extravagant fruit and flower. It would be impossible to starve in the tropics. Tropical fruit in abundance, dropping most of the harvest on to the ground—pawpaws, papayas, mangoes, bananas, custard apples, passion fruit, melons, many new varieties she didn't even know the name of. Every backyard had a macadamia tree, indigenous to Queensland and named after the Australian doctor John Macadam. This fine source of protein the aborigines had been enjoying for tens of thousands of years. Sated on fruit and nuts, one only needed to throw in a fishing line to avail oneself of some of the best seafood in the world.

The sparkling Coral Sea wasn't visible from the ground floor, but there was a breathtaking view from the upper story's balconies and more stupendous again, though a bit chancy in high wind, the widow's walk. Zizi had always listened when Alyssa made up her endless stories about "The Captain." It was a secret between the two of them. Her mother regarded Zizi as an endlessly fascinating eccentric, eccentricity being a perfectly acceptable part of the artistic temperament. Mariel, on the other hand, was of the firm opinion that her sister had lost all track of reality.

Neither woman visited Zizi much anymore. Mariel, as strong as a horse, always cited a growing number of psychosomatic ailments—high blood pressure, tachycardia, stress headaches and the like. She claimed she couldn't abide the tropical heat, which was probably true, though she lived in subtropical Brisbane. Stephanie, though deeply fond of Zizi, was a topflight barrister who had little or no spare time to visit a place that required half a day just to get there.

An only child, Alyssa had grown up knowing her parents hoped she'd follow them into the law. She had bowed to their expectations, completing her law degree and working for three years as an associate in the firm. That was where she'd met Brett Harris, handsome, clever, ambitious. In those days he used to hang on her every word!

She hadn't been unhappy at the firm. Most of the work allotted to her she found interesting and sometimes challenging, but her heart wasn't in it. She actually preferred her voluntary work at the women's refuge, where she'd made good friends and been truly effective. Zizi, realizing that she was floundering in her legal career, had come out of her shell to have an old friend of hers, the highly respected art critic Leonard Vaughn, take a look at the best of Alyssa's work, which she'd painted while staying at the plantation.

The two of them worked wonderfully well together in Zizi's large, airy, light-filled studio, which smelled of paint, turpentine, linseed oil, varnish, glue, fixatives and always the salty scent of the sea and a million tropical flowers. Alyssa continually strived to match Zizi's brilliance. The irony was, within a few years she was receiving the critical acclaim, the hefty prices and certainly the media exposure that had eluded Zizi for most of her working life.

Her great quest was to persuade Zizi to give at least one showing. There were so many wonderful works of hers the public should see, if only she could persuade Zizi. So far, despite the fact that Zizi loved her dearly, she'd been unsuccessful. Zizi was adamant that her work would remain hidden from the world.

When I'm gone, my darling, maybe…

Alyssa couldn't bear to think of the time her great-aunt would go out of her life. She comforted herself with the knowledge that Zizi was fit and healthy. Zizi might be seventy, but she easily could pass for a woman in her late fifties. And a beautiful one at that. Alyssa wanted her beloved great-aunt to live forever. There was simply no one who could replace her.

IT WAS A BRILLIANTLY fine Saturday morning three uneventful weeks later. Alyssa was extremely grateful for this hiatus, although she feared it was only the eye of the storm. Indeed, for days now she'd been tormented by a vague sense of unease she couldn't shake off. Now she sat on her deck re-reading Yann Martel's *Life of Pi* when the phone rang. The kitchen extension was closest. She swung her legs off the recliner, put her book down on the glass-topped table, then went inside to answer it.

She expected it to be Zizi. She'd called her the previous evening and again earlier that morning, getting only Zizi's charming, cultured voice saying, "I can't come to the phone right now, but please leave a message after the beep." She had done so. The older Zizi got, the more she intended to keep in touch with her, a daily call as opposed to twice a week. An old saying kept reverberating in her head. *Live alone. Die alone.* That couldn't be allowed to happen to Zizi.

It was her mother, whose voice was so similar to Zizi's Alyssa often mistook one for the other.

Strange, how her mother, a beautiful woman, looked and sounded more like Zizi than she did her own mother, Mariel. Mariel had lacked Zizi's beauty, although she was undeniably a force to be reckoned with.

MUCH LATER Alyssa would say she'd known at some level what her mother was going to tell her the instant she picked up the phone. Hadn't she been experiencing those shivery little premonitions?

Her mother, the supremely calm, professional woman, sounded distraught. "It's Zizi," she said, with a sob. "There's no good way to tell you this, darling, but she's gone. We've lost her. A neighbor, an Adam Hunt, couldn't raise her on the phone so he went to the house to check on her. He found her dead in the bathroom. Apparently she'd fallen while getting into the bath, cracked her head, and—" Stephanie choked on her tears.

Alyssa half fainted into a chair. "Mom, what are you saying? Zizi always took a *shower!* It couldn't have happened that way. Zizi *never* used the bath. She'd slipped once and nearly broke her neck. She always took a shower after that."

"Try to stay calm, darling," her mother urged when she was anything but calm herself. "I'm so sorry. I know how much you loved her. We all did, but you two were especially close. Your father's very upset. He took the phone call. So, of course, is poor Mother. She's tremendously agitated. I had to call her doctor to the house but thank God he didn't find much wrong with her. Your father can't get away, so you and I will have to go up. This is an absolute tragedy. Zizi's so *young* for her years. God, *was* so young. Why did I wait so long to see her?" Stephanie berated herself.

Alyssa tried to offer comfort. "Your heavy work schedule, Mom," she said, fighting down her own grief until she got off the phone.

"Why did she choose to live so far away from us?" Stephanie lamented. "No one was happy about it. That bloody place, it's beautiful but it's so remote. I've always agonized that she might die alone." Stephanie's teary voice betrayed the extent of her grief. "I can't believe Zizi's left us."

"Neither can I!" In the golden heat Alyssa found herself shivering convulsively.

THERE WAS AN AUTOPSY. Everyone accepted the coroner's verdict. The blow to the head wasn't the cause of death, although it was the major contributing factor. Zizi had drowned. She would've become dizzy, lost consciousness, then slipped beneath the water. It was all too tragic.

Once her body was released by the coroner, the funeral quickly followed. Zizi had expressed the wish to have her ashes scattered in the Coral Sea, but Mariel as next of kin wouldn't have it. She overrode that wish, insisting on having Zizi's casket flown to Brisbane where she could be buried in the family plot so "we can keep an eye on her."

Such an odd way to put it!

It was a small, private family funeral, although Mariel had been too upset to come. No notice had been placed in the papers. Yet when Alyssa accompanied her parents back to the car after the short service, she saw Brett, dressed in a black suit with a white shirt and black tie, standing some distance off. The sight of him chilled her.

"Isn't that Brett?" Stephanie asked. "I expect he feels dreadful."

"How did he even know about Zizi?" Alyssa looked at her father. "Did *you* tell him, Dad?"

"My dear, Brett has left the firm," Ian Sutherland answered.

"When was this? Why didn't you say anything?" she asked incredulously.

"We felt you had enough to contend with. Brett handed in his resignation. I accepted it. I could see he was deeply distressed by the breakdown of the relationship. I don't think there's any question that he was—is—madly in love with you. I was sorry to lose him, but it's better that way, the situation being what it is. He won't have the slightest difficulty getting into Havelock Hayes. I told him I'd put in a word for him. Brett's certainly clever, but I have to tell you now that the relationship is over, your mother and I feel relieved. We weren't all that happy about you and Brett."

Alyssa looked from one to the other, having difficulty taking it in. "You never said."

Ian Sutherland smiled wryly. "You're twenty-six years old, Alyssa. Your mother and I left it to your own good sense, didn't we, darling?" He glanced down lovingly at his wife. "You deserve someone with a more open nature," Ian Sutherland said, picking his words carefully. "More openhearted. I don't know *exactly* what it is in Brett, but no doubt you do. There's something… secretive about him."

Alyssa tried to calm her thoughts. "Things bothered you both and you didn't tell me?"

"Actually, darling, we were on the brink of expressing our concern." Stephanie put an arm around her daughter and gave her a little hug. "But just as your father said, you handled it yourself. Trying to put up with someone who constantly needs attention is difficult. That's going to be a problem for Brett. In a sense he's his own worst enemy."

Alyssa fell silent. She was too distressed to pursue the subject.

"Well, there you go!" her father exclaimed, as though that settled it. "Best acknowledge the poor chap. It was decent of him to come, although I always got the feeling he saw Zizi more as an opponent than a friend. Still, no reason not to be kind to him. Your mother and I will wait in the car."

Alyssa felt no desire to acknowledge Brett. Had her parents known he'd struck her, things would be very different. Brett's certainty that she wouldn't tell them was evident in his coming here. He had plenty of self-confidence, the in-grained belief that he was always right, and she'd come to suspect he enjoyed danger. Why was he really here? It wasn't to pay his respects to Zizi. It could have been sadistic curiosity. That was more in keeping with his character. Or perhaps he was trying to demonstrate to her what a *civilized* person he was.

She moved toward him but stopped halfway, forcing him to join her on the path. No way was she was leaving her parents' sight.

"What are you doing here, Brett?" He appeared thinner than usual in his elegant Italian suit. There were dark shadows beneath his eyes as if he hadn't slept. He wore an air of dejection, but that, of course, could be an act. She realized Brett had the ability to play many roles.

He seemed surprised by her question. "I came

to pay my respects, of course," he said in a subdued voice.

"How extraordinary, given your attitude toward Zizi."

His smile was more of a grimace. "I wanted this chance to tell you I can never forgive myself for the things I said about her. I never meant a word of it, Ally. That was my jealousy talking. I've never loved a woman like I love you . I regret my behavior more deeply than I can ever say. I beg you to forgive me. I love you so much. I'll never stop loving you."

Alyssa nodded slowly. "I used to hear that all the time from men who beat up their wives and girlfriends," she said. "*I love you. I can't live without you,* followed by *I'll kill you and the kids if you don't come back to me.* Some of them did. You didn't think you could get away with it, did you? With *me?*"

"I went *crazy!*" Brett said, abandoning that dull voice. "I've never struck a woman in my life before."

"Somehow I have the feeling you have," Alyssa answered, playing a sudden hunch. "I bet if I had the firm's investigators make some inquiries, they'd come up with something. I'm reasonably sure I'm not the first female to suffer your aggression."

Panic flashed across his face so quickly she would have missed it if she hadn't been studying him intently. "You wouldn't."

"No, I wouldn't." She shook her head. "But you have a violent streak, Brett. You didn't keep it hidden for long. My advice is to seek help. I mean that. What would you have done if the crack to my head had been more serious? Would you have called a doctor, an ambulance, my parents? Would you have relied on me to lie for you? I wouldn't have."

"Yet you haven't betrayed me, have you?" A flicker of triumph came into his dark eyes as he stared at her.

Alyssa stared back in stupefaction. "I kept quiet for the sake of what I *thought* we had, Brett. Also, I'm giving you a chance to seek professional help. I have no wish to harm your legal career, but if I ever hear you've attacked some other woman, I'll come forward to back her story. So watch out!"

He took a step toward her and despite herself Alyssa felt her blood freeze. "Ally, that will *never* happen."

She was in control again. "Don't touch me, Brett." She wondered why she felt such alarm. He didn't look threatening, but appeared to be buckling beneath the weight of remorse.

He drew back, smiling at her so tenderly it made her ill. "Sweetest love, will no amount of repentance wash away my sin?"

Another person, another role! "What are you

playing at now, Brett?" she asked. "As far as I know, you have no links with any religion."

He looked puzzled. "I believe in good and evil, Ally," he said with absolute conviction. "I mightn't believe in God, but I believe in the devil."

"Maybe that's because you've seen him!" She had no idea where that remark came from. "But you can't have one without the other. If there's a devil, there must be a God. Pick which team you want to be on." She was on the verge of walking away from him. "I won't thank you for coming today, bearing in mind your attitude to Zizi. It was just a pretext to see me."

"I admit it." Persuasion poured into his hypnotic eyes. "Perhaps you'll see me some other time?" he asked, his voice full of a touching hope.

Alyssa didn't reply.

"I give you my word I'll seek help. I love you, Ally," he repeated passionately. "I want to be with you. You were never in any danger that awful night."

"On the contrary, you *enjoyed* punishing me." She spoke with intuitive certainty. "And you wanted a whole lot more. You wanted forced sex."

He drew a hand across his mouth as if wiping away a bad taste. "I just snapped, Ally. It was the way you seemed to be abandoning me for your aunt."

She felt furious and humiliated. "That was all

in your own mind, Brett. Don't say any more. It isn't working. We've buried Zizi today."

"And my heart goes out to you, Ally." He assumed an expression of deepest sympathy she knew perfectly well was feigned.

"That does nothing whatever to comfort me, Brett."

She walked away.

She didn't look back.

CHAPTER TWO

THE INTERIOR DOORS were never shut. Not unless there was a cyclone. Yet several of them were closed. Perhaps the police had shut them? Or Adam Hunt, the kindly neighbor. She intended to call on him. She and her mother had not made the long trip north following Mariel's decision to have Zizi's casket flown back to Brisbane. No family member had entered the house until now.

Flying Clouds was hers. She was her great-aunt's sole beneficiary, excluding some things Zizi had willed to her niece and goddaughter, Stephanie. That included the beautiful portrait of Stephanie painted shortly before her marriage. It now hung in a place of honor above the white marble mantelpiece in her parents' elegant living room. Alyssa had often wondered why Zizi, the most generous of women, hadn't given it to her mother all those years ago. But for whatever reason, Zizi had decided not to part with it. What was puzzling was the fact that Mariel hadn't even been mentioned in the will. Obviously Zizi had thought there was no need to make provision for her as Mariel was sitting on her late husband's millions.

"It makes sense *logically,*" Stephanie said, herself puzzled about Mariel's omission. "And yet, they were sisters…."

ALYSSA HAD BEEN too depressed to avail herself of a nap on the long flight. Nothing improved her mood. In the weeks after Zizi's funeral, she'd found herself unable to sleep. Sometimes she imagined Zizi sitting on the side of her bed watching her or standing at the window watching her, as if she wanted to tell Alyssa something. The feeling was so incredibly strong that one night her heart had almost seized. Not in fright but in the actual belief that Zizi was showing herself.

"Zizi?" she'd cried out, unable to stop her tears, but silvery Zizi had faded from sight. Such was grief. The living often saw their beloved dead. Maybe the recently dead stayed around for a time, watching, neither side able to completely break off communication.

ALYSSA HAD RENTED a car that had been waiting for her at the airport. It was parked in the garage now. Tears flowing, she'd let herself into the house. The key had always been "hidden" among the spectacular psychedelic colored leaves of a potted caladium on the front veranda—silly place to hide it. They both used to laugh about it. That was probably the most likely place anyone intent on breaking in would think of, but Zizi had never had the slightest bother in all the years she'd lived there. Occasionally they'd driven into the town together, leaving the front and back doors unlocked.

For many years Zizi had kept dogs for company, usually two Labradors, so each would have a friend to play with. But since the death of old age of her beautiful golden Labrador, Molly, Zizi confessed she hadn't the heart to buy herself another pet. Of course there was Cleo, Zizi's sleek Abyssinian, who not surprisingly greeted Alyssa ecstatically and now accompanied her on her tour through the house, every so often snaking around Alyssa's legs.

She had to find some way of properly thanking Adam Hunt. Her father had spoken to him several times on the phone and formed an excellent impression. What a shock Adam must have received coming on Zizi as he had. She'd imagined the neighbor as someone Zizi's age, but her father said he sounded much younger. Whatever his age, her father had taken to him and apparently so had Zizi. The really strange—and, she had to admit, *hurtful* part—was that Zizi had never mentioned him to her. That was decidedly odd, given that she and Zizi talked about anyone new in their lives. She tried to brush the hurt aside. Zizi would've had a reason. Perhaps he was too recent to the area? A fellow artist? No, Zizi would've said something. A would-be property developer was more like it. It was boom-time North of Capricorn. Yet this stranger or near stranger had attained such a degree of intimacy with Zizi that she felt comfortable with his looking in on her.

Zizi, the self-styled recluse, must have liked him a lot. Alyssa couldn't see Zizi trusting just anyone. Maybe Hunt was an art scholar planning a book that included a section on Elizabeth Jane Calvert. But wouldn't Zizi have said? She definitely had to meet this mystery man. What exactly had drawn him to seek Zizi out? Pure coincidence? Perhaps they'd met while doing some shopping at the village. Alyssa told herself to put aside all the questions buzzing around in her head until she felt more able to cope.

How different everything was without Zizi! She supposed the raw grief would lessen with time, but right now the sorrow was practically unbearable. She inspected the labyrinth of rooms downstairs. It was a huge house, but she knew it so well she could've found her way blindfolded. Afterward, she mounted the cantilevered staircase that led to the upstairs bedrooms and sitting rooms. She glanced into Zizi's bedroom—ivory and pale-green with a lovely canopied bed and an antique writing desk covered in informal family photographs in silver frames. The portrait Zizi had painted of her shortly before her twenty-first birthday hung over the mantel.

Who'd made the bed? It was Zizi's practice to turn down the covers before taking her bath. So many questions to be answered, Alyssa thought, her shoulders hunched in a sob. She avoided the adjoining bathroom. Just thinking about how Zizi had met her end was like an icy cold hand squeezing her heart. She knew she'd have to get around to it sometime. Not now.

In her own bedroom, the one she'd chosen all those years ago, redecorated as she passed from childhood to adolescence to adulthood, she unlocked the French doors and let herself onto the veranda. Her spirits lifted as she was enfolded by the breeze with its delicious tang of salt.

Another glorious day in the tropics. The sky was a cloudless electric blue, the sea like turquoise satin. She stood there, holding Cleo to her like a talisman. The cat had been fretting. It was obviously very glad of her company, although Abyssinians were usually standoffish. The grounds—the roughly thirty acres that was left—

didn't look at all abandoned. Zizi must've had someone in to do some slashing, although there was still a tidal wave of jungle in rampant blossom—oleander, hibiscus, frangipani, gardenia, allamanda, strelitzias, golden rain trees, angel's trumpets—beyond the mown areas surrounding the house. There were always snakes in the undergrowth but neither she nor Zizi had ever been bitten. Unless one actually trod on a snake, they took good care to keep out of the way, except for the one Zizi had nicknamed Cairo, who liked to slide along the front railings. Cairo, mercifully, was harmless and even frightened of Cleo, who used to speed him on his way with many a hiss and a spit.

"We miss her, don't we, Cleo?" Alyssa murmured, stroking the cat's amber coat. Cleo meowed loudly in acknowledgment. Everyone knew cats had special powers, and in Alyssa's opinion. Cleo was more gifted than most.

She had stopped in the village, where she was well-known, to buy herself a few basic provisions—milk, fresh bread, butter, eggs, a few slices of succulent ham—intending to return the following day to place a larger order. People had come up to her, expressing their sympathies before taking themselves off. It would've been evident to them that she was very upset. Eccentric Zizi might have been, but these people had loved her and guarded her privacy. It seemed that they were about to pass their loyalty on to her.

Alyssa sat down in one of the old chairs on the deck, cuddling Cleo, while she rocked gently back and forth. As always, the warm perfumed air of the tropics had a lulling effect, so in spite of her unhappiness, she drifted off….

SOME TIME LATER—she didn't know exactly how long—she was jolted awake by the sound of a heavy vehicle driving onto the property. She sat up in confusion, startling Cleo, who registered her disapproval by digging in her claws.

"Ouch, Cleo, that hurt!" She tipped the cat on to the timber deck, then made her way back into the house, briefly checking her appearance in the mirror. She *looked* composed enough. She quickly ran down the staircase, to the entrance hall. There wasn't a soul for miles around. Very few people ever ventured along the private road unless invited. For one dismal moment, the luxuriant jungle that enfolded the house now seemed like prison walls. Her father hadn't wanted her to come until someone could go with her. Who knew when that would be, considering her parents' heavy workload and her grandmother's "illness."

Alyssa's first thought was that her visitor might

be the local police chief, Jack McLean, checking on her. She knew him and his assistant, Constable Bill Pickett, well. Or it could be a neighbor? Maybe even *the* neighbor? She moved out onto the front veranda, seeing an unfamiliar dark-gray Range Rover pull beneath the canopy of trees, the ground beneath them carpeted with wind-stripped scarlet blossom.

Moments later a man climbed out, turned and looked toward the house.

He was tall, certainly over six feet. Even from a distance she recognized something *dynamic* about him. He was simply dressed, in a navy T-shirt and jeans, but his superb physique made the casual outfit look classy. Burnished by the blazing sunlight, his sweep of hair gleamed a rich mahogany. Thick and wavy, it was worn fairly long. None of the fashionable short spiky cuts for him. He walked like an athlete, loping along on the balls of his feet. Hero material dropped from the heavens, she thought cynically. After her experience with Brett she was feeling pretty wary of men.

This had to be Adam Hunt, Zizi's mystery friend. A mystery to be solved, she reminded herself. It was important to her to get to the truth of people. She had taken way too long to get to the truth of Brett, in the process shaking her view of herself and her own judgment. She felt no fear of her visitor, yet her hand on the balustrade was trembling. She couldn't have said why that was, but she made an urgent effort to steady it.

Her visitor covered the distance between them in no time. He was standing on the graveled drive a few feet away, looking up at her with a curious air of intensity. His eyes were startling in his tanned face, a true aquamarine like the shoals of the Reef waters. They compelled her into an extraordinary awareness of him. A sudden vertigo took hold, and she felt dizzy enough to pitch over the balustrade and into the gardenia bushes. That should get her even more attention.

He smiled faintly. "Miss Sutherland." It wasn't a question. He already knew the answer.

She realized belatedly that they were united in the intensity of their appraisal, matching glance for glance. He had a good voice. Voices were important to her. "Adam Hunt," he said. "I've spoken to your father several times. I hope I'm not disturbing you."

She couldn't manage a proper smile. Not yet. Besides, there were too many loose ends she had to sort out. "Adam Hunt, of course. Please come up." She knew she sounded very formal, but she wasn't about to jump into the deep end of instant familiarity—despite that odd moment of…recognition?

"Thank you. I won't stay long." He turned his head back toward his vehicle. "I have some provisions for you in the car. I really should get them out first. Some of them will need to go in the fridge."

"How did you know I'd be here? I didn't tell a soul."

"You told your parents."

"Surely Dad didn't call you?" she asked in dismay.

He nodded, an amused glint in his eyes. "Fathers generally like to keep an eye on their daughters. It's very lonely here, very isolated." He gestured about him as if he wouldn't recommend the remote plantation to any woman on her own.

"He asked *you* to keep an eye on me for him?" she asked, her tone incredulous.

Now she was treated to his full smile. It was a smile of enormous attractiveness, sexy yet wonderfully open. He would find it very useful when dealing with women. "Trust me, he loves you."

"I know that, Mr. Hunt." She had a desire to put him in his place.

"Adam, please."

She inclined her head. "I'm well able to look after myself, *Adam,*" she assured him, sounding more confident than she felt. "Nevertheless, we're in your debt. I know my father's thanked you but I want to add my own thanks for being on hand when you were. It must've been an extremely upsetting experience."

He made no attempt to deny it. "I couldn't believe it. I don't need to tell you Elizabeth was always so bright and alert, remarkably youthful for her age. I'm surprised it happened the way it did, and so very sorry. We were just getting to know one each other."

"May I ask *why* you wanted to get to know her?" It came out more bluntly than she'd intended.

"Certainly. She didn't tell you?" He kept his eyes trained on her, more than a touch of skepticism in his expression.

"What do you mean?"

"I thought Elizabeth would've told you. I understand you were very close."

"As close as we could be," she answered without hesitation. "But for some reason she neglected to mention *you*. You were saying?"

A sardonic pause. "A close relative of mine wanted me to look her up. He knew her back in the old days."

"And your relative has a name? Perhaps I've heard it. Zizi and I had no secrets from each other." Actually they did. *Him!*

"Julian Wainwright," he said.

"Julian Wainwright! Of course! Several of his paintings are in the house. They belonged to the same artists' colony in the early sixties. His paintings are splendid, especially the seascapes."

He nodded his agreement. "Julian had to abandon his artistic career for business. He always said he regretted it. You probably know he continued to carry a torch for Elizabeth all his life."

Was this a joke, or was a huge chasm opening beneath her feet? "I'm sorry, I didn't know any such thing." Even to her own ears, her voice sounded defensive.

"You didn't know that at one stage they intended to marry?" He maintained the look of skepticism.

For a moment she felt the reality of her life might be stripped away. "Forgive me, but I have only your word for it. Is Julian Wainwright still alive?"

"Barely." He shrugged, regret on his handsome face. "His doctors have given him no more than six or seven months."

"I'm sorry." Love for her great-aunt and a feeling of apprehension were inextricably entwined. If this was true, how much more had Zizi kept from her, from them all?

"Julian is four years older than Elizabeth," he was saying. "He's been in ill health for the last ten years. He was devastated to hear of her death."

"You told him?"

"Of course." His tone was clipped. He looked back at the Range Rover. "I should be getting the cold things into the fridge."

"Can I help? I'm stronger than I look!" This time she managed a shaky smile.

His glance, brilliant as the gemstone, touched her lightly. She was still wearing the outfit she'd traveled in—a white tank top over navy straight-legged pants. "You look fine."

"A girl does her best!" She spoke flippantly, to combat the heat that washed over her. It irked her to feel more like a flustered teenager than an experienced woman. "Would you like a cup of coffee?" She leaned over the wrought-iron balustrade to call to him. A cluster of white trumpet flowers from the vine-wreathed pillar tickled her cheek, its perfume entrancing.

"I won't say no," he said over his shoulder. "Elizabeth always made me a cup."

Did she indeed? She had to wrestle with that picture. Adam Hunt and Zizi sharing friendly cups of coffee?

Zizi, whatever were you up to?

For the first time in her life, Alyssa began to realize that her great-aunt must've had a life about which she knew little or nothing. She was starting to feel desperately hurt at being kept in the dark.

CHAPTER THREE

A BIG MAN, he filled the kitchen. He left Alyssa, who was above average height, feeling small. And it wasn't only his height and breadth of shoulder that made him so powerful, but a kind of blazing *energy*. The two of them worked in fraught silence while they packed the provisions away. She took care of the things that went into the refrigerator. He'd brought her more fresh bread, butter and milk, and in addition a carton of cream, vanilla ice cream and some small tubs of fruit yogurt. From the excellent village delicatessen he'd thrown in some King Island Camembert, a chunk of Havarti, New Guinea coffee beans and a half-dozen little pastries. It was more than enough to keep her going.

She'd noticed him putting away a small bag of locally grown baby potatoes and some red and white onions, about the only things Zizi hadn't grown herself. Alyssa hadn't checked on the vegetable garden yet, but she had a feeling he would've given it some water as well as fed Cleo. He looked that sort of man.

"You seem to know your way around." She couldn't help the dryness creeping into her tone.

"Elizabeth showed me all over the house the first time I came here," he explained as he emerged from the large pantry. "It's a marvelous old place, incredible atmosphere. The widow's walk is quite unique in this part of the world. I'd heard about it, of course."

"From Julian?" She was having difficulty coming to terms with Zizi's late-blossoming friendship with *him,* let alone a supposed romantic involvement with Julian Wainwright. "What *is* your relationship, by the way?"

"Ah, a woman who wants answers!" he jibed gently. "Julian's my great-uncle. Think back. Surely she mentioned their close friendship at some point? Perhaps you've forgotten?" There was an unmistakable note of challenge in his voice.

Alyssa stood staring at him. "I assure you I wouldn't have forgotten."

"So, what *did* she say about him?"

Alyssa felt ill at ease beneath that probing gaze. "She did speak of him, but only as a friend—a colleague—of her youth. There was never any hint of romance. Zizi never spoke of any romantic attachment to *anyone*. Don't you find that extremely odd if what you say is true?"

His expression was reflective. " I do find it odd, but it would seem Elizabeth was a woman for secrets. She was beautiful at seventy. Imagine what she was like in her twenties. Very much like you, I'd imagine, except for the eyes."

She bit her lip, feeling bewildered and upset. "That's true. Zizi's eyes were a definite green. No one else in the family has eyes like mine—with gold flecks. My mother's more like Zizi than I am, but I see what you mean. Zizi was bound to have many admirers. So how far did this involvement with Julian go? Were they thinking of getting engaged?" She felt a flare of antipathy and it showed.

"Didn't happen. Elizabeth lost her heart to someone else."

"Another suitor?" she asked with a brittle laugh. "Your great-uncle gave you all this information?"

"He can give it to *you* if you like." He registered her every passing expression. He'd seen her portraits in the house and enough photographs of her in Elizabeth's scrapbooks to know in advance that she was beautiful. None of them did her justice. One had to see her in the flesh to fully appreciate the exquisite complexion, the delicately sculpted bones of her face, that cascading hair, the lovely mouth and those distinctive eyes. The body matched the face, willowy and graceful. She was the kind of woman a certain type of man hungered for. The kind of woman that man could only dream about. "That is, if you want to risk hearing what he has to say," he added, dragging out a kitchen chair for her. "Why don't you sit down? You've lost color."

She obeyed him, waiting until the darkness at the edge of her vision receded. "Why have we never heard of Julian Wainwright in all these years?" Impatiently she pushed a long coil of hair over her shoulder.

He watched her do it, fascinated by the femininity of the movement. She was a natural ash-blonde, as her great-aunt had been. But whereas Elizabeth had worn her hair shorn like a small boy's, she wore hers center-parted and falling in loose waves over her shoulders and down her back. He studied her; she was either a superb actress or what he was saying was a shock.

"Let me get you something to eat first," he suggested briskly. "Then we can talk. What about a sandwich with the coffee?"

She waved a distracted hand. There was a firmness and strength about him, a masculinity that would turn any woman's head. Wasn't it a good thing hers was now firmly screwed on? "Would you mind answering the question?"

"Sure." His handsome mouth compressed. "Let me grind the coffee beans first."

"Please, don't worry about the coffee." She wanted to move forward with this.

"It's no problem."

She gave up. So many chaotic emotions were running through her. Shock, pain, confusion and a sense of wonder that he was moving so authoritatively around her kitchen. Had he done this with Zizi? She had to admit he was very deft in all his movements. In no time at all, the percolator was on the hot plate and turkey-breast sandwiches, neatly cut into four triangles, were in front of her. "Surely you're going to join me?" She was starting to feel quite... *unreal.*

"Delighted to," he said, taking a chair opposite her. "Elizabeth and Julian corresponded for years. You didn't know?"

"Why do you continually doubt me?" He watched the sparks in her eyes flare brightly.

"Because it's hard to believe Elizabeth kept all this from you."

"It is," she acknowledged, her tone bleak.

"He used to visit her often after Langford was lost at sea."

She was forced to take two big steadying breaths before answering. "Are you about to tell me she was friends with Richard Langford, the yachtsman?"

There was a quick flash of impatience in his eyes. "You *have* to know about Langford."

She struggled to control her temper. There was flat disbelief in his voice. "Look, just take my word for it, will you? All I know is what Zizi told me. She bought this house when it came on the market. This was *after* Richard Langford was lost at sea. As I understand it, he took his yacht out in very dangerous conditions. The locals thought the house was haunted, so Zizi got a bargain. It *is* haunted, by the way."

"I wouldn't be a bit surprised," he said without any trace of humor.

"I only have *your* word for all of this," she reminded him. "Zizi and I were as close as we could be. I spent all my vacations with her since I was seven. We talked about everything and everyone."

"Except Richard Langford and Julian Wainwright," he retorted bluntly. "Both of whom were her lovers."

She had to put a hand to her heart, it gave such a lunge. "Well, well, well! Why didn't I see that coming?"

His features tightened. "You're not going to say you didn't know that, either?"

"It's not possible." This man was a stranger.

Zizi was her much-loved great-aunt. Why should she believe one word he said? For all she knew, he could have a hidden agenda.

"But very easy to prove." He spoke more gently this time. "Elizabeth and Julian were seriously involved. Then Langford came into her life."

She sat there, speechless, almost in a trance.

"Alyssa?" he prompted.

She made a huge effort to respond. "This is a far cry from the encounter I expected to have with you." She began to rub her temples, which ached.

"I know and I'm sorry. The fact is, Langford deeded this house to Elizabeth a year before he died. He also presented her with her little sailing yacht, the *Cherub*."

All at once Alyssa felt a great surge of anger. She leaped up, unwilling to accept a word of it. "For pity's sake, stop! Zizi *bought* this house. She bought the yacht. Either you've got your facts wrong, or you're making it all up. Zizi would never have lied to me. She was a woman of integrity!"

He seemed unimpressed, although his tone was calm. "Please sit down again. I'm sorry to upset you. You may have been led to believe otherwise, but Richard Langford deeded the house to Elizabeth. The yacht, too, was a gift."

The air thrummed with electricity. "That can easily be checked out." She spoke sharply, but resumed her chair. "Why didn't you tell my father any of this?"

"It wasn't the time to talk to him about Elizabeth's affairs. It was *you* Elizabeth was most focused on. She told me she was leaving you the house."

"Do you have anything else to tell me?" she asked coldly, struggling with unfamiliar pangs of jealousy that Zizi could have been so drawn to him, confiding even that piece of information.

He seemed to realize it. "She spoke about you at length. How gifted you are, how much she loved you. How you both loved Flying Clouds. She was more than happy to speak freely about you, but it was extremely difficult to get her to talk about herself."

"Why should she?" she asked angrily. Her heart was hammering away.

"Because of Julian," he said, rising abruptly. "Julian deserves some consideration. Julian is the issue for me. Here, let me pour the coffee." The rich fragrance pervaded the kitchen. "There's no question that was a very painful area of her life. She was loath to talk about it, although I think she accepted that she'd soon have to."

An awful suspicion came into her mind. "You're not a writer, are you? I shudder at the thought of some unauthorized biography of Elizabeth Jane Calvert, full of shocking disclosures."

He didn't answer until he'd placed her coffee before her. "It could happen," he said with a shrug. "It's quite a story, but it won't be written by me. I'm an architect."

Something clicked. "Hunt Hebron?" She referred to a Sydney-based firm, multi-award winners for many years.

He nodded, setting his own coffee down on the table. "My father, Philip Hunt, heads the firm since Uncle Julian retired."

"I daresay you've won a few awards of your own." She allowed her eyes to rest on him, struggling to keep the slow burn of hostility and a perverse awareness out of her voice, although it must have been obvious. Brett had always told her she was hopeless at hiding her feelings.

"A few," he answered, "with better to come, I hope. I've checked out your work, although I've never managed to get to Brisbane to a showing. It seems to me that you're on your way to matching and—who knows?—one day surpassing Elizabeth."

"I doubt it. Zizi was wonderful."

"And *you* aren't?" A smile curved his lips.

He'd shared that smile with Zizi. No wonder she'd softened toward him. Alyssa had no difficulty picturing the two of them sitting here in the kitchen as *they* were doing now, sharing a cup of coffee. She could see Zizi letting him make it.

Alyssa shook her head, trying not only to conceal her reaction to this man, but also to push it away. "Not yet," she answered. She picked up another sandwich, scarcely aware of what she was doing. "Does your father know any of this? If it's *true*."

"Everyone in the family knows that Julian was madly in love with Elizabeth Jane Calvert when they were young. We also know it was serious between them. Everyone expected a wedding, but in the end nothing came of it. Julian never married."

"Neither did Zizi. So what? Perhaps they were genuine loners. There are people like that. Zizi was reclusive. She was eccentric—I can't deny that— but she was the most lovable woman in the world."

"And one of the most secretive, it seems," he said with quiet irony.

Alyssa shook her head once more. "Provided what you're telling me is true," she repeated. "We've only got *your* great-uncle's word for it. Artists are highly imaginative people. Perhaps he dreamed up this epic love affair? Perhaps the love was all on his side? He wouldn't be the first or the last to get it all wrong."

"You wouldn't say that if you knew him." He swallowed a mouthful of coffee. "Besides, there's more."

Her laugh was slightly hysterical. "Of course

there's more! Next you'll be telling me there was a child, in the true tradition of soap opera."

"Which nevertheless manages to echo real life." His voice was so grave it gave her a jolt of foreboding. "Why don't you finish those sandwiches," he urged.

Her skin flushed. "I must really look like I need reviving."

"You do. More coffee?"

"Yes, please."

He refilled her cup, topped up his own, then sat down again. "There's no easy way to go about any of this, Alyssa. Not for you, not for me, certainly not for Elizabeth. Not for Uncle Julian. Or for that matter, the Langfords."

Her tenuous control snapped. She set down her coffee cup so forcefully, it clattered against the saucer. "What on earth have they got to do with it?" she asked. "They're ancient history. I assume you're talking about *the* Langfords, as in LCL?"

He nodded, a glitter in his eyes. "Richard Langford had a great many shares in the family company, as you might imagine."

"So? They would've passed to his heirs. Why have you *really* come here, Adam? To stir up trouble?"

"I told you." Muscles bunched along his firm jawline. "I came as my great-uncle's emissary.

He desperately wants to know before he dies if Elizabeth's child was his or Langford's."

Shock flooded her. She opened her mouth to protest, but no sound emerged. For an instant she feared she might faint. Her brain seemed totally dislocated from her heart. *Elizabeth's child?*

"Alyssa!" He was on his feet, shoving back his chair. "Here, put your head down." He placed his hand on her nape, his touch gentle but nonetheless compelling.

For a full minute she obeyed, then when she felt better, she shook off his hand. She was angry and afraid of his effect on her. She'd felt that touch of his hand not only on her neck, but in her breasts, the pit of her stomach, between her legs. If she put all those sensations together, what did she get? She fought to compose herself. "I'm fine."

"Just sit quietly for a moment," he advised, himself so affected by a moment so intimate he wished now he hadn't touched her. Was it possible she truly didn't know about Elizabeth's baby?

I've got to stop this, Adam thought. Start again another time.

"This is a shocking conversation, isn't it?" she lamented. "Zizi never had a child. I'm sorry to have to say it, but Julian Wainwright must be crazy. There's a name for it, isn't there? Erotomania, something like that. The poor man must be fantasizing, especially if he's pumped full of drugs."

He looked at her with compassion. "If Elizabeth told you so little—after all you were a child when she was already a middle-aged woman—surely someone else in your family knows. Her sister, Mariel, perhaps?"

"No way! Zizi never married. She never had a child. Do you seriously believe we wouldn't know if she had?"

He sat back, staring at her. Her emotional upheaval appeared real. "It's happened before," he mused. "All families have secrets, even from one another. The thing is, secrets don't always remain buried. My aim isn't to shock or upset you, Alyssa. I see I have, but you must trust me on this. Elizabeth *did* have a child. What Julian's desperate to know is who was the biological father. Julian's a very rich man. He's made his will, but it's obvious to us all that he doesn't feel he's put his affairs in order. Over the years he begged Elizabeth for the truth. She always said the child died within twenty-four hours of its birth. We now know that's not what happened."

"We?" she cried. "Who's *we,* your dying uncle and you? It's all hearsay in your case. And it's not *true! None* of it is true! I hate when people make up lies. I hate *you.* Zizi must have hated you."

He gave a half smile. "I think Elizabeth braced herself the moment she laid eyes on me. I'm told I look very much like Julian as a young man. Elizabeth, for reasons of her own, appears to have led a life of deception. In doing so she turned her back on fame and fortune, a full life, a successful career. All the things most people would give anything to have. I think some part of her was greatly relieved it was all coming to an end."

Every nerve in her body was jittering. "Was she going to rejoice that all the skeletons would come tumbling out of the closet?" She didn't hide her outrage at the insult to Zizi's memory.

"Can't *you* see it as a release? Elizabeth didn't bar me from the house. The truth is, she was comfortable with me. Unfortunately I'd barely begun my voyage of discovery before she had her fatal fall."

"Are you sure you weren't there at the time?" It simply stormed out of her before she could claw back control.

"I'll forget you said that." His expression went taut.

"I'm sorry." She rested her aching head on her hand. "I hardly know what I'm saying. But why should I sit here and listen to you destroying all my illusions about the Zizi I loved?"

"The closer the link, the more intense the pain,"

he said. "Elizabeth Calvert was a riddle. Secrets were her way of life."

"Secrets and secret lovers!" Alyssa laughed bitterly. "I'm sorry, but it's all too far-fetched for me. Sadly Zizi's not here to defend herself. Julian Wainwright might well be delusional. It's not uncommon. Even so, lovers are one thing, but saying Zizi was an unmarried mother not even sure of the identity of her child's father is quite another. Zizi may have been *different,* but she was much loved by her family. They would've looked after her. They would have protected her. She had her sister, as you seem to know—my grandmother, Mariel. Do you really believe Mariel would have let Zizi go through a pregnancy by herself?"

"Very possibly Mariel didn't know about it," he suggested. "Based on the little I saw of Elizabeth, I'd say she would try to see it through by herself. Again, not uncommon."

Alyssa found herself grinding her teeth. If all of this *was* true, nothing could restore her faith in Zizi. "There's never been *one* word about any unwanted pregnancy."

"Who said it was unwanted?" he asked.

Anger spurted again. Had Zizi really had such a tempestuous past? *What was I really?* she thought wretchedly, as doubts started to pour through her breached defenses. *The perennial seven-year-old who implicitly accepted whatever Zizi told her?* Of course she was.

"Elizabeth was only starting to open up," Adam Hunt was saying. "She'd committed her youth to the deepest vault. I suspect that whatever happened to her so traumatized her, she withdrew from the world. The further tragedy was her accidental death."

Alyssa lifted her hands helplessly. "Something I just don't understand. Zizi didn't use that bath, not since she had a near-accident some time back."

He shook his head. "I wouldn't know anything about that. There was no hint of anything untoward. It was a tragic accident. One that's quite common in that age group."

It was difficult to deny. "That must have been awful for you." Her beautiful eyes welled with tears she blinked away.

"Devastating," he said, still seared by the memory. "When I first entered the bathroom, for some reason, suicide came to mind."

Alyssa drew back obviously, astounded. "Suicide? I can't consider that for a moment. Zizi wasn't the type."

"Is there a type?" he asked. "Might she have thought of it as a way out?"

"Out of *what,* damn it!" Alyssa exploded. "I think I'd like you to leave."

"I don't blame you." There was a grim under-standing in his voice. "In my own defense, please remember that I'm carrying around my own burden of shock and bitterness. Julian held fast to his secrets, too. Only his impending death has fully opened up the past."

She had to concentrate. "You believe this story about a child?" she ventured.

"You'd better believe it, too," he said, his voice oddly harsh. "Julian called in a private investiga-tor. You would know that the Freedom of Infor-mation Act changed things overnight. Julian could never quite accept Elizabeth's story. He now knows the child lived."

Alyssa shut her eyes, appalled. "And no doubt his whereabouts. Are you going to share this big secret with me?"

"Certainly, but not today." He stood up, pushing in his chair. "I can see the anguish on your face. We'll talk again later."

"I don't think so," she said coldly, rising to join him.

"I do!" He spoke as though it was a foregone conclusion. "I can't leave here without the truth. I explained that to Elizabeth. Now I'm telling you. I look on it as a duty to my great-uncle, a good man, a *dying* man."

"And you're expecting to get this supposed

truth out of *me?*" She laughed as if he'd made a bizarre joke. "I don't know *anything.*"

"There must be letters, papers, documents," he suggested. "Some sort of written confirmation. It would be a first step."

"It's a wonder you haven't gone in search of them," she snapped. "You would've had the run of the house before I arrived."

Anger was apparent beneath the calm. "I doubt anyone but you could get away with talking to me like that. I'd been hoping we could work this out together, Alyssa. Time is running out for Julian."

She released a breath. "If you know the identity of Zizi's child, why don't you just go and speak to him?"

"Her," he corrected.

She looked at him sharply.

"Elizabeth had a daughter, not a son. DNA testing would confirm the identity of the biological father if certain people were prepared to cooperate. No one can be forced. As I said, the *whole* story was news to me until very recently. Julian had always clung to the idea that the child was his, not Langford's. There was apparently some incident that made him think so."

"Good God!" She was swamped by feelings of utter unreality. "I don't know what to make of all this. I'd hate to have to live with the thought that

Zizi kept such secrets from us. I'm certain my mother knows nothing. She'd be horrified. So would my grandmother."

"Are you sure?"

"Of course I'm sure!" She made an effort to calm down. "My mother wouldn't keep something like that to herself. As far as we all knew, Zizi had no all-important man in her life." Even as she said it, she realized it sounded absolutely ludicrous. Zizi would have been a beautiful vibrant young woman. She was bound to have had some sort of sex life, even if things went drastically wrong.

"That's unbelievable and you know it," he said. "Elizabeth may have elected to live alone after Langford was lost at sea, but Julian told me she was brimming over with life when she was young. She was the honeypot for the bees. Men fell for her in droves, and why not? She was very beautiful and very gifted."

"And she *lied* to us all?" Bombarded with information, she couldn't figure it out. "Why? Zizi wouldn't have been abandoned by her family. They loved her. Come to that, I have no proof that you're who you say you are. I don't know whether to see you as friend or foe. You could be a journalist poking your nose into an old story. You could be part of some art conspiracy. Maybe you know that I've wanted to arrange a showing of Zizi's paintings. I'm positive it would be an enormous success even without publicity stunts. People play so many devious games."

"No games," he said, shaking his head. "You're welcome to check me out. My license is in the car."

"I'll come out with you," she said, walking toward the kitchen door. "What do I owe you for the groceries?"

"Nothing. Just a friendly gesture."

"Except we're not friends nor are we likely to be. I'd prefer to pay you."

"As you wish. The bill's in my wallet."

"Where exactly are you living?" She turned to confront him, hating him for making so many allegations. She was being asked to take in so much information yet given no time for the information to settle. She couldn't pretend she wasn't also drawn to him. Was the attraction real, or were her defenses down? Never for a moment had she pictured anything like this.

"I've rented the old Gambaro farm," he said.

She nodded curtly. "I know it. How long have you rented it for?"

"I had to take it at the agent's three-month minimum."

"Well, you can't squeeze blood from a stone," she told him, moving out to the hallway. "I'll be of absolutely no help to you. You might as well turn around and go back to Sydney."

"I'm staying," he said. "I had a break coming and I'm taking it. This is a glorious part of the world. But there's a dying old man in Sydney who needs a few answers before he goes. When you've had time to process all this information you claim you don't know, you may feel inclined to help."

She shook her head grimly. "Not at this point." Not ever!

They had reached the entrance hall before he spoke again. "Elizabeth told me you worked pro bono for a women's refuge. That makes you a compassionate person. Unless Elizabeth was totally paranoid about her past, in all probability she kept letters and papers that would confirm the truth. She wouldn't have had time to arrange a bonfire. She didn't know she was going to die, after all."

Would the grieving ever pass? "And what if these mystery documents open up a Pandora's box? Have you thought of that?" Her lips were trembling. "Families stand to get desperately hurt. What good is the truth when there could be a huge scandal? I don't think the Langfords would thank you."

He took a deep breath, keeping his hands rigidly by his side. "Some things demand clarification," he said. "Julian only wants to know if Elizabeth's child is his, a child she led him to believe died soon after birth. If this person is shown to be his daughter, she's going to inherit a great deal of money."

She looked at him with scorn. "And how should she take that, like a rain of diamonds out of the sky? What's Julian after, exactly? Does he want to set the record straight once and for all? Does he want revenge? And more to the point, what do *you* get out of this?" she challenged. "You, the favorite great-nephew? Won't you come out of it second-best? Wouldn't it benefit you to simply go away? Concoct some story for your dear Uncle Julian? What if this mystery daughter would rather not know? After all, she must've been put up for adoption. Zizi didn't keep her. This daughter, if she exists, has lived her life thinking she was one person, now your uncle wants to tell her she's someone completely different? Can't you see that this could turn out to be a total mess? The safest course might be to keep quiet." She felt tears well in her eyes again.

"I'm sorry, Alyssa." He moved quickly to the front door, in case he did something crazy, like sweep her into his arms. He had never in his life felt such *desire* for a woman. "Life isn't simple," he mused. "If you were adopted, wouldn't you want to find out who your biological parents were?"

"I'm actually familiar with *two* cases when the

people involved were devastated to discover that the parents who'd reared them weren't their biological parents at all. Both took the truth very, very badly. Better to live in your comfort zone than know the brutal truth."

"*I* would need to know," he said somberly.

She was terribly afraid she would, as well. "Coming here was a bad idea of yours."

"Elizabeth didn't think so."

"Only she isn't around to back that up." She frowned at him with accusing eyes.

He smiled. "Why not try finding whatever documents Elizabeth might have put away? Apart from that, she had many paintings stored here. Maybe there are some portraits. Who knows? I'm sure you haven't seen them all."

"Perhaps not." She had never felt free to delve into Zizi's large body of work. Zizi had showed her only what she meant to show her, she now realized.

"Will you tell me if you find anything?" he asked.

She shook her head. "I don't want to see you again."

"Why don't you look at me while you say that?"

It wasn't a challenge. It was more an overt acknowledgment of their mutual attraction.

Betraying color came into her face. "I can't make any promises."

"I rely on your integrity, Alyssa."

She nodded curtly. "Wait here. I'll get the money I owe you." She walked toward the staircase, desperate for him to leave, yet knowing if she never saw him again she'd always remember him.

"Do you feel safe here?" he asked abruptly.

In the act of mounting the staircase, she turned to look at him, one hand resting on the banister. He had taken up a position in the entrance hall beneath her, his aquamarine gaze keen as a laser. It seemed to go deep inside her; much deeper than *she* dared to go. "I've been coming here all my life," she said in a deliberately offhand tone. "I'm rooted to the place. Besides, I'm not afraid of things that go bump in the night. No old house is without its resident ghost."

He nodded, a vertical line between his brows. "Who, I haven't the slightest doubt, is Richard Langford."

Alyssa felt her throat dry up. She'd always accepted that, but now wondered if the original Captain Richard Langford who'd built the house was the only one who haunted it. Perhaps the more recent Richard Langford, the famous yachtsman, had joined his ancestor. "Did your uncle hate him?" she asked.

He continued to stare up at her. "Deep in his heart he did. He was madly in love with Elizabeth. Forget all the years in between. Talking to him now, the years were as nothing. He might have been talking about yesterday. She was the love of his life." He shook his head. "I find it almost too much to grasp, but maybe there *is* such a thing as everlasting love. Julian blamed Langford for everything that went wrong in three lives. He even blamed Langford for his own death."

She couldn't have been more unnerved. "But… that makes no sense at all."

"Langford was a married man with two small children," he said tonelessly.

Something like shame burned in her cheeks. "Zizi would *never* have had an affair with a married man," she protested, affronted by the very idea.

"Blame it on passion."

Passion in the past. Passion in the present? Alyssa had a presentiment that life-changing emotion was waiting for *her.*

With a shiver she continued up the stairs. Richard Langford had been Zizi's lover and possibly the father of her child? A married man, an adulterer? And Zizi had never told a soul? Had she been too ashamed? Zizi had supposedly let her child go, not knowing how that child grew up, if she was all right, no doubt praying she had love and security and all the things a child needed to be happy.

Who did that child look like? Zizi? Had she inherited Zizi's talent? Questions without end. Someone must have known about Zizi's pregnancy at some point. It wasn't something a woman could hide, especially toward the end of her term. Then again, Zizi knew all about going into hiding. Was that where she'd given birth to her baby, in hiding? Had the child died within twenty-four hours of delivery as she'd supposedly told Julian Wainwright?

Zizi was fast turning into an enigma. Zizi, who'd been extraordinarily beautiful in her youth, not only beautiful, but with some *magic* about her.

Whatever the true story, Alyssa knew her perceptions of her beloved great-aunt had been altered forever. History might have to be rewritten.

CHAPTER FOUR

SHOCK SETTLED OVER Alyssa in the week that followed. She went over and over her long conversation with Adam Hunt, questioning every word, every allegation. She had difficulty holding herself together. Who could solve such a mystery with two of the main protagonists missing? She'd always known Zizi was deep—what gifted artist wasn't?—but Zizi had always been so open and cheerful when they were together, the best of company for a young person. She had never even considered plumbing what lay hidden beneath the calm surface. Of course the big age difference was a major factor. Understandably Zizi would have kept things from her during childhood and even later, when she was an adolescent. At university and afterward, as a practicing lawyer, she no longer had as much time to spend with Zizi. She'd taken several holidays abroad but had always found opportunities to fly to North Queensland.

Maybe Zizi had wanted to talk to Alyssa the

woman, but didn't know where to begin? Maybe she couldn't bear to explain what had happened to her in her youth? A passionate affair with a married man… *If* Zizi had given up her child for adoption, there were laws in those days governing confidentiality. Those laws no longer applied. As a lawyer, hadn't she been an unhappy witness to the consequences of full disclosure? Not everyone wanted to know.

When Zizi had first laid eyes on Adam Hunt— given that he was supposed to closely resemble Julian and assuming that all these revelations were true—wouldn't she have felt caught in a trap?. What should she have done, anyway? Ask for absolution? Was that message she'd wanted relayed to the man who'd loved her so much and in vain? What incident was so seared into Julian Wainwright's memory gave him reason to believe that Zizi's alleged child could be his? Why would Zizi have claimed such a child had only lived for a few hours? Alyssa gave up in despair. Was Zizi's supposed history a complete fiction?

AT NIGHT SHE LAY wide-awake, listening to the usually soothing sound of the sea and staring out at the great clusters of stars that gathered in such brilliance over the sea. The Southern Cross was clearly visible over the tip of the roof, the Milky

Way a broad blur of diamonds. Outside in the grounds, the night wind set the great fronds of the coconut palms clattering. Fruit bats added to the nocturnal din as they plundered the cornucopia of mangoes, pawpaws, custard apples and bananas.

Despite all the familiar sounds of the plantation at night, she'd never felt so *alone.* In fact, she was trying hard to fight down her nervousness as she lay with the top sheet pulled up to her chin. As a child, she'd believed if her leg slipped off the bed someone would grab it. She still vaguely felt that way. The house certainly didn't feel the same. There was a sense of disturbance where previously there'd been comfort and shelter. Now she felt something sinister in the very air. She'd never felt it before. To be on the safe side, she had a golf club handy beside her bed, should—God forbid— she need a weapon against an intruder. She'd never thought to ask who'd owned those clubs. To the best of her knowledge, Zizi had never played golf.

Best of her knowledge! *What* knowledge? By now she'd decided, as Brett had been fond of pointing out, that she wasn't terrifically bright. She hadn't stopped believing in Zizi, she would keep loving Zizi no matter what. But there was no getting away from it—she was badly shaken. Zizi hadn't been calm waters at all. The waters may have *appeared* crystal clear, but that had only fooled her into underestimating their depths. There was no excuse for her as a seasoned sailor. Sailing *Cherub* around the crystalline Reef waters, she knew perfectly well that details could appear as distinct at forty feet as five.

She was glad of Cleo's company. They were becoming very friendly. Aristocrats like Cleo weren't given to friendliness. But there the cat was, lying at the foot of the bed, making a whirring noise. It wasn't exactly a contented *purr,* more like an engine idling. She interpreted it as Cleo making her presence felt to any would-be invaders. The cat was wakeful, wanting, her tail shuddering.

Who exactly were they waiting for anyway? Zizi and her resident ghost? Two ghosts now? Zizi and Richard Langford, united for eternity? Maybe the two of them would visit her bedside. Alyssa sighed; she'd always had too much imagination. Sometimes it was a nuisance. Australians were a pragmatic lot, and when asked about ghosts most would say, "There's no such bloody thing!" She, on the other hand, would have to admit she'd spent her childhood vacations in their company.

She had to blame her restlessness on Adam Hunt's disclosures. They'd provided Zizi, the committed single woman, with a passionate sex life. It was so *dark* outside, except for those glorious stars. The aboriginals believed the sky was home to the great Beings. There was Orion, the mighty hunter, with his upraised club and jeweled belt; Sirius, the watchdog of the sky.

Abruptly Cleo turned up the volume of her whirring. Alyssa raised herself on her elbow, still clutching the boronia-scented sheet to her neck. Were those footsteps she heard on the widow's walk?

"What's that?" she hissed at Cleo. It was some relief to have the cat for company and moral support.

In answer, Cleo made a rasping sound, then padded up the bed and curled into her side. Obviously she'd heard those footsteps as well. In fact Cleo was following Alyssa's fixed upward gaze to the roof.

After a moment of intent listening, Alyssa lay back, with Cleo taking up an even closer position, her whirring noise as loud as snoring. What she'd heard might have *sounded* remarkably like footsteps, but Alyssa told herself it was nothing more than creaky old boards—or maybe Captain Langford, taking a stroll. But the captain had never meant her any harm. In any case, she'd shut up the house as tight as a drum. Not that a determined intruder couldn't get in under four minutes. Would breaking in to the home of a young woman be more exciting to a certain type of criminal than breaking in to the home of an elderly lady? But Zizi hadn't looked or moved like an elderly lady. Zizi who'd led an enormously secretive double life.

Alyssa punched up her pillows and began thinking about Adam Hunt. He'd caused a terrible shift in her life. It was not a restful idea; it set her tossing and turning, her mind in turmoil, her body wired with sensations difficult to explain away as nonsexual. She thought about him until the digital clock read 2:45 a.m. He wanted her to look for letters and documents. God knows Zizi had never thrown anything out. She'd been a hoarder, but everything had been hidden away in cupboards and cabinets and lovely little antique desks with secret drawers. The place was like a museum where the most private papers weren't on display. Zizi had never shared what was in all those repositories, not even with her. Her own fastidious instincts had always told her not to pry. Well, tomorrow she had to begin prying in earnest.

And what about the stacks and stacks of paintings? A lot of them were in unreachable places like the attic. It was the most enchanted room full of treasures from Southeast Asia—furniture, sculptures, carvings—all manner of beautiful objects, including Oriental porcelain and bronzes, Coromandel screens, Persian carpets. Where had it all come from?

"With the house, my darling. Nobody wanted it but me."

She had accepted without question everything Zizi had told her at age seven.

All through her childhood she'd been allowed to open the old sea chests, which emanated the most intoxicating fragrances, to find costumes. There were silks and satins, chiffons and velvets and lovely day dresses, shoes and bags and adorable hats one could wear to the Melbourne Cup.

"Who wore all these beautiful things, Zizi?" she had asked in wonderment. The Zizi she'd known dressed like Katharine Hepburn in shirts and trousers, hitched together with a leather belt.

"Believe it or not, my darling, I did, when I was young." She had made it sound like an eternity ago.

"But where?" Alyssa, the child, had leaned into a trunk burying her face in emerald satin the color of Zizi's eyes. It was an evening dress, with a mere scrap of a bodice that must have revealed tantalizing glimpses of bosom, decorated with exquisite beading.

"When I went on holiday. I loved Hong Kong, Shanghai and Bangkok. Once I managed to get as far away as San Francisco."

"Did you go on your own?" She had looked up, eagerly awaiting Zizi's answer, but Zizi had

dropped to the wooden floor beside her, resting a loving hand on her head.

"Listen, little darling, I didn't always lead a quiet life. So don't go feeling sorry for me."

That had made her sad. The truth was, she *did* feel sorry for Zizi, sorry for the might-have-been, the waste of a potentially brilliant life.

She woke with Cleo sitting Sphinx-like on her chest, gently pawing her nose. Alyssa turned her head to check the bedside clock, frowning slightly. "Listen, Cleo, I've got to tell you it's only six o'clock."

There was definitely something disdainful in Cleo's expression. She'd been penned in the house long enough. The sun was up; brilliantly plumaged lorikeets were making a raid on the garden, dive-bombing the unending source of tropical nectar. Cleo wanted her breakfast and she wasn't one to wait. Zizi had spoiled her dreadfully.

Alyssa swung her bare feet to the floor at the same moment Cleo, now satisfied to see some action, jumped onto the rug. "Today we have to look for some answers."

But could she actually bear to? Did she really *want* to know?

She didn't have to remind herself that someone far wiser had once said, *"The fruit from the tree of knowledge can be bitter to the taste."*

BRIGHT SUNLIGHT flooded in through the windows of the shower recess, despite the tall, jungly screen of banana plants outside that were bearing bunches of creamy sweet fruit. She'd have to cut them down before they ripened and hang them under the house. She dressed for the heat in a yellow ribbed singlet, a pair of white shorts, white sneakers on her feet and her hair pulled back in a ponytail. At least she was the one looking into Zizi's past, not some prying journalist intent on vandalizing Zizi's memory. Zizi had been one of the country's finest artists, arguably the best woman painter they'd ever had. Despite her eccentric facade, the asexual mode of dress and the ultrashort hairstyle, she'd been a deeply sensuous woman.

Zizi had loved good food and fine wines. She loved the sun and the surf. She loved beautiful things. Alyssa recalled the way Zizi's long, paint-stained fingers slipped over objects, absorbing their feel and their shape. Zizi had been a very tactile person. How incredibly naive of her to go along with the idea that Zizi had never known a man's love. She'd seen her great-aunt through a *child*'s eyes, loving and honoring her, proud to be family. Was there a large part of Zizi she didn't know? She had to acknowledge the strong possibility.

BREAKFAST WAS FRUIT, a slice of papaya spritzed with lime juice and a couple of passion fruit. Afterward she took her coffee upstairs to savor the veranda. Cleo joined her in the old squatter's chair, launching herself companionably onto her lap. This morning the sea was an electric blue, almost the color of a gas flame with a million glittering needles of light dancing over the surface. Could she blindly accept what Adam Hunt had told her? What did he have to gain? As far as she could see, nothing. In fact, he stood to lose.

Did she trust him? *No.* She wasn't ready to abandon her trust in Zizi. His great-uncle could well be suffering from the early stages of dementia, when fantasies became reality. It was possible that Adam Hunt was so close to his great-uncle, he'd chosen to believe everything he'd been told. Unless Adam had actual proof Zizi had borne a child? Zizi couldn't have kept the birth quiet if she'd gone to a hospital. What information had that private investigator uncovered? She would have to see it herself before she believed a word of this extraordinary story.

And yet… Underneath all the doubts, belief was shaping.

Inside her bedroom, the door of the magnificent antique French armoire banged shut, the noise ricocheting so loudly around the walls, it might as well have fallen over. She jumped, sliding back into nervousness; Cleo unwound a paw and dug her claws in.

"Hey, cut that out!" Nevertheless she let the cat stay on her lap. She had no recollection whatever of opening the armoire. Despite her resolve, she found it scary. As a child, she'd received any number of scratches climbing inside; she'd believed the armoire led to a tunnel that went underground across the plantation and onto the beach. It was a way for the captain to come and go.

History could be fascinating and a burden. Zizi, in one of her rare moments of talking about herself, had once confided that she'd almost lost her life on one of those not-so-distant coral cays. She'd been stung by a stonefish when exploring the coral gardens at low tide. Zizi had often gone off by herself for days or even weeks to paint.

"So what happened?" she'd asked, enthralled. She'd known all about the dreaded stonefish, with its many venomous spines. Its main habitat was on coral reefs north of Capricorn. *"How did you get off the cay? Wouldn't you have been in terrible pain?"*

"Excruciating," Zizi had said not with a shudder but a smile that instantly revived her youthful beauty. It might have been some marvelous incident enshrined in her memory rather than a near-tragedy. *"A passing yacht sighted me*

on the beach. Something—divine intervention perhaps—alerted the skipper that I was in trouble."

"So he saved your life?" Alyssa, the child, found this thrilling, so much so she spent a good deal of time after that, reenacting the drama with the ghost of Captain Langford standing in as hero.

"It was like a dream," Zizi had said. *"I recovered and he sailed away."*

"Did he never return?" she'd asked regretfully.

Zizi just lifted her shoulders philosophically. *"He had to go home to his wife."*

Richard Langford, the yachtsman, had a wife. And two children. It would be very disturbing indeed if Richard Langford had been Zizi's rescuer. She'd treasured that incident like a beautiful dream. Had Richard Langford been the object of her passion? Had she fallen deeply in love with him when she'd already promised to marry Julian Wainwright?

Zizi had kept Julian's paintings in the house. Why, when Alyssa had admired them, had Zizi not said, "Julian and I were once very close." Zizi had a remarkable facility for playing her cards close to the chest. It wasn't that she had been fobbed off with falsehoods; she simply hadn't been told the *truth*. But wasn't that the definition of a lie?

Oh, Zizi!
Alyssa sighed deeply. Even idols had feet of clay.

ALL WEEKEND she worked feverishly, hauling reams of stuff out of cupboards and cabinets and then shoving it back. From time to time she sat on the floor poring over things that opened up the floodgates of old memories. Zizi had actually kept her school reports. Not one of them without a glowing comment from the headmistress, she saw with a wry smile. Her parents had expected her not only to work hard but to come out a winner. There'd been no such thing as failure for the Sutherlands' only child.

Cleo, too, was caught up in the nostalgia, delicately circling the strewn papers, not randomly, it seemed, but with some hidden purpose. Sometimes she paused to stretch out a paw to pin one or other paper to the ground. Having done that, she pondered it first, then set about rearranging all the pieces as if she was puzzling out a jigsaw. In the end her efforts looked remarkably like the map of Tasmania!

"Clever girl, Cleo!" Alyssa applauded, trying to remember if Zizi had ever mentioned visiting Tasmania. Everyone knew about cats and their psychic powers. Maybe Cleo would hit on some clue.

But alas, no luck for either of them.

They went through a stack of old leather-bound photo albums together. There were endless pictures of her at all stages of development. Old school photographs year after year until she graduated at the top of her class with an astonishingly sweet and vulnerable smile.

A heavy silence brooded in the house. They sat on the sofa staring at all these mementos of years past. They weren't in any kind of order or chronology, except for her school photographs. Zizi liked to go at things methodically—it was her nature and her training. She'd lived a life of selective chaos. Nobody could have called her *tidy*. In fact, she'd been seriously disorganized.

When Alyssa was ready to put the album back in the cupboard, out slipped a couple of photographs stuck together. The one underneath was of Zizi, holding a beautiful, platinum-haired toddler in her arms. It could've been herself as a baby, but Alyssa knew perfectly well it was her mother, Stephanie. Mariel, her strong-boned face unsmiling, was standing alongside, one arm flung big-sister fashion around her younger sister's slender shoulders. Zizi looked absolutely, heart-breakingly, beautiful.

And it seemed plain to Alyssa's artist's eye, *tragic*. Surely Zizi should have been overjoyed for her sister? Mariel had always declared herself the happiest woman alive when Stephanie was born. Mariel had had great difficulty getting pregnant. Stephanie was her only child.

Cleo, rasping heavily, laid her head over Alyssa's arm, staring fixedly at the old photograph as though Alyssa's attention was in danger of wandering.

"What is it, Cleo?" Alyssa stroked the silky amber head, feeling quite tender toward her. "You see something special about *this* one?"

Alyssa's mind began racing at full tilt. It was odd, discovering a beloved relative was in many ways a stranger. She'd run out of excuses. Revelations she'd been trying hard to process suddenly assumed new meaning. Her hand froze on the photograph as Cleo tilted a questioning head to look at her.

"It *couldn't* be! It's not possible!" Alyssa closed her eyes as the shock waves began to hit. Her heart flew to her throat. There was a pounding in her temples. Adam Hunt's words echoed and reechoed in her head. *Julian knows who the child is.*

She heaved herself up with Cleo in her arms and walked through to the kitchen, where she made herself a cup of coffee and gave Cleo a saucer of cream. They had to keep their brain cells working.

IN LATE AFTERNOON, when the cloudless blue sky was turning to shades of indigo, purple, gold and pink, they abandoned their search in the house and went out to Zizi's studio, a converted barn just across the paved court from the kitchen and adjacent to the old servants' quarters. Access to the loft, where Zizi worked, was by an either internal or external fight of stairs.

She hadn't intended to visit the studio so soon. It was a special place, though she realized now that she'd never spent any time in it alone. Zizi had always been with her. She felt raw with grief, but all these revelations forced her to keep going.

She opened the lower door, flooding the interior with sunlight. Both she and Cleo hesitated as though afraid to go in. "Come on, let's face it together." She tried a bracing tone that sounded pathetically hollow.

Cleo, up for the challenge, stalked ahead, tail held unnaturally high. Alyssa followed. It took a few moments to realize all those ragged breaths were coming from *her,* not the cat. Cleo was moving farther and farther away, her movements suggesting she was trying to track something down.

Settle down. It's probably a mouse. They'd had an invasion of field mice ages ago.

The atmosphere inside the barn was dense, the golden sunbeams swarming with minute specks of light like gilded dust. Everything looked just the same. The ground floor was far more exotic than her own studio. There was a treasury of gleaming Thai furniture that would probably cost a fortune if shipped in today. After Richard Langford's untimely death, why hadn't the Langford family claimed the riches that lay inside Flying Clouds?

Because Richard Langford gave it all to Zizi, that's why! the voice inside her head answered. Had the Langford family even known about Flying Clouds or had it been Richard's private retreat? So many unanswered questions. Had Richard's wife known about the existence of a mistress? One would hope not.

Cleo, back from her investigations, jumped onto an exotic nineteenth-century bed that had marble insets in the carved panels. As a girl, Alyssa had spent countless hours there reading while Zizi worked, bolstered by the pile of Thai silk cushions. Cleo looked splendid posed against those cushions of indigo and gold silk. She decided then and there to paint Cleo into one of her interiors. A valuable collection of red and black lacquerware was displayed in a tall cabinet at the far end of the room. She'd bring it into the house.

She could do it, if she chose. All of this was hers! She was only beginning to realize the scope of the fortune Zizi had left her. Basically Zizi's taste was her own. She loved the arts of Asia, so prominently on display at Flying Clouds. The collection had most likely begun with Captain Richard Langford in the late 1800s, added to by successive heirs.

Alyssa walked toward the stairs that led to the loft. Cleo, eyeing her closely, leaped off the bed and raced up the stairs before her, meowing loudly to alert any two-dimensional—or four-footed—creatures hanging about that she knew a way to deal with them. Alyssa followed her furry guide, one hand on the banister, her mouth dry. She could almost hear Zizi's voice. *Come up and see what I've done, darling. I need your opinion.*

She hadn't, of course, but she'd always made it sound like she did.

There was a loud rustle in the roof that made her spin around suddenly, her unease escalating. Cleo sprang onto a tallboy, turning a highly suspicious gaze upward.

"Birds," Alyssa whispered by way of explanation. There were parrots, pigeons, lorikeets and pink and silver galahs flying about—all kinds of rustlings, squeaks and sighs.

Why was she so nervous? She'd loved Zizi so much, yet she felt tremendously unsettled, as though her great-aunt could materialize at any moment. The dead didn't simply disappear; their shades could never be annihilated. Neither could the peculiar feeling she had of being shadowed. The air vibrated and it seemed that something on the periphery of her vision moved too swiftly to be seen. The studio was the ideal place for such feelings.

There were canvases stacked everywhere; against the insulated walls, structural beams, work benches. Others were tied together up high, where she'd need a ladder—and, better yet, a *man* to get to them and lift them down. They would be heavy.

Adam Hunt? She pondered that one. She had his phone number. She knew where he lived. Why not catch him as unaware as he'd caught her? When she had a chance, she would have him checked out by one of the law firm's investigators. She might be powerfully attracted to the man, but that was no reason not to be wary of him.

With Zizi gone and so many allegations against her, she had no hesitation in taking a close look at the stacks of canvases she *could* reach. If only she could paint like this! She had a duty to have Zizi's work shown, she thought, flooded with admiration. There was one magnificent semiabstract painting of floating tropical orchids she'd definitely take into the house.

Zizi had been a marvelous portrait painter, but

she'd veered off into semiabstract and abstract painting for some years. No matter how often Alyssa had urged Zizi to return to portraiture, it was to no avail.

"Who's around to paint?" It was always said with a wry laugh.

"Famous people would stand in line to have you paint their portraits, Zizi. You'd only have to come to the city, but just for a while."

"The only way I'll leave Flying Clouds is in a box."

And she had. But they'd taken the body, not the soul.

A few minutes later, Cleo gave such a loud melancholy howl, Alyssa had to struggle not to let out a scream. "Cleo, will you *stop!*" she flared, at the same time feeling very foolish. The spirit of Captain Richard Langford had never bothered her in the least. In fact, for years she'd believed that *anything* could happen at Flying Clouds. So why all this uneasiness now? Was it just part of the ongoing trauma of a death in the family?

She watched as Cleo took a flying leap atop a gilded birdcage with two tiny mechanical birds inside. One was sitting on a perch, the other sitting on the floor of the cage. When the handle on the side was turned, the birds fluttered about too realistically for Alyssa's liking. Birds didn't belong in cages.

"I told you before, Cleo. They're not *real* birds." Alyssa walked toward the cat. "What else are you looking at?"

She followed Cleo's solemn gaze, somewhat surprised to see an easel tucked away in a corner with a large canvas standing on it. The canvas was covered by a dark cloth.

She would never have lifted the cloth without Zizi's permission. This time she walked purposely to the easel and lifted the cloth, hooking it over the apex of the stand.

A blast like one from Antarctica blew over her. She stood rooted to the spot, her body freezing yet breaking out in a cold sweat.

Who was looking back at her?

Excruciating pain overwhelmed her. The subject of the painting was too familiar. What she had to deal with now was not the annihilation of death but an annihilation of trust. All the connections came together, each locking into the other with mechanical precision. She had thought she knew Zizi—heart, mind and soul—but she hadn't known the real Zizi at all. She only knew the face Zizi had presented to the world.

Loss. Sorrow. Utter disillusionment. Had this

painting been destined to be hidden away or destroyed like so many others?

Alyssa stood in utter silence, the artist in her fighting the wounded woman and child. Her mouth was so dry, she couldn't seem to swallow. Her face was set in an expression of mourning. Today she'd learned far more than she'd *ever* wanted.

It was a portrait. The first, to her knowledge, that Zizi had attempted in many years. It wasn't of anyone she actually *knew,* familiar or not. But she *did* know him, even if she'd never met him or ever laid eyes on him. The portrait was of a man in his prime, head and torso. His steadfast gaze was fixed on her as though he'd been waiting for this moment for such a long time. It was more than just a handsome face. It was a wonderfully captivating face, one with a swashbuckling aura. To suit the image, he wore a billowy white shirt half-open down the front. His light eyes set against the bronze of his skin and the crow-black of his hair and brows had enormous impact. The artist's acute observation—of the facial structure, the intensity of expression, the exposed arms and hands, the white fabric of his shirt—was masterly. Not *only* masterly. In so capturing the essence of her subject, the painter had almost dissolved into it, revealing herself to be profoundly, emotionally involved with her subject.

How many years after his death?
This had to be Richard Langford.

SHE WAS GRIPPED with a desperate sadness and
her heart flipped like a hooked fish in her chest.
The painted eyes—so lifelike—looking directly
into hers, were large, liquid, gold-flecked, the
color of rain. People had always asked her,
"Where did you get your eyes?" She'd never been
able to answer. Until now.

This knowledge had been waiting for her all
her life. Had Zizi never planned to tell her? Alyssa
felt tears streaming down her cheeks and running
under her chin, attended by a grief so intense she
had to grope blindly for a chair. She slumped into
it. Cleo jumped onto her lap.

*And to think that Mariel, who knew this secret,
had never even considered telling anyone.*

Why would she? To the formidable, straitlaced,
childless Mariel, it would've been both a heaven-
sent opportunity and a scandal never to be brought
to light. The coppery taste of betrayal, of a profound
disillusionment, was in Alyssa's mouth. The
woman she'd loved and admired had been unwilling to trust her or, more importantly, her mother,
Stephanie, with the truth. They had the *right* to
know. Or did Zizi have no concept of the pain and
shock it would cause if her secret ever got out?

Stephanie was Richard Langford's daughter. She, Alyssa, was his granddaughter. This *had* to be Richard Langford. It wasn't Julian Wainwright, since Adam Hunt was supposed to resemble him. They were two completely different men, different features, different coloring. Under the shock simmered a mounting rage. Zizi wasn't her great-aunt. Elizabeth Jane Calvert was her grandmother. She didn't have irrefutable evidence of it, but one would have to be blind not to see the extraordinary similarity between Richard Langford's eyes and hers.

There had been a huge conspiracy between Zizi and Mariel to keep the truth hidden.

She agonized silently, her face wet with an endless stream of tears. One door opened onto another. Her mother had no capacity for conspiracy; the truth had been kept from Stephanie as well.

Mariel, not Zizi, had decided what course to chart. Mariel, who'd made lying an art form. Mariel, the supreme manipulator.

And now Adam Hunt. That hit hard. Adam Hunt had come to Flying Clouds to confront Zizi on Julian Wainwright's behalf. He'd come knowing the identity of Zizi's child. Had he confronted Zizi with it or hadn't he been given enough time? She felt a cold hard anger in her chest. She'd have to pay Mr. Hunt a visit.

What precisely was his agenda? To prove that Julian Wainwright had *not* fathered Zizi's child? It was in his interests to do so. He would, in all probability, be one of the beneficiaries of his great-uncle's estate. No doubt he had assumed, up until recently, he would figure largely. What a *huge* disappointment his great-uncle's disclosures must have provided. She'd never encountered a single soul, no matter how well off, who'd refuse a financial windfall.

Except that Julian Wainwright *wasn't* her grandfather. Adam Hunt wasn't her cousin. She didn't want him for a cousin, anyway.

Why precisely?

That voice in her head started up again but she ignored it. Richard Langford had been the love of Zizi's life. A crucial piece of information Zizi had dared not reveal. All trace of him had been hidden from sight, until *now,* and only because Zizi's death had been a tragic, unforeseen accident. Zizi had spent her last days on earth painting her secret lover's portrait, a work in progress because Alyssa could see it wasn't quite finished. Remarkably, she was even considering how she could finish it, ideas automatically flitting into her head. Zizi had begun a painting of a man long dead, but far from dead to her. Now *she,* Zizi's granddaughter, was planning to *finish* it? It wasn't all that unnatural, she told herself. It was something artists did.

Cleo cradled in her arms, Alyssa rocked back and forth, a woman in pain plunged into a great dilemma. The sense of belonging so crucial to one's well-being had been stripped from her. Her whole world had imploded. The past was never properly buried, it was just waiting to be exhumed.

CHAPTER FIVE

SHE PARKED THE CAR in the shade of a magnificent poinciana, some thirty feet tall and more than twice as wide. Its great branches were so laden with bright scarlet flowers they curved into a perfect umbrella. She and Zizi had often painted these magnificent tropical trees, the showiest flowering trees in the world, but this was one of the finest specimens she'd ever seen.

The old Gambaro farmhouse perched high on timber stilts, once a pristine white, was now a weathered gray, the paint flaking badly in some places. Bouganvillea, allamanda and trumpet vines sprouted everywhere, and a yellow, red-splotched spider orchid, normally a tree dweller, had taken up residence in the gutter, spilling twelve-foot spikes over the roof. At least the estate agents responsible for the rental and sale of the property had kept back the encroaching jungle. There was a broad half-moon of thick, lush green lawn directly in front of the house.

She remembered the Gambaro family well. Italian in origin, they'd come to Australia in the late 1940s to work the North Queensland cane fields. The sugar industry owed a great debt to the Italian community, who'd formed the backbone of the workforce. For many years these sugar families had prospered, but when the industry suffered reversals so, too, did the fortunes of the farmers. Both Gambaro sons had abandoned life on the land for business careers in Brisbane. Mrs. Gambaro had gone to live with her daughter in New Zealand after her husband died. The old farm had been on the market for some time now.

She climbed the front steps, fully expecting to find Adam Hunt at home. The front door was wide open, as were the French doors leading onto the veranda. Cream lace curtains billowed out from the living room, cavorting in the breeze. The brilliant sunshine that poured across the veranda shone into the entrance hall. It was floored in gleaming black marble.

She didn't venture in, but called, "Is anyone home?"

No answer.

She tried a loud knock, alarming a school of tiny silver lizards that scattered into the woodwork.

"Hello?" Her voice echoed back at her.

Where *was* he? She hadn't called ahead; the intention was to catch him off guard. He had to be at home. She made her way down the steps again and around the side of the house where a prolific lavender-blue morning glory all but enveloped the two water tanks. Bats, she saw, had taken their fill of the custard apple trees and dozens of mangoes were lying on the ground. The air was heavy with the smell of overripe fruit.

"Hello?" Her voice seemed swallowed up by the density of the huge mango trees that formed the boundary of the garden. The branches were pulled down by the weight of the fruit. He had to be some-where, damn him! There was a big agricultural shed in the backyard as she recalled. A tree snake sidling along one of the branches above startled her into a mild expletive before it disappeared into the thicket of narrow dark-green leaves.

She rounded the corner of the house just as he was coming out of the shed, flicking at his bare back and chest with a hand towel. The sight of him, stripped to the waist, wearing an old pair of shorts, almost caused her to panic.

What's the matter, Alyssa? Too sexy for you?

Whatever she felt, it was suffocating. For long moments she couldn't catch her breath. She reminded herself that he had a perfect right to be walking about stripped of most of his clothes.

"Why, hello there!" He spotted her rooted to the

ground, like Daphne pursued by Apollo, turning into a tree. It made her feel extremely foolish. "Why didn't you tell me you were coming?"

Her answer was cool. "I decided to come on the off chance."

"Really?" He was moving ever closer, so physically splendid her blood fired. She dragged in a quick breath, feeling a strong urge to shield herself from his attraction, which was very, very *physical*.

"Anything of interest in the shed?" she asked, more as a cover-up than anything else. She thought he might have been shifting bags of plaster. His body, hard with muscle, was dewed with sweat and a fine white dust. He'd toweled his rich mahogany hair into a riot of waves and curls. If he'd worn a gold ring in his ear, he would've looked like the dashing pirate-hero she'd dreamed up for her childhood adventures.

Adam studied her in turn. She was beautiful, even in brilliant sunlight. No makeup that he could see, her mouth lightly glossed. He was fascinated by the way her ash-blond hair didn't fall straight; neither did it form into curls. It sort of swirled around her shoulders and down her back in long, loose, sinuous waves. He envisioned her as a model for a sea siren. "I'm using it as a studio while I'm here," he explained.

"Studio?" Her brows arched in inquiry. "Just as I suspected. You're a would-be painter."

"Not a painter," he said, gazing back at her.

"What then?" The way he was looking at her was causing odd little flutters in her heart and her stomach.

"Come and see."

She followed him across the thick springy grass, noting it, too, had been mown. "Did you do this?" She gestured around her.

"What?" He turned his head.

"Mow the grass?"

He shrugged, amused at the sternness of her tone. "I had to protect myself somehow."

"The snakes?"

"What else? I let out an involuntary yelp three or four times a day."

She had to smile. "They won't hurt you unless you're unlucky enough to tread on one. We have a pet snake called Cairo at the house. It's very fond of sliding along the banisters on the front veranda."

"I've met Cairo," he said drolly. "It was a real thrill."

"I suppose you cut Zizi's grass as well? I seem to recognize the half-moon pattern."

His face softened into a smile. "I like curves."

"Most men do." She gave a tiny derisive laugh, cursing herself for not realizing he was the one who'd cleaned up the grounds at Flying Clouds for Zizi. He was that kind of man.

A cacophony of birdcalls accompanied them to the shed, almost obliterating their attempts at conversation.

"What was the origin of the name Flying Clouds?" he asked. "It wasn't original to the house."

She waited until they reached the open doorway of the shed before answering, dangling one perfect fragrant gardenia she'd plucked from a nearby bush. "Zizi told me it was from a Thai poem. Something about the almighty sky not hindering the white clouds in their flight."

"So Elizabeth named the house?"

She sighed and glanced away so acutely conscious of his half-naked body anyone would think she'd never seen such a thing in her life. "Actually, she told me she didn't, but we both loved the name. We used to watch the flying white clouds from the widow's walk. When I was a child, coming to stay with Zizi was like living in a fairy tale. There was magic, enchantment and, to top it off, the spirit of Captain Langford walking the plantation."

"You're intensely imaginative, aren't you?"

His voice sounded oddly tender, causing something that had been tightly furled inside her to start to unravel. "Zizi and I had a remarkable facility for fitting in with the spirit world at Flying Clouds. Once when I was about twelve, I suggested we hold a séance in the old drawing room, hoping we could contact Captain Langford. Zizi really surprised me when she refused point-blank. Anyone would've thought she expected him to come at our call."

"He or one of his descendants," he said dryly. "You've found something, haven't you?"

"Why would you say that?" What was she, an open book?

"Come inside and tell me. It's too hot in the sun."

She remembered what Zizi used to say when she came into her bedroom in the mornings. *Wake up, little darling, before the sun burns a hole in you.* Curious, she preceded him into the cool interior that still smelled of rich tropical fruit.

The shed was huge and empty, except for long built-in benches that lined the walls and—

She gasped in amazement. Momentarily her eyes flew to him, then away again. "Why, you're a sculptor! This *is* your work?"

He smiled at her obvious delight. "I'm the merest amateur. I had the rare opportunity to work with a *real* sculptor, Mario La Spina."

"Mario La Spina? That's the truth?" Mario La Spina was world-famous.

"Of course. I don't lie."

"How did you manage it?" Smoothing her hair off her face, she moved toward a powerful abstract sculpture or sculptures—two pieces, one much larger than the other—in high-quality white marble. They were displayed on a broad black onyx plinth. She began to examine them, thinking they would look splendid in a big beautiful garden or a park. The taller sculpture rose protectively above the smaller one, which was lying on the plinth. To her eyes it represented some marvelous marine creature, perhaps a whale, guarding its young.

His large well-shaped hand dropped onto the bigger piece. "Mario's back from Italy. As you probably know, he studied and worked there for years. He's opened a studio in Sydney, an excellent facility with lots of space. I like the monumental nature of sculpture. I especially like working in marble. It's ideal for carving. I prefer to work in the traditional way, hammer and chisel—it hasn't changed since Michelangelo's time—rather than using modern techniques and tools."

"Very different from being an architect." She stared in fascination.

"It started as relaxation. Sometimes when the pressure of work got a bit too much, I needed to do something physical. Hammering away at a block of marble trying to discover what's hidden inside is a form of therapy." He laughed gently. "Therapy, I'm discovering, can become all-consuming."

"And you've done all this since you were here?" She fixed an intense gaze on him, watching him nod.

"No wonder La Spina took you on," she said, her eyes moving to the solid block he must have been working on when she arrived. Again it was high-quality white marble, more than six feet in height with enough depth to carve a human figure. "I'm impressed. What do you intend to do with this block?" she asked.

"I was waiting for the stone to tell me what to do." He answered seriously. "Now I'm sure."

"Are you going to tell me?" She risked a glance into his aquamarine eyes.

"No. I'll *show* you when it's finished."

Some expression in his eyes made her draw a shaky breath. She didn't quite understand what was happening to her, and so quickly. She'd always thought this level of attraction, virtually at first sight, was a wild exaggeration. "I'd love to see it," she managed, taking a few paces away. "Is there any reason you didn't tell me you were a sculptor?"

"I preferred to surprise you."

The note in his voice triggered another ava-lanche of sensations. The conversation was normal, yet it felt incredibly erotic. "So you knew I'd come?" Unconsciously her hand was caressing the texture of the marble.

"Almost certain," he admitted with a half smile. "You discovered something, didn't you?"

Watch out for him, her inner voice said. Good advice. "It just so happens I *would* like to show you something at the house if you have the time. That's why I came, but you've totally broadsided me with *this!*"

He raked back his sweat-darkened hair. In the heat it had set into crisp curls frosted with white marble dust. For a searing minute, Alyssa imagined him naked, splendid as the marble statue of *David,* whorls of curls clinging to the fine shape of his skull. "It was Elizabeth who brought us together," he said.

His presence was so magnetic she forced herself to step back. If she didn't, she thought she might do something incredibly foolish and *touch* him. Like Zizi, she was a tactile person. His body, so beautiful to the eye, would be wonderful to touch. "Did Zizi know you were a sculptor?" Her right hand gripped the raw marble block, as she tried to maintain her self-control. "Had she seen any of your work?"

He banished that notion with a wave of his hand. "As much as I might have wanted her to, Elizabeth and I didn't get that far. I never told her I was a part-time sculptor. She never came here. As I said, we were only beginning to get to know each other. I think we're in agreement that Elizabeth was a very difficult woman to know."

Alyssa frowned. "She showed you only what she meant you to see," she said, absorbed in painful memories.

He nodded. "She played out her life as a mystery."

Zizi had taken a huge step step backward in Alyssa's mind. "All I ever knew of her turns out to be next to nothing. It makes me think she didn't truly love me."

"Then think again. She adored you."

She hugged herself impulsively, unable to conceal her hurt. "But as a *child*. Not a woman she could trust with her secrets. Strangely, I never saw even a shadow of grief in her. It was exhilarating being with Zizi. There was no sense of melancholy. At least not with me. I suppose hiding her grief was one of her skills." Alyssa shifted her gaze back to the finished sculpture. "This has a lot of power," she commented, deliberately changing the subject, "but a poignancy, too."

His face took on a serious expression. "Thank you. Yours is an opinion that matters." He placed his hand on the taller sculpture and their fingers briefly touched.

It was a touch that traveled to her toes.

Keep calm, keep calm, her inner voice warned. *You don't know if you can trust this man!*

There was a silence between them that went on too long. She could feel her whole body becoming pliant. It astonished her. Was it the way those blue-green eyes met hers? There was a key to her heart that had never been turned, and this man was giving every sign of reaching out for it. Such profound attraction was mysterious; it had the quality of a dream. How could she feel like this about a man who'd so recently entered her life and under such grim circumstances?

The voice inside her head answered: *Easily!* Everyone was trying to find a soul mate, the one person who could complete them. Zizi had lived her life thinking she'd found hers. And now Alyssa couldn't deny her attraction to Adam Hunt. He possessed a sexual radiance any woman would find impossible to ignore. It would be easy enough to abandon herself to a brief affair. It might even be therapeutic. Maybe she'd discover reserves of sensuality in herself she'd never known she had?

Instead she did the smart thing. She moved her hand, thus breaking the spell.

Adam broke the silence, thrusting a hand through the thick waves of his hair. "I'm having a shower." His manner was brisk. "I'm covered in marble dust, as you can see. Come back to the house. Why don't you have a cup of coffee while you wait."

WHEN HE RETURNED, fresh and clean, he stood unobserved for a moment watching her. She was relaxed, head back, eyes closed, sitting in the old squatter's chair he'd painted white. A single beam of sunlight fell on a long lock of ash-blond hair, glittering like liquid sunshine.

An almost unbearable sensation of joy seized him, a joy he sometimes felt with his sculpture. The dress she was wearing was very pretty, very feminine. It was sleeveless for the heat with a low oval neckline revealing the upward curves of her breasts. The gauzy fabric was the color of the sky, patterned with pink and yellow flowers. Behind her, as a background, was a passion-fruit vine that covered the lattice. The purple and white flowers were out in all their glory, giving off the heady sweet-tangy scent of the harvest to come. It was a painterly composition. Such beauty inspired tenderness. He felt as if he was drowning in it.

Soon after he'd moved into the farmhouse, he'd done some work on the veranda. There were dozens of empty pots and planters stacked away in the shed, now filled with luxurious plants. A cool green haven, much like he imagined the Gambaro family would've had it. Ferns fanned prolifically out of pots and hanging baskets; philo-dendrons grew in wicker baskets. From the cor-rugated iron roof he'd hung flights of the beautiful butterfly orchids and several species of dendrobi-ums, including the lovely deep purple Cooktown orchid, the state floral emblem.

Alyssa's eyes suddenly flew open, as if she was aware of being watched. Abruptly she sat forward, turning her head. Their eyes met and she felt acutely conscious of strong feelings that flooded through her. She felt powerless to prevent it. Their instant intimacy shocked and even alarmed her. Attraction was far more complex than friendship. Her reaction to him made her feel she'd been ambushed.

"You've done a remarkably good job of turning this back into the old fernery." She made an effort to reduce her excitement. Excitement was conta-gious around him. "Mrs. Gambaro would love you. I can still see her watering all the hanging baskets."

"They effectively cool the house. All set to go?"

"I am." She stood, bending to pick up her cup and saucer.

"Leave it," he told her. "I'll collect them later. I'm anxious to find out what you've discovered."

"Why wouldn't you be? Isn't that what you wanted?" How could she be so infatuated with him and yet so uncertain of his agenda? He looked extraordinarily vibrant in the heat that made others wilt. He'd washed his hair and thrown on a short-sleeved white cotton shirt and khaki slacks. If his uncle Julian had looked like this, Zizi must've had one heck of a time deciding between lovers.

"I'm doing this for *Julian*," he said, his tone quiet but intense.

"Don't get up your hopes," she warned.

They were at the front door a moment later when they saw a blue four-wheel drive parked a few feet away from Alyssa's rented car.

"That'll be Gina," he said.

She felt the oddest sensation she hoped had nothing to do with jealousy. "Just say the word if you want me to leave."

His eyes pinned her. "Don't jump to conclusions. Gina works for a real estate company."

"Aaaah!" She took a drawn-out breath. "Are you married, Adam?" She should've asked long before this. Why hadn't she? Had attraction made her blind, deaf and dumb?

Amusement softened his expression. "What would you do if I said yes?"

"I'd ask what are you doing up here without your wife. And kids?"

"Have a heart," he groaned.

With a wash of relief, she interpreted that as confirming he was a bachelor.

A very attractive brunette, on the voluptuous side,

slid out of the 4WD and began to sashay toward them. "Adam!" she called in a honeyed voice.

The only thing missing was a Carmen-like rose behind her ear. "I could come back another time," Alyssa muttered.

"Let's see what she wants."

"I would've thought that was obvious," she answered dryly. "She wants to see you. Why don't I go home? You can follow when you can."

"I have to follow you up, anyway," he was swift to point out. "You won't want to be driving me back here."

"True, but I was prepared to do it."

Gina, now at the bottom of the steps, hesitated fractionally. "Hi, Adam. I was passing by, so I thought I'd pop in and say hello." She glanced at Alyssa as she spoke. "I know you, don't I?" she asked. "Ms. Calvert's niece?"

"Great-niece," Alyssa corrected with a smile. "We've never met, but I know your face, too."

"Gina Rossi. I'm from around here. I tried life in Brisbane for a few years, but I'm back home again. I work for Haven Homes."

"I'm sorry, Gina," Adam smoothly intervened. "Don't stand out there in the hot sun. Please come up. We were just leaving but it's not urgent."

Gina, her thick glossy hair shining a dark plum in the sun, was clearly disappointed.

"Look, why don't you come over later?" Alyssa was already walking to the steps. "You really don't have to make it today. Tomorrow would do." Her tone implied pure business.

"Today's fine." He fixed his eyes on her briefly.

Gina mounted the steps on high heels that showed off her shapely legs. She wasn't tall, but deliciously curvy, with lustrous dark eyes and glowing olive skin. She was dressed very smartly in a tomato-red outfit with a black trim. Perhaps a bit too smartly for a country estate agent, but there were very few men who wouldn't be pleased to see her.

"Nice to meet you, Alyssa," Gina said, spoiling it with a message Alyssa was meant to catch. *Hands off!*

SHE SAW THE OLD vagrant again as she drove home. She'd first sighted him the day she'd arrived and once or twice since. This time he wasn't shambling along the road out of town, unseasonably dressed in a tracksuit with the hood pulled over his head—no doubt to protect himself from the sun—but standing in the middle of a field sown with a million yellow wildflowers. She almost waved, but then thought better of it. He might find his way to Flying Clouds. The tropical North was the ideal place to lead the vagrant life. At least he'd never starve and he could always wash himself in the sea. She wondered briefly what had started him on his path.

CLEO WAS WAITING for her when she got home, staring at her with omniscient eyes.

Didn't come with you, eh?

Alyssa actually found herself answering. "It wasn't like that. One of his girlfriends turned up." She retrieved the key from the flowering pot and then unlocked the door, prompting Cleo to leap off the planter's chair and slip into the house.

IT MUST HAVE BEEN a short visit because he arrived some thirty minutes later. Perhaps they'd agreed to meet that evening. There was an excellent little Italian restaurant in the village. Alyssa let him ring the doorbell twice before she went to answer it.

"Ah, there you are!" She eyed him coolly. "Much earlier than I expected."

He raised his hands in a parody of conciliation. "I had no idea you were so interested."

"*I'm* not interested, Gina is. She's very glamorous for a country estate agent."

"I think she's hoping to move up in life." His tone was dry. "May I come in?"

"Certainly." She stood back from the door. "We

need to go out to the studio. There's something there I want you to see."

"Splendid! Lead the way. Is it a painting?"

That stopped her in her tracks. She lifted her chin, eyes narrowing suspiciously. Perhaps he'd already explored Zizi's studio at his leisure.

"Well?" He didn't look away.

Hear him out, the voice in her head said. But she answered in cool, barely pleasant tones, "I'd like to trust you, Adam, but somehow I *can't.* Did Zizi show you her studio or have you availed yourself of the opportunity to take a look around yourself?"

"It was neither," he told her. "The only paintings I've seen are the ones in the house. I think you owe me an apology."

Her laugh was humorless. "Not yet. Maybe not ever. You have to prove yourself to me first."

Cleo, having cleverly sensed the strained atmosphere, chose that moment to bound into the hallway. "Ah, Cleo, here to protect me!" Adam bent to scoop up the cat, cradling her in his arms. "How's it going, girl?" he asked, brushing a hand over the Abyssinian's sleek head.

So, Cleo had ousted her in favor of *him!* "I assume you fed her," Alyssa said, as though that explained Cleo's nod of approval.

"Someone had to," he returned mildly. "Cleo and I are pals."

They moved out the back door, walking beneath the covered walkway with its canopy of Thai gold bouganvillea. "How do you manage at night here all alone?" he asked.

She clicked her tongue. "God, you sound like my father. I suppose you've already talked to him?"

"No, ma'am, I'm leaving that to you. You know he's not happy about you being here on your own."

No way was she going to tell him that for the first time in her life, she felt uncomfortable at Flying Clouds. She didn't tell him about her disquieting sense of being *watched,* or the way she and Cleo had taken to listening for footsteps at night. "Don't worry. I've got plenty of ghosts to protect me." Her voice echoed her irritation. "No one comes near the place. The sign clearly says Private Road."

"You feel that's enough to keep intruders out?"

Heat was in her bones, in her flesh. Sunlight danced in front of her eyes. The birds shrieked and darted from tree to tree in a whir of brilliantly colored feathers. "Are you deliberately trying to make me nervous?"

"Of course not, but I share your father's concerns. Why not invite a friend to stay with you?" He caught up with her. "Elizabeth told me about…Brett, isn't it?"

"What *didn't* Zizi tell you?" she asked crossly. "She knew very well that Brett and I had split up."

He appeared pleased. "I wasn't sure. Some instinct told me Elizabeth thought he wasn't half good enough for you. What about a girlfriend?" he suggested.

"*No*," she said shortly. "My friends have jobs. Maybe you mean well, but my safety isn't your concern. I'm perfectly all right on my own."

"So you're not bothered by the aloneness."

"I'm *not* alone. Cleo is no ordinary cat. She could stab you with her whiskers." She turned to face him. "Surely you're not getting around to asking me if you can sleep over?"

A smile broke out—it was a long time since she'd seen a smile like that. It lit up his whole face, like a brilliant sun dispels dark clouds. "I assure you, Alyssa, you could count on me to act like a perfect gentleman. You can see how Cleo trusts me."

"She remembers all those gourmet dinners," Alyssa responded tartly. "Anyway, you might want to pack up and go home once I show you what I discovered."

"Sounds significant."

"It floored me," she said simply. "But then, I don't imagine you'll feel the same way."

"What's that supposed to mean?" They stood confronting each other outside the barn door.

"Aren't you the one with all the inside information? Most of which you're keeping to yourself."

He didn't deny it.

Her back curved, Cleo sprang out of his arms, stalking into the barn. Adam stood back to allow Alyssa to enter, then followed, his eyes moving quickly all around the interior. His whistle when it came was low and appreciative. "This is a veritable Aladdin's cave!"

"You're absolutely *sure* you haven't checked it over?" she asked, her tone unashamedly blunt.

He continued to stare. "You're the most suspicious woman I've ever met. I *told* you I haven't. Let that be an end to it." He paused. "Elizabeth took an awful risk, especially at her age, living alone with all these treasures. There are more than enough in the house, but look at all this. Langford left it all to her."

"She knew him—just like you said."

"Like *Julian* said," he corrected her sharply. "I know he truly believed that with Langford dead he would realize his dream of marrying Elizabeth."

"Except she loved Richard Langford. Dead or alive. I'm sorry about Julian, but Zizi longed for one man and one man only. That was her tragedy. We have to go upstairs to the loft."

"Lead on," he invited. "She could've had a brilliant career. Julian would have given her every encouragement. He was so proud of her. He swears she loved him—but that was before

Langford sailed into her life and ruined it, or so Julian claimed."

"I think you're right," she agreed somberly. "If you look like your great-uncle, he must've been a handsome man."

"Does this mean you find *me* attractive?" he asked.

She didn't reply until they were on the upper level. "Handsomeness, in the sense of good regular features, and *attractiveness* don't necessarily go hand in hand."

"So, you're saying I don't have it? I think *you're* beautiful. If I overlook your suspicious nature, I could even find you attractive."

"It's over here," she said with lofty disdain.

"Are you sure Cleo can't talk?" he asked, as the cat leaped up beside the ornamental Parisian birdcage, turning to check on Adam's progress.

"She hasn't as long as I've known her. But we do have a telepathic rapport." Alyssa moved to the covered easel, waited until he joined her, then threw back the enveloping cloth, making a huge effort to keep herself under control. No way in the world was she going to crumple in front of Adam Hunt.

The silence was absolute.

In a world full of fluttering, darting, shrieking birds, there wasn't a single sound. Even the dancing dust motes seemed to fall still. When

Adam spoke, his voice vibrated across the loft. "I'm shocked." He turned and stared at her.

"Imagine how *I* felt. I nearly fainted."

He reached out to gently touch the painted surface. "It's got to be Langford. What a guy!"

"That doesn't necessarily mean he was a *good* guy."

"This portrait says he was everything in the world to Elizabeth. I'm sure she not only captured a remarkable likeness, but I feel as if I can see the man's *soul*. I think he might've been in hell, caught between two worlds—separated from Elizabeth for long periods so he could return to his family. In all likelihood he loved them as well and felt duty-bound to support them. He couldn't have known he was going to meet Elizabeth and fall madly in love with her."

"Then love is a madness?" she asked quietly, obscurely envious of such a grand passion.

"Obsessive love, yes. It would be akin to being put under a spell with no hope of finding an antidote. Two people captive, unable to imagine life without each other." There was pity mixed with his fascination. "The painting is recent. Not quite finished, either."

"The background mostly," she said.

"So this is the man who won Elizabeth's heart and soul," he said—for the first time without condemnation. "The old photographs don't do him justice."

"Old photographs?" Alyssa faced him. "Did Zizi show you photographs?"she asked in an impassioned voice.

"Richard Langford wasn't only one of the Langford dynasty, he was a famous yachtsman. I've been sailing Sydney Harbour myself since I was a boy. I've seen photographs of him taken with his crew."

"Well, good for you!" She was almost totally discomposed.

"Don't make matters worse, Alyssa," he said. "You have absolutely nothing to fear from me. Actually *I'm* the one in danger."

"How is that?" She directed her anger at him.

"I could fall in love with you. Ever thought of that?"

She turned her face away. "I'd feel sorry for you if you did. I'm off love."

"You mean you saw the error of your ways with Brett?"

She swung back, the color mounting to her face. "Absolutely none of your business."

"I stand reproved. I can't say I'm off love, but I've never loved any woman to the extent that I'd give up my bachelor status."

"You're probably too set in your ways," she

answered tartly. "It's a cautionary tale, this illicit love affair, but Zizi loved Richard Langford until the day she died. Is there anything really wrong with loving?" she asked, looking closely at the portrait. Richard Langford's striking gaze met her own. He was so lifelike, he might have been trying to escape from the canvas.

"I suppose there could be when it involves hurting other people," Adam said. "I have to say that from this portrait—and it tells us a great deal—he looks like the kind of man who'd inspire everlasting love. Even Julian concedes he was a larger-than-life character, very much the charmer, handsome, rich, a renowned yachtsman. But *married* with two children. Julian says they should have kept away from each other, instead of chasing after catastrophe. Poor old Julian!" He gave vent to a sigh. "The saddest thing is that Elizabeth might have married him if Langford hadn't come into her life."

"Maybe," Alyssa said, raising her eyes to the portrait.

"You resemble him," Adam said quietly.

"Yes, I do."

"No one could miss it. Least of all, an artist. Even without DNA testing, it looks very much like Richard Langford was your grandfather. *Not* Julian."

She felt an urge to lash out at him, not understanding why. "You must feel a lot better now that's settled. You came here armed with all sorts of inside knowledge. You knew my mother, Stephanie, is Zizi's child. The only thing you didn't know was whether or not Julian's her father. Did you confront Zizi with this?"

He shook his head, eyes returning to the portrait. "No time. I intended to at the right moment, but I never got the chance."

"I'm supposed to believe you?" She drew away.

"I think at the moment you've got too much going on in your head to believe anybody."

She couldn't deny it. Her body language betrayed her agitation. "So now we know. Or we're almost certain we do. Julian wasn't the father of Zizi's child. That was the role of her secret lover, Richard Langford. So there's no need for you to worry about your inheritance anymore. It's safe. My mother *isn't* Julian's daughter. I'm not your—"

That was as far as she got.

"Stop." Before she could move or say another word he hauled her into his arms, his face taut with anger and an arousal he couldn't hide.

She made no attempt to ward him off. Her heart leaped and next thing, his mouth covered hers, drawing her headlong into the kind of passionate embrace she had never before experienced or even known existed. Her blood fired, her body quickened. Under her thin dress she felt naked. There was a dull roaring in her ears. Her body was melting, fusing against his, showing him how frantically she wanted this contact. She couldn't *think* at all. She could only absorb the pleasure.

The kiss was fierce. It was something they both wanted, both craved. A mad mingling of hostility and blind arousal. Then, astonishingly, it was transformed. The hunger and passion remained but the sense of conflict became a ravishing tenderness.

"Oh, God!" She pulled away shaking, almost losing her balance.

"Steady!" He caught her, deliberately holding on. "Don't expect me to say I'm sorry. Kissing you was the only way to stop you."

"I don't think I could bear you to do it again." She had the strangest sensation in her chest.

"But you know I will."

She could scarcely speak. "Can't you understand how I feel? I hate you for starting all this, you and your precious Julian. I hate you for keeping things from me. I hate all the deception."

His voice betrayed a parallel level of emotion. "I don't blame you, Alyssa, but isn't what I told you more than enough to deal with?"

She didn't answer, so violently aroused she felt she was only making a fool of herself. Anger was an antidote to desire. "How could Zizi have kept so much from us? I feel like the ground's given way beneath my feet. What am I going to do now? Your job is over. Mine has only begun. Where do I go with this? I swear my mother knows nothing. My grandmother—damn it, *Mariel*—knows it all. She took Zizi's baby. She reared my mother as her own daughter. The two sisters, they tricked everyone. That was *their* secret. I swear the man I knew as my grandfather had no idea, either. Lewis was treated like a fool, just like the rest of us. I have one question—why was Julian so sure Zizi's child might have been his? They must have been lovers."

He stepped back, as though putting a safe distance between them. "Alyssa, please *stop*. I don't want you to think badly of Julian. He loved Elizabeth. Maybe Elizabeth put up a fight for a normal life. Maybe she knew in her heart that Langford would never leave his wife and children. He probably told her just that. Apparently one of the children was handicapped in some way. Maybe she tried to make a go of it with Julian, maybe she desperately needed comfort. Julian loved her, and I know she had deep feelings for him. What she felt for Langford was the stuff of fiction, love that goes beyond the grave. But that sort of love can destroy lives along the way. You saw what happened to Elizabeth. She subordinated her talents to the memory of Langford. She turned into a recluse. She simply shut down."

Alyssa couldn't control the tears that welled in her eyes. "What I can't understand is how she could give her child away. She wasn't in desperate circumstances. Why did she *do* it? She had the child of the man she loved. Maybe he wasn't about to break up his marriage but he could have supported her through it all. I don't understand how Zizi could give her baby up. It goes against everything she was. I thought Zizi was as open and bright as sunlight when she was as murky as…as hell." Her voice broke.

Adam tried to ease her pain. "Langford's death destroyed her. She must have been in a terrible state. Survivors of tragedy often suffer a peculiar sense of guilt. She must have felt she didn't have it in her to rear a child. She could even have thought she'd be a bad mother. Who knows what went through her mind? I understood from Julian that she had some sort of breakdown. That would go a long way toward explaining it. Her sister, on the other hand, was desperate for a child. Elizabeth must've believed Mariel would be a good mother. Obviously, the two of them colluded to make it appear Mariel had given birth. Everyone accepted it. Mariel would've had to stay with

Elizabeth toward the end of her pregnancy, and together they stage-managed it."

Yes, they were guilty of that. Alyssa turned away feeling chilled to the bone.

Adam's voice was steady enough. "Julian would have married her even knowing she was carrying Langford's child. He *adored* her. He still does. Most love affairs are fairly fragile. Elizabeth inspired grand passion."

Alyssa gave a wild little laugh. "And yet for all the grand passion Zizi settled for *crumbs*."

"Only she considered those crumbs the greatest banquet of her life," Adam answered quietly. "Love isn't rational. It can happen when one least expects it. Hearts are given on sight. Irreversible decisions are made. That's what happened with Elizabeth and Richard. Richard couldn't navigate his way around it. He loved his wife and children, but he couldn't find it in himself to give Elizabeth up. He had lost himself in her and she in him. Even with Richard drowned at sea, Elizabeth couldn't put that love to rest. Take this painting. Her last thoughts were of him."

Alyssa gave a moan of agreement. She turned back to the portrait, meeting the painted gaze. "There's no remote possibility we're mistaken?"

He shook his head. "Those eyes and the arch of the brows speak volumes."

"Do you suppose that if Zizi hadn't died so unexpectedly she would've told you the true story?" she asked sadly. "She could've sworn you and Julian to secrecy. She was good at that. After all, Julian only wanted to know whether Zizi's child was his."

"You don't think the truth should see the light of day?" he asked.

"That kind of truth can destroy lives."

"But doesn't your mother have a right to know?"

"Oh, Adam!" She appealed to him. "Easy enough to say! My mother's spent her entire life as someone else. It may seem odd to you, but I was even closer to Zizi than Mom was, although they loved each other. Mom told me once that Mariel didn't encourage their relationship. Mariel has a very jealous streak. The whole situation has potential for great harm. Surely you can see that?"

"Of course I can," he said gravely, "but if you don't tell your mother what you know, the truth may be lost forever. The choice is yours, Alyssa. You have nothing to fear from Julian. Or me. Elizabeth's secret is yours to keep—or to share."

She raised stricken eyes to him. "You seem genuinely concerned, but I've come to the conclusion I'm a very poor judge of people. From the way you've spoken, Julian will be bitterly disappointed, not to say devastated, to learn that

Zizi didn't have *his* baby. What did happen between them to make him think there was a possibility?"

"God knows!" Adam shrugged. "Perhaps Langford was away at the crucial time. He was a public figure with many responsibilites."

"And an adulterer." Alyssa was trying very hard to come to terms with that. "As you said, he probably had no intention of leaving his wife and children. He used Zizi. Used up her youth and robbed her of a wonderful career."

Adam sighed. "We keep going around and around in circles. That was *her* choice, Alyssa. Langford was her world. When she lost him, it's as though she lost herself. He haunted her until the day she died. Now they're both gone."

"Where are his love letters? She must have received some. She would've kept them. Zizi threw out nothing, let alone something so important. She kept the beautiful dresses he must have bought her when they went on their travels. Shoes, hats… I'll bet there's jewelry stashed away somewhere, too. There are just so many places to look!" she added forlornly.

Adam glanced at the paintings stacked high up the walls. "There must be a ladder around someplace?"

"Of course!" She wanted his help and yet she didn't. "How did Zizi get all those paintings up there, anyway? She couldn't have managed it herself."

"A handyman could have done it for her, possibly Mr. Gambaro. Elizabeth spoke fondly of the family. In fact, she told me she'd given them a couple of her paintings, probably for favors rendered."

Although she'd done nothing to warrant it, Alyssa felt exhausted. Her whole body was trembling. How could she ever think of Adam as a stranger again? The passionate kiss they'd shared had been a revelation.

It seemed to cement a powerful connection that had traveled down the years.

CHAPTER SIX

SHE HELD HER BREATH while he lowered the first stack of paintings, all large, onto the top of a teak cabinet, and then one by one, transferred them to the floor where Alyssa set them up. There were a dozen canvases—a jewel-like interior of the house, tropical landscapes, a series of island paintings, three of the rain forest lit by white orchids. The last was a lovely painting devoted to a view from the widow's walk. The depiction of the sparkling turquoise sea was so realistic one could practically dive into it.

"Why don't we take a break?" she suggested. "You must be tired." Up and down the ladder, covered in dust, no word of complaint.

"Not at all!" he responded vigorously. "Well, no one can say Elizabeth didn't work hard. I suppose it kept her sane. An icy cold beer would go down well."

She pulled a little face. "I'd like to tell you I have some in the fridge, but I don't drink beer."

"Anything cold," he said carelessly. "I'd like to

keep going for a while if that's okay with you. I thought we could have dinner at Renato's later."

Excitement spurted. "That would be nice, but we might have a bit of trouble getting in. It's very popular. This part of the world never lacks for tourists."

"I've taken the liberty of booking a table." His answer was just slightly dry.

"Have you really!" He had no business being so sure of her.

"Does it matter? Now what about that drink? I'm the one up on the ladder."

When she returned with two tall frosted glasses of homemade lime cordial topped with sparkling mineral water, she found him bent over a stack of canvases he'd propped up against the legs of tables and chairs. Cleo was circling the area, giving every appearance of being deeply excited by this latest batch.

"What have you got there?" Alerted, Alyssa quickly set down the tray. "Adam?" He seemed to have fallen into a trance.

"You tell me," he muttered, his tone odd.

Her heart did a curious flip-flop in her chest. "I hope they're not shocking."

"They're not nudes if that's what you mean. Well…partly." His face showed no trace of amusement.

She fell into a kneeling position beside him on the rug. He put his hand on her shoulder. "Behold—Elizabeth the mermaid!"

There were four paintings in all. Without a trace of whimsy, all were charged with enchantment. It was Zizi's face so beautiful when young. There was the swirl of long blond hair, the tilt of small naked breasts, the human female torso merging into the long iridescent silver-green tail of a fish. She was depicted floating or swimming, or—as in one painting—riding a milk-white steed with a snowy plume and tail, in the deep blue depths of the ocean. In the background of each painting was the wreck of a yacht listing on the seabed. Its name was clearly visible. *Miranda*. Richard Langford's yacht. In each painting the mermaid wore a garland of pearls and miniature seashells around her head, but around her neck she wore a beautiful necklace of diamonds from which hung a large emerald teardrop that fell between her naked breasts.

"These are *extraordinary,*" Alyssa whispered. "Zizi always did have magic in her. I'm not surprised she painted a fantasy realm."

He nodded, his expression reflecting her delight. "They have an air of brooding about them, don't you think? Mermaids have been around for centuries. They're part of the mythology of many cultures. Artists, painters, sculptors haven't been able to resist their lure."

"Writers, too." Alyssa was carefully studying the painted sea vegetation. It was botanically accurate as she knew from her open undersea exploration of the Reef area.

"But why Pegasus and not a dolphin?" she asked. "It *is* Pegasus, the winged horse?"

He slanted a mock-chiding glance at her. "Have you forgotten your Greek mythology? Poseidon, the god of the sea, who controlled all the waters on earth, was also the god who created horses. His most beautiful creation was the untamed Pegasus our mermaid is riding here, although I seem to recall that only Poseidon was allowed to ride him. But never mind, these paintings are extremely appealing. Look at the sparkle she gets into those diamonds and the depth of color of the emerald. I'd say that necklace was painted from life."

This was something Alyssa had already considered. "You think it could be hidden away somewhere in the house?"

He shrugged a broad shoulder. "You know better than I do that there are countless places to hide a velvet pouch or two."

"You're also assuming Richard Langford gave her that necklace?"

"Why not? He gave her plenty else. He was a rich man. Besides, doesn't a man give jewelry to the woman he loves?"

She nodded, her mind awhirl. "It's sad about the wreck of the *Miranda*."

"Yes," he said in a clipped voice.

"You sound as if you don't like Richard Langford, the man."

"Alyssa, I need to be on Julian's side," he said. "He loved Elizabeth, too. Without measure or constraint. I was primed to believe Richard Langford was the monster who took Julian's woman from him when—as a married man—he had no right to." He released a pent-up breath. "Julian insists Langford should've left, resisted temptation. Instead he took advantage of Elizabeth and in the end turned her into a recluse. In Julian's book, Richard Langford destroyed the woman he professed to love."

"But Richard Langford was my grandfather." The portrait had changed everything for her. She could no longer harden her heart against him.

"At least that means *we're* not related," Adam said with a sigh of relief. "That's the only plus so far as I can see."

"A big plus. Your inheritance is safe." She raised challenging eyes to him.

"And not the only one," he muttered. "I wouldn't

want to be driven by desire for my *cousin,*" he said in a low voice. "I wouldn't want to go around wanting to kiss her, to touch her, to get to know and understand everything about her. No, Alyssa, it's much better that you're *not* my cousin."

With his eyes on her, she could feel the air being sucked out of her lungs. It was like being underwater for too long. She dared not move. She dared not speak. He drew her to her feet, his arms enveloped her. It was marvelous to be held close by him; it was also rash. Things were happening much too fast. At the same time, that made it easier to understand how a powerful attraction had ambushed Zizi and Richard.

"Can a man be damned for desire?" Adam asked her gently, his chin resting on the top of her head.

"*You* damned Richard just before."

"So I did! That was my head speaking. My heart says desire makes us very vulnerable."

His mouth on hers was as perfect a sensation as she had ever known and so natural it thrilled her to the core. It was as though he'd divined her hidden cravings and was acting on them. Was this the legendary bolt of lightning she had read about but never believed in, or had he planned on seducing her? Her recent experience of being manipulated by Brett should have urged caution. Instead she'd leaped. The parameters of her world were no longer stable. They were bending outward and upward, fluid in their motion…

A SUDDEN GUST of wind blew one of the barn's double doors shut with a resounding clatter. Both of them pulled back, startled out of their lovemaking. Air rushed across the downstairs space, knocking something over that fell with a noisy crash.

Alyssa was forced to wait for her heartbeat to slow. "I suspect someone did that on purpose," she said, trying unsuccessfully to laugh away the high emotion. "A warning that this is all going too fast?"

"Does it worry you?" he asked. His hands slid caressingly down her back, molding her body to him.

"It should worry you, too. Anyway, how do I know you're not manipulating me in some way?"

"You're not over your fiancé."

"Yes, I am." She stared back at him. "But there's some ambivalence in you, Adam. You could be looking for revenge, for all I know. Richard Langford took Zizi from Julian. So you take me."

"You really think I'm capable of that?"

"Yes."

"The *taking* part I admit to." He bent to kiss her. "I want you to desire my touch so much you can't resist me."

"I'll bet I could!"

He stepped back, holding up his hands in mock surrender. "Is this when you ask me to go?"

"No!" She shook her head so vigorously her hair slid around her throat. "I happen to need a man around right now, and that's you. You've put yourself squarely into this. There are so many heavy things that need lifting and you're strong. Besides, two of us can explore more quickly than one."

"So, I'm allowed to make myself useful?" He laughed quietly.

"That's right." She moved past him to check on what had fallen downstairs. "You're as obsessed with this as I am!"

WHEN THEY ENTERED the restaurant, the first person they saw was Gina Rossi. She was seated at a central table with an impressive-looking older man, dark hair in retreat from his forehead. Her father? Not with the way she was dressed, or her body language.

Gina, facing the lobby, had actually seen them first. She gave a brilliant smile—that might or might not have been false—and a little wave. They responded before being whisked off by a waiter to a quiet corner table. "I think we'll see more of Gina before the evening's over," Adam predicted.

"Just so long as you didn't drop her for me," she said dryly.

"No date was made. The guy in the Armani suit is Dave Belasco."

"The property developer?" Alyssa waited until they were seated at their table to ask. She looked around at their surroundings with pleasure. The table was covered with a crisp, spotlessly clean white cloth. The white napkins had been stiffened into bishops' hats. There was a small posy of native orchids as a centerpiece, a white tapered candle in a silver candlestick beside it.

"I told you Gina was dead set on going places."

"He's not married? He must be in his fifties."

"There is such a thing as divorce, you know," he murmured. "If Dave proposes to Gina—which I somehow doubt—she'd become wife *numero tres*. Are you hungry?"

"Now that you mention it, starving. You said *Dave*. Do you know him?"

His nod was casual. "Our firm's done work for him in the past. My father designed his luxury resort on Angel Island. I was Dad's assistant. I'll say hello before we leave."

"It's a small world," she observed. *Too* small.

"It always is with the major firms," he said casually. "The best architects work all over. You can be based in Singapore or Hong Kong and still get plenty of commissions back in Australia. For that matter, I could work up here in the North."

"Would you consider it?" she asked in surprise.

He lifted one shoulder. "I could picture it. I've learned a great deal working for my father, but I'm ready to cut myself free. Dad and I don't always see eye to eye on design. I have my own ideas. He's more traditional. As far as he's concerned, I'm *assertively* modern. His words. Sculptural, I call it. I'm really a sculptor at heart, though Dad was very proud when I won the Nathan-Gordon award for domestic architecture last year."

"As well he might be," Alyssa said, familiar with the prestigious award.

"Very rich clients wanted a beach house, but not your usual beach house. They wanted something very elegant with plenty of private space and accommodation for half a dozen guests. The place had to be sensitive to the environment and yet take full advantage of the spectacular views. The views aren't quite as good as yours," he conceded. "Flying Clouds is a marvelous house, very atmospheric."

"That's because of the ghosts," Alyssa said lightly.

"And living beside the sea is always seductive."

She nodded. "The sea's always had a powerful influence on me." Changing the subject, she said, "I thought we got through a lot this afternoon. But nothing that really helped. No love letters, no private papers, no velvet pouches full of sparkling jewels."

"And you'd never have done it without my help." He gave her a quirky smile.

"Agreed. The seafood here is wonderful. Local, of course. I think I'll have lobster. Seared scallops with white truffle butter to start."

"It's nice to meet a woman who enjoys good food." His eyes moved over her with a flame of pleasure. She was wearing a silk dress patterned in a swirl of amethyst, teal, turquoise and emerald. The candlelight changed the color of her eyes to violet. He was bowled over by the sheer exhilaration of being with her. "Now what shall we drink?" He opened the wine list, holding it in his tanned hands.

Hands that could draw complicated designs and sculpt objects of beauty and power out of marble, Alyssa thought.

"A Sauvignon blanc?" he suggested. "Or would you prefer something else?"

"Sauvignon blanc is fine." Despite all the recent shocks, she had a fervent wish to make the most of these few hours. Time enough to find answers to the moral dilemma that plagued her. Time enough to confront her family. And yet she was plagued by the worry that there might be more wisdom in letting the past stay hidden.

Once Pandora's box was opened, it could never be closed.

THEY LEFT THE restaurant well after ten. Alyssa stood admiring the striking flower arrangement that brightened the foyer, while Adam had a word with Dave Belasco. This gave Gina—Alyssa had caught her watching them closely throughout the evening—the opportunity to cross over to where Alyssa was standing.

"No need to ask if you enjoyed yourself." She smiled brightly. "I could see your face."

Despite the smile, Gina made "it" sound like a crime. "And you? You enjoyed yourself as well?" Alyssa asked, determined to be pleasant. "The food here has always been good."

"So it is. A bit expensive." Gina was sizing up what Alyssa was wearing. "Has Adam found what he's been looking for?"

Alyssa felt a decided jolt. "I didn't know he was looking for anything in particular. He has quite a lot of vacation time, I understand. This is a glorious part of the world. I daresay he'll get around to exploring the offshore islands and the Reef."

"No need to tell me!" Gina laughed brightly. "But it *was* Ms. Calvert he came to see, wasn't it?" She swept on. "Such a sad thing, her accident! I expect you'll be returning home soon? Maybe you're even thinking of putting the property on the market." There was a speculative expression on Gina's face. "I could find you a buyer in no time.

Just between the two of us—" she cupped a hand to the side of her mouth "—Adam's shown an interest. Or perhaps he's already told you? I have a hunch Dave's after him to build his dream house, and your place would make a great base for Adam. I hear Ms. Calvert acquired a lot of beautiful things. According to rumor, anyway." She rolled her dark eyes. "It's the most exotic house in the whole region, though I have to say it has a rather *eerie* feel to it."

To her credit Alyssa didn't betray the anger that was coursing through her. "I had no idea you'd ever been to Flying Clouds?"

Gina looked her right in the eye. "Well, I haven't been *inside,*" she elaborated, "although I think Adam would have shown me if I'd pushed it. But I've been all over the grounds. It was a real jungle. I half expected to see Tarzan swinging through the trees. Adam and I had gone for a swim, then a long lazy lunch. I asked him to show me around."

A chill was running through Alyssa's body, moving from her fingertips to her toes. "He took you on a tour of the grounds?"

Gina's near-black eyes glistened like a bird's. "It doesn't bother you, does it? After all, I am in the real estate business. Look here, I wouldn't want to get Adam into any trouble." She hesitated uncertainly.

"He's been so nice to me." She smiled as though there was no need to spell out what *nice* meant.

"Be that as it may, Gina, it's a pity you didn't ask first," Alyssa managed to say. "I wouldn't advise taking or giving any more tours without permission." Although her voice sounded calm enough, some of her anger must have showed on her face. "Flying Clouds is private property. I assure you it's *not* going on the market. I'll say good-night now." She started to turn away.

"I'm sorry if I've offended you!" Feline claws sank into Alyssa's flesh. "It was never my intention. Will you let me know if you ever change your mind?"

Alyssa looked pointedly at Gina's hand on her arm. "I'm not selling, Gina. You can take that as final."

THEY'D LEFT THE village well behind. A strained silence rode with them.

Adam finally broke it, flicking a glance at her set profile. "What's the problem?"

"No problem." She suddenly felt like crying and despised herself for it. The wine, she supposed, and the stress of everything. Once again her judgment was called into question.

"You seem to have stopped talking since your little chat with Gina."

She couldn't deny it. "Gina's a very pushy person. Just like *you*."

He shot another glance at her. "Hey, you might explain that."

"Certainly." Her voice had a sharp edge. "What did you think you were doing, taking her on a tour of the house?"

"Wh-a-a-t?" He braked as a lone wallaby, caught in the headlights, took a moment before continuing its foolhardy bound across the road and into a grassy paddock. "Do you trust me about *anything?*" he asked.

"Maybe my trust has been eroded," she said, turning her head deliberately to gaze out at the cane fields. Above and beyond them were the shapes of houses, lights winking from within. Some of the fields lay fallow. Others were empty, save for a thick carpet of wildflowers. Some were cultivated, some fenced for horses. It was a full moon, the great copper moon of the tropics, and the countryside was drenched in radiance. Farther off to their left, the sea glittered so brightly it might have been molten silver. The infinite stretch of beach was smooth, clean, shining white sand. On a jutting promontory, luxury houses clustered, the yachts moored out front tied up to pontoons. It was so beautiful and so romantic. Or it *should* have been, only there were always outside forces to contend with. This one was called Gina.

Adam groaned. "I don't understand why Gina told you that. It's not true."

"Want me to jog your memory?" She felt horrible, yet couldn't stop herself. "You had a swim, then a long leisurely lunch on the beach and then she asked you to show her around the property."

"In her dreams," he said tersely.

"You don't remember?"

"I don't remember."

In the light from the dashboard she could see the flare of anger on his face. "Why would she be so silly and malicious as to lie?"

He reached out to grasp her hand, holding it tight for a few seconds. "Perhaps she thought you wouldn't tell me. Perhaps she doesn't like the idea of the two of us being friends."

"We're *not* friends," she said.

He moved his hand back to the wheel. "Have it your way. Maybe we could start being friends when you decide to trust me. I've never gone swimming with Gina, although I'm sure she looks great in a bikini. I've never had lunch with her, for that matter, but I do have to own up to a cup of coffee. Apparently it's mandatory when you sign a lease. Happy now?"

She shook her head. "You're perfectly free to do as you please. It's not mandatory to seduce *me*."

"I'm not trying to seduce you. You'd have far too many complaints."

"I most surely would."

The evening that had gone so well was ending badly. She hadn't even begun to ask if what Gina had said about his interest in the house was true. She could understand if it was. Dave Belasco was apparently thinking about commissioning him to design his new home. Did Adam know that? Was he two, maybe ten, jumps ahead of her? Her mind was flooded with suspicions and herein lay the danger. She could be moving down yet another crooked path. If she was wrong about one thing, she was probably wrong about others.

THEY WERE ALMOST through the tunnel of trees that formed Flying Cloud's long drive when the next shock wave hit her. She was sure she saw movement on the widow's walk. She didn't want to believe it, but she was convinced it wasn't a trick of the headlights.

"Did you see that?" Her voice was taut with nerves.

"See what?" He swung his head toward her at the note of panic.

"I thought I saw someone up on the widow's walk?"

He didn't scoff or try to persuade her she was seeing things. He stopped the car and turned off the lights, staring up at the widow's walk as though trying to pinpoint her supposed sighting. "The only way anyone could get up there is through the house. You stay here. Lock the car after me. I'm going to take a look."

"I'm coming, too."

"Oh, no, you're not!" His response was prompt. "If it *is* someone—and let's hope it isn't—I don't need *you* to worry about. I suppose you've left the key in the same silly place?"

"I'm afraid so. But it wouldn't be that easy for an intruder to find. There are dozens of potted plants on the veranda. You'd have to know which one."

"Or you'd need time to search them all. Please stay put, Alyssa. Promise me."

"All right." An eerie composure fell over her. He was a tall, splendidly fit man. Besides, he'd picked up a heavy flashlight presumably to use as a weapon if the occasion arose. She watched him move off, veering toward the cover of the trees.

What if someone attacked him? What if that someone had a gun? Never mind the very strict gun laws; things still happened. What if she was mistaken? Enough disturbing things had happened to make her a bit paranoid. In the back of her mind lurked a terrible fear that it could be Brett. However determined she was to overcome her recent past, he remained on the edge of her consciousness. Could he possibly be stalking her? Obsessions didn't disappear overnight. She found herself wondering if Brett could have followed her North. Ever since she'd arrived she'd felt a sense of unease. She remembered his saying he'd never let her go. It was the sort of threat she'd heard many times as a lawyer, threats that had too frequently been carried out.

Brett knew where the front door key was hidden. Brett knew the layout of the house. All her instincts screamed his name.

Agonizingly long minutes elapsed. Adam was inside. The house was now ablaze with lights, the exterior lights illuminating a broad expanse of the front and side gardens. The brilliantly flowering poincianas stood out dramatically. She'd be able to see anyone who ran out of the house unless he took the back door. God knows it would be easy enough to get swallowed up by the jungle at the rear of the plantation. There was a large area still under sugarcane.

Without much difficulty she maneuvered herself into the driver's seat, switched on the ignition, then drove the 4WD right up to the base of the front steps. She'd given Adam her promise to stay put but she couldn't just *sit* there. Not when her body was throbbing with anxiety.

Adam had heard about Brett. She wondered how much Zizi had told him. At least Zizi hadn't known about the dark places in Brett's soul. That had been *her* secret, to keep Zizi from worrying.

Could there be a struggle going on in the house? She couldn't stay here paralyzed with fright. Finally her agitation became so great she leaped out of the car onto the graveled drive. She had to find Adam. She was up the steps and into the entrance hall before he appeared.

"Don't you ever do what you're told?" he shouted down at her.

She could tell he was angry with her but she wasn't contrite. "Any sign of someone being in the house?"

"Well, no one's here now," he said flatly. "If there was someone he's been scared off. This is a very big house with far too many entries and exits." He shook his head worriedly.

"Did you check the back door? Could someone have gone out that way?" Knowing he was safe, she felt a measure of calm returning.

"Headed where?" he asked reasonably. "I wouldn't like to fight my way through that jungle at night. That cane's probably full of snakes. The back door was closed, but it wasn't locked. Did you lock it before we went out?"

"I'm not sure." Her voice was strained.

"Come and have a look around yourself," he said. "You know the house far better than I do. Elizabeth told me she never had a moment's worry in all the years she lived here."

"That's true." Her voice had dropped to a whisper. "I've never felt the slightest fear at Flying Clouds. Until now."

"What about that boyfriend of yours?"

His question stunned her, putting her immediately on the defensive. "What do you mean? Have I ever said I was afraid of him?"

He looked down at her troubled face. "I got the idea he was crazy about you, *crazy* being the operative word. There's a good deal of evidence to support the theory that obsessive men are dangerous."

"He wouldn't come up here," she said, although she didn't really believe it.

"Why not?" he countered. "All he has to do is jump on a plane."

"And stay where? Even with all the tourists around he'd be easily spotted—new man in town, tall, dark, good-looking. Gina would be the first to notice."

"I thought *I* was the one she was interested in," he said with faint sarcasm. "Maybe he's disguised himself. All he'd have to do is change the cut and color of his hair, wear contact lenses, dress differently. He doesn't have to be living anywhere near the village. He could be hanging out in some isolated old farmhouse."

She shook her head. "I must've been mistaken. I was seeing things that weren't there. I've always been too imaginative. Everything that's happened lately has built up into some kind of paranoia. I'm far from calm these days."

"We'll search all the same." He put his arm around her, guiding her up the stairs.

The second search was more thorough than the first.

Nothing. No one. Another mystery unsolved.

"What now?" Adam asked, obviously noticing how pale she'd become. "I think I'll invite myself to stay over. I'm not leaving you on your own."

"Sure you didn't plan it this way?" They were in the garden room, which housed a luxuriant indoor garden. Alyssa sank into an armchair, her silk dress floating around her.

He took a seat opposite her. "Why would I swap my comfortable bed at the farm for a very exotic but fearfully uncomfortable Thai bed over here?"

"You're making me feel like a helpless woman," she complained. "I don't think of myself as helpless."

"In certain circumstances any woman could be."

"Where's Cleo?" she suddenly asked, sitting up straight.

He stood up at once. "I'll take a stroll around, call her name."

"Be careful," she begged.

She was still sitting in the same place when he returned with Cleo in his arms. "What was she up to?"

He glanced down at the cat. "Cleo and I haven't arrived at the stage where she actually talks to me."

"Cats see things invisible to the naked eye, you know." She paused. "Doesn't it seem odd to you the way she's purring?"

"It would be odder still if she wasn't," he said. "But maybe it *is* a bit plaintive. I'm always ready for a late night but you look like you need your bed."

"As a matter of fact, I'm exhausted," she admitted. "You really should go home, you know."

To her enormous relief he shook his head. She wasn't feeling particularly brave. Even Cleo looked panicked and Cleo wasn't afraid of anything.

"No, I've made my decision. I'll bunk down here." He indicated the big sofa, custom-made to fit the spacious dimensions of the room. "Cleo might keep me company."

"You're not worried about the ghosts?"

"They can rattle around all they like," he said with complete unconcern.

"See how you feel at three a.m.," she warned. "There are beds upstairs, you know. I can find fresh linen."

"Better if I make myself comfortable down here."

"Then I'll grab a couple of pillows and find you a cotton throw."

"What more could a man want?"

She was walking away when he asked, "You're not in love with this Brett character anymore?"

"Not if I can fall into *your* arms so easily," she said.

"Elizabeth held two men in the palm of her hand."

She took seconds to answer. "I'm sure Zizi did truly love your uncle Julian, Adam," she said gently. "Both of you will have to forgive her. What she felt for Richard Langford took over her life. Right to the very end she couldn't get free of him."

"But why?" He spoke with a kind of angry bewilderment. "It would have been natural to grieve. Langford lost his life when he was in his prime. She obviously loved him. But to mourn him the way she did for the rest of her life? Does that make sense?"

"It did to Zizi." Alyssa shrugged helplessly. "The heart's very complicated. We don't love to order. Neither can we turn it off when we want. Zizi never forgot him."

"Like poor old Julian. He never forgot her, either," Adam said regretfully. "He could've had his pick of a dozen women. Instead his heart closed up."

She cleared her throat. "When are you going to tell him?"

He held her eyes. "As soon as we're absolutely sure of the truth."

"I thought we already were."

" Julian wants *proof positive*."

"Poor Julian! The portrait alone would give it to him." Melancholy set in. "Report what you like, Adam, but I have to think very carefully about all of this. There's my mother to consider. My father, my family, even the Langfords have a right to know."

"Would you be prepared to meet Julian face-to-face?" he asked.

"To what end? It could only upset him. I look enough like Zizi when she was young to do that. And I resemble Richard Langford, as well, the man who stole Zizi from him. It won't work, Adam."

He shook his head. "Julian wouldn't let his enmity toward Langford cloud his judgment of you."

She turned away, trying to control her sadness. "I don't think I should get involved."

"You couldn't be more deeply involved than you already are," he reminded her.

Alyssa stopped short, turning to face him. "You aren't planning to introduce me as someone significant in your life, are you?"

He gave her a look that made her heart knock wildly against her ribs, but didn't respond.

FULLY EXPECTING to toss and turn, she fell asleep almost as soon as her head hit the pillow. Adam had acquired the art of making her feel secure. She was a little put out that Cleo had stayed downstairs with him. It must've been all those gourmet dinners he'd fed her. She comforted herself with the thought that Cleo would stay with him for a little while, just to be sure he was okay, then come upstairs and take her usual place on the bed.

Hours later, she and Cleo woke to the sound of footsteps on the widow's walk. Cleo's padded paws hit the floor first. Adam would've heard those footsteps, too, Alyssa reasoned, hurriedly pulling on her robe. They were loud enough to wake the dead.

Sunlight was streaming across the veranda; the curtains were dancing to a stiff breeze and a thousand birds were calling to one another in the garden.

How had she slept so late? And she wasn't the only one. Cleo, who never let her sleep beyond seven before pawing her nose, hadn't stirred, either.

"Right, then, Cleo," she said briskly. "We'd better investigate." She didn't wait to dress. Her robe, bought in Hong Kong, was yellow silk, richly embroidered with birds and flowers, perfectly presentable.

With faint trepidation, the two of them made their way downstairs. No sign of Adam. The pillows and throw were stacked neatly at one end of the sofa.

"To the roof!" she said to Cleo, who took off on command, bounding up the stairs and on to the attic.

The wind was up catching at her robe, making it flutter and cling to her body. She pulled the tasseled belt tighter. What she saw was a peacock-blue sky, deeper blue sea, seagulls wheeling over a patch of glittery water. She could detect a new scent on the salt-laden air, unbelievably fragrant. She recognized as coming from the enormous dangling flowers of the datura growing in a sheltered copse beneath her.

She didn't have to search long for the owner of the footsteps. Adam, who'd been hidden from her view by a chimney, now hove into sight.

"Oh, it's *you!*" she said in relief, bringing up a hand to hold back her streaming hair. It had broken out of its night-time braid.

He let his eyes devour her. Everything about her had a special magic, a special grace for him, but he'd never expected to see her in a twist of yellow silk the wind was fusing so erotically to her body. Not so soon anyway. "It's too gusty up here." He moved swiftly toward her.

"You didn't find anything?"

"No, and I've had a good look 'round."

She had to pitch her voice higher. "After breakfast, we should go down to the beach, check for footprints."

"It's not a private beach, Alyssa," he pointed out, positioning himself so his body acted as a buffer between her and the force of the wind. "People can walk on it."

"It's a secluded bay," she said. "There's a major bay beyond the headland with endless miles of beach to walk on. Not many people venture down here."

"Okay, we'll go look," he agreed, even though he didn't want to look at anything but *her*.

The wind got its playful fingers beneath her robe, whipping it loose. It flew from her shoulders like a cape, exposing her willowy body in its yellow nightgown to his view—delicately sculpted shoulders, the deep plunge of the neckline revealing the curves of her breasts.

"We'd better go below," Adam said, before he lost all self-control and scooped her into his arms. He bent to pick up the silk tassel that had tied her robe, shoving it into his jeans pocket.

She didn't answer, but turned around slowly, letting the stalwart Cleo, almost overwhelmed by the wind, go first. The wind, gaining strength by the moment, tossed her long blond hair, sending skeins of it flying every which way, a silken rope to bind him.

The seduction was complete.

THEY WERE BACK in the attic. After the bluster of the open, all was silence, stillness, the whole area lit up by sunlight pouring in through the shuttered side windows.

"You know you're torturing me?" His voice came from deep in his throat. More vulnerable to a woman than he'd ever believed possible, he wrapped his arms around her, drawing her into a locked circle. It felt to him as if he'd never held a woman in his arms before, never known the magic, the excitement, the *thrill* of it. "Come closer to me, Alyssa. Closer!" The scent of her skin and her beautiful hair was in his nostrils. All sense of calm had left him. He could feel the sparks in his electrified blood.

Blindly he bent his head and took the lobe of her ear into his mouth. Then he let his mouth roam to her cheek. She wasn't drawing back, he thought with exultation. He drew a deep aroused breath, sliding her robe down from her shoulders until it pooled at their feet. He was astonished at how quickly and deeply he'd fallen in love with this woman. He would take what she offered. Everything she had to give.

CHAPTER SEVEN

THE MARINA WAS FULL of boats of all kinds and shapes and prices—yachts, ketches, tour boats, glamorous motor cruisers, catamarans, fishing boats, runabouts with outboard motors, even an old wreck in the process of being restored to its former glory. Seagulls and cormorants perched atop tall masts. Flags and pennants crackled, water slapped against hulls, ropes strained in their efforts to hold back the graceful racing yachts, restlessly at anchor. The water in the basin was a translucent green, shot through with iridescent lines of royal marine blue, turquoise, burgundy, white and yellow, reflecting the painted hulls.

It was an idyllic scene, except for the pillar of gray-black smoke that rose into the air over Pier 8. A small crowd was assembled there, the police chief and his deputy at its center. Jack McLean, the police chief, had rung Alyssa to tell her to get down to the marina as quickly as she could. *Cherub* had burned almost to the waterline. It was, without question, arson, the accelerant being the methylated spirits used for the old stove.

There had never been an incidence of arson at the marina. Other boat-owners, naturally concerned for their vessels, were already demanding the arsonist be found and locked up. Police Chief McLean was under pressure to act fast.

"Is there anyone you can think of, Alyssa, who might want to do this?" the chief asked. "Someone who held a grudge against Ms. Calvert or yourself?"

Alyssa glanced back at the wreckage in numb despair. Her beloved *Cherub,* what was left of her, was swinging to her mooring with the lapping tide. She remembered her very first voyage, when she was seven. Zizi had taken her out to a beautiful coral cay she always called *Sun Kiss* where they'd anchored and had a picnic on the beach.

"I can't imagine who'd do such a thing," she whispered. "It's a nightmare."

"It is indeed!" McLean agreed. Nothing much happened around the bay the chief didn't know about. If things went missing, just about everyone knew who'd "borrowed" them. Generally such matters were easy to sort out. This was different.

"Anything remotely suspicious *you* can think of, Adam?" McLean transferred his gaze to Alyssa's companion.

Adam shook his head. "Nothing specific.

Alyssa and I had dinner at Renato's in the village last night. When we got back to the house, Alyssa thought she saw someone on the widow's walk."

McLean shot a glance at Alyssa, gesturing to his constable to take note of that.

"It could have been a trick of the light," Alyssa hurried to mention.

"Or not," Adam said. "I left Alyssa in the car, then went to investigate. I searched the house thoroughly, then again with Alyssa. Nothing."

McLean scratched his head. "The locals say Flying Clouds's haunted, not that I believe in any of that nonsense myself. Be absolutely certain we'll find who did this, Alyssa. The fact that you thought you sighted someone up on the widow's walk can't be ignored. It's such a great barn of a place. Couldn't you arrange for someone to keep you company?"

"I'll be taking over that role until a member of Alyssa's family arrives," Adam immediately volunteered that piece of information.

McLean digested it without comment. "What was done here seems to have been premeditated, not a random act of destruction. I'd say it was someone who knew the marina, the boat and its layout. Knew about the stove and where the fuel was stored. Not a professional, however. More like someone with revenge on his mind. We don't have any answers yet, but we'll get them. So far as I'm aware, Ms. Calvert had no enemies around here. People were protective of her and her privacy. No complaints from her, either, over the years—no strangers wandering onto the property and so forth. At this stage it's a mystery."

"I want whoever did this to be found, Chief," Alyssa said, tears glistening in her eyes.

"Leave it to me," McLean said, nodding his head firmly.

On the way back from the marina they stopped at the farm so Adam could pack a few clothes. While he did that, Alyssa tried to reach first her mother, then her father on the phone. Both were in court. She left messages with their secretaries. Next she put a call through to the woman she'd always called "Gran."

"Alyssa, dear, thank goodness!" Mariel answered on the second ring. "I've had so many worrying dreams about you, my dear. What's happening up there? I've told your mother, it's a bad place for you to be. Can't you bring yourself to sell it, my dear? There are far too many ghosts."

The familiar rich contralto held undertones of more than ordinary concern. Alyssa instinctively felt that Mariel was frightened at some level. "I know all about the ghosts, Mariel," Alyssa said, feeling the terrible sadness of betrayal. She'd never called Mariel anything else but Gran. That alone would alert Mariel.

"I thought you might." Mariel's tone altered within seconds. It turned to flint. "I knew something was coming," Mariel said brusquely. "What with Elizabeth dying so unexpectedly. You've found her journals, no doubt?" She didn't sound resigned, but filled with anger. Mariel had always been a formidable woman. She still was, Alyssa reminded herself. Mariel obeyed rules and laws of her own.

"I found a portrait Zizi was working on," Alyssa said, without answering the question. "An unfinished portrait of the man she loved. It was Richard Langford, wasn't it, Mariel? I have his eyes. But you know that."

The line rang with distorted laughter. "Of course I do!" Mariel snapped. "What I don't know is what you intend to do about it. No one else has any idea. No one but you and me. Not even poor Lewis. I never could figure out how my late husband could be so brilliant at business then downright dense at home. It was a pact between Elizabeth and me to be kept to the death. I would strongly remind you, Alyssa, *I'm* still here."

Alyssa's heart beat painfully. "Of course you are. Still getting away with it, too. And Lewis wasn't dense at all. He was an old-fashioned gentleman, who for some reason that escapes me, wanted to keep the marriage intact. Even now I can't believe you kept this secret, Mariel. Why did you do it? Why did you *both* do it?"

"Because it *had* to be done, you stupid girl!" Mariel let her anger rip. "We were two desperate people. Desperate situations call for desperate measures. There was no other way. Elizabeth had lost her mind. She used to talk to him as if he wasn't dead. If that's not crazy, then what is? I doubt she and my beautiful Stephanie would have survived without me."

Could that be true? "Your beautiful Stephanie is your *niece,* Mariel, not your daughter." Alyssa was overtaken by pity and revulsion in equal measure. "I have to talk to you, Mariel. You must tell me everything. Only then can we decide what to do."

"Don't tell me what I must or mustn't do," Mariel thundered into the phone. "I'll do the deciding around here."

"Like you did with Zizi when she was at the breaking point?" From somewhere Alyssa found the courage to retaliate. "You manipulated her, Mariel. She trusted you and you used her."

"Where are you calling from?" Mariel demanded.

"Don't worry. No one can overhear me. It's my mother who has to be considered here."

"In a few seconds Stephanie's whole idea of herself could be shattered," Mariel said fiercely.

"She's a brilliant, confident woman but even she can't reinvent herself at will."

That was Alyssa's own concern yet she persisted. "Zizi was her *mother,* Mariel. Doesn't that mean anything to you? Shouldn't Mom know?"

"*I'm* her mother, Alyssa." Mariel sounded frighteningly harsh. "She loves me. *I'm* the one she's looked to all her life. Elizabeth gave her up to *me.* I spent the best years of my life loving her, looking after her. Stephanie is *mine!*"

"I'm sorry," Alyssa said. "That may be the way you see it, but no one *owns* anyone else. Who am I supposed to be?" Alyssa took in a gulp of air. "You never did treat me like a granddaughter, did you?" Alyssa had battled with that knowledge over the years, watching her own friends with their loving grandmothers.

Another harsh laugh from Mariel. "It doesn't take a genius to work that out. You're *not* my granddaughter. It's not easy keeping up a facade." Then, a new tone emerged, more conciliatory. "But I am fond of you, Alyssa, although I wish you'd stuck to the law instead of trying to make a living as a painter. That was Elizabeth's legacy. *You* were her baby. She just skipped a generation. Fifty years ago, Elizabeth was in no state to look after Stephanie." Mariel had returned to her normal lofty tones. "She couldn't even look after herself. Langford was the worst possible person she could have fallen in love with, married with children and so well-known. It was scandalous! But that was Elizabeth, a law unto herself. She was so beautiful and so talented she thought she could get away with anything. But that all came to an end with her breakdown. When I said I'd take the baby and raise her as my own, Elizabeth agreed. I can't and won't talk about it anymore, Alyssa. Certainly not on the phone."

"You're quite right. I'm sorry. We shouldn't discuss this on the phone. Perhaps you'd consider coming up here?" Alyssa kept her voice steady. "Strange things are happening, Mariel. Zizi's yacht, *Cherub*, was destroyed in a fire. The police are treating it as arson."

"What does this have to do with me?" Mariel asked. "It must be some local firebug, problem teenagers. It was falling to pieces, anyway."

"It wasn't!" Alyssa replied sharply. "Brett— have you heard anything of him?" Mariel had been quite taken with Brett, always so charming and solicitous toward her, commenting on her "marvelous" jewelry and "amazing" hats.

There was complete silence for a moment then Mariel said, "I had a courtesy call from him after you'd broken up, a couple of calls actually. He knew I could offer him good advice. Such a mistake you've made, my girl. He told me he was leaving for London, where he hoped to find work. Needless to say, I was quite sympathetic toward him. I considered Brett Harris an excellent catch. He told me he wanted a complete break after what happened between you. He loved you, Alyssa. Losing you was very painful for him. I liked him, but no doubt he'll be better off with someone else."

"You *didn't* know him, by the way, although he worked very hard to ingratiate himself with you. Brett was another one who kept his real self hidden." She took a deep breath, trying to compose herself. "I'm going to ask Mom to come up here for a few days. It would be a good idea if you came with her. We do need to talk."

Mariel laughed shortly. "Talk can ruin lives, Alyssa. Talk can *take* lives. Have a care before you cross me."

Alyssa felt a sick jolt. "Is that supposed to scare me?"

"I won't allow you to destroy the family peace," Mariel ventured back.

"Are you going to hire a hit man?" Alyssa asked wryly, thinking it couldn't be entirely ruled out.

Mariel was showing her steely core. "I'm relying on your common sense, Alyssa," she said, not bothering to bank down her fury. "It's not a crime to keep one's private life private. All you have to do is hold on to one solid fact. Elizabeth loved you. You brought love back into her life. She was never all that close to Stephanie. Stephanie was *mine.* You're young. You'll get over it."

"Will I?" Alyssa asked ironically. "I don't expect that to happen, at least not for many many long years. Please make an effort to come. We should talk face-to-face. You're the only one now alive who knows the whole story. But I have to warn you, there's someone else who wants to get to the truth. His name will be familiar to you. Julian Wainwright."

Mariel's gasp was genuinely shocked. "Wainwright?" she cried so loudly Alyssa had to hold the phone away from her ear.

"You don't have to shout, Mariel. You must know the past is never truly buried. Julian Wainwright's great-nephew, Adam Hunt, is the one who found Zizi. He'd traveled up here to speak to Zizi on behalf of his great-uncle. Julian Wainwright is dying."

Far from registering dismay Mariel's voice vibrated with callous relief. "Thank God for that!"

"It's not going to be as easy as all that. Before he dies, Julian wants to know if Zizi's child was his."

Mariel's laugh was like the crack of a gunshot. "On what grounds?"

"Zizi had *two* lovers," Alyssa said tonelessly.

"And probably a dozen more!" Mariel returned with disgust. "But she *did* love Langford. And he did love her."

"You were jealous of Zizi, weren't you, Mariel?" Alyssa asked quietly.

"Always," Mariel said. "There wasn't a man who could look at her without wanting her, even my own fool of a husband. I've never met a man yet one can trust."

WHEN ADAM RETURNED he found her on the rear veranda, her face pale and strained. "What's wrong?" He'd heard the low murmur of her voice from upstairs but continued his packing.

She responded with a heavy sigh. " I couldn't contact my mother or father but I did put a call through to…to…"

"Okay." He took over. "Your ex-grandmother?"

"Yes." She gave him an agonized look. "Oh, God, Adam!"

"That conversation hit you hard?" He took her hands and rubbed them gently. Despite the heat her skin was cold.

"It went badly, but that's always been the case if you say something to Mariel she doesn't want to hear. I asked her to come up here." She stared into his eyes as though she could find all the answers she needed there.

"So what did she say to upset you?"

She sighed. "It went both ways. I upset her. I called her Mariel, for one thing. I've never called her *Mariel* in my life. That gave everything away. I suspect she's been dreading this—the mysteries of the past coming out. She mentioned Zizi's journals."

"So they exist," Adam exclaimed. "I'll bet they hold the missing pieces."

"If only we could find them. You're being entirely honest with me, Adam?"

His gaze was unflinching. "I came as Julian's emissary, Alyssa, nothing more. What else could there be?"

She could have introduced Gina's theory of business reasons, but let it go. It was a potentially explosive area and she already had too much to cope with. "Mariel wants me to leave well enough alone. She was far angrier and more aggressive than I expected. She even threatened me in a way."

Adam was shocked. What kind of woman was this? "Well," he said slowly, "she has a great deal to lose. Remember, she's lived the last fifty years as a mother and grandmother. It doesn't sound like she was the model granny to you, but what about your mother? She must love her?"

"She dotes on her," Alyssa said. "I learned over

the years that I didn't really count. My mother ful-filled all of Mariel's maternal instincts. Besides, I have *his* eyes. Maybe that made me unworthy of her love. Mariel is very unforgiving. Your great-uncle has an unexpected ally. Mariel hated Richard Langford. I heard it in her voice. I accused her of being jealous of Zizi and she admitted it. So she must've hated Zizi, as well, or at least felt the classic love-hate. And she told me Zizi did have a serious breakdown."

That didn't surprise him. "You know Lang-ford's death at sea has long been regarded as a mystery?"

She looked at him in surprise. "He took his boat out in high seas." As far as Alyssa was concerned, that explained it. A master mariner Langford might have been but she knew how dangerous the Reef waters were, especially during the cyclone season. Richard Langford would have known, too. Maybe he didn't care.

Adam, an experienced sailor himself, said, "Julian's version was that Langford committed suicide."

The full weight of his words hit Alyssa like a blow. "Now I think *I'm* going mad."

"No, you're not." His grip tightened. The tremors in her hands were spreading to the rest of her body. "You're coping well at a very difficult time. And I'm here to help you in every way I can. So, is Mariel coming or not?"

"I don't know. I hung up on her after she admitted she was jealous of Zizi."

"Well, don't despair." Adam tried to transmit strength to her through the warmth of his hands. "I'm betting you'll get a phone call to tell you she's coming. She's got too much to lose. Is she well enough? She must be well into her seventies?"

Alyssa gave a brittle laugh. "Don't get the idea that Mariel's a frail old lady, Adam. Mariel is one tough cookie. She's always ruled the roost. My 'grandfather'—and I loved him, he was a very nice man—simply let her. Anything for a little peace. I'm convinced he didn't know or didn't *want* to know the truth. It seems an awful thing to say, but it's a good thing he's dead."

Adam was busy reevaluating his perception of Mariel. "This threat, what form did it take?"

"Nothing specific. What could she do, anyway?"

Adam thought about that for a second. "She could try to frighten you off Flying Clouds. She could've had someone set fire to the boat. I don't know this woman."

"I don't know her, either," Alyssa said with a heavy sigh. "She's not a bit like Zizi, I can tell you that. You don't mess with Mariel."

"She did manipulate Elizabeth at the lowest

point in her life," Adam said in a disgusted tone. "That proves she's a ruthless person. Is there any possibility she had someone set fire to *Cherub?*"

Alyssa shivered. "I wouldn't want to believe that of her. Not that she wouldn't have it done if she thought it would help her. But she didn't know I'd found the portrait of Richard Langford until I told her."

"But you *were* in the house," he said. "She knew you'd be going through it and she might reason it was only a matter of time before you uncovered Elizabeth's journals. It must've been weighing very heavily on her mind. Was she against your coming up here?"

"You bet she was! Now that I think about it, she was downright vehement. She didn't want *any* of us coming up to Flying Clouds after Zizi died. She pushed for the place to be sold. I had the feeling she wouldn't have cared if it burned down. We all knew I'd inherit it. There was never any secret about that."

"If your family couldn't persuade you to sell, could Mariel have considered trying to frighten you off, or is that too far-fetched? It's one way to deal with the problem. It's a method that's worked well in the past. I could tell you many instances of people being frightened off their property because some developer wants it."

"Like Dave Belasco?" Her voice sounded hollow.

His expression tightened. He dropped her hands. "I can't see Dave Belasco trying to terrify anyone, let alone a woman on her own."

"How well do you know him?" Her voice gained strength.

"I suppose I could say very well. Leave Dave out of this, Alyssa. I can assure you he's never been involved in any criminal act."

"So we're back to Mariel."

"Mariel, or someone in her pay. In the end, motivation is the key. Mariel has a motive."

"So could *you* for that matter." She tried to pass it off with a laugh.

"You mean *I* want Flying Clouds now?"

She didn't back down. "How do I know you and Dave Belasco don't simply want to take it over?"

"Then what?" he asked grimly.

She shrugged. "The plantation is a very valuable parcel of land. It has wonderful sea views."

"True. You're sitting on a fortune. The North is booming. But Dave isn't the only big developer. I could name another four off the top of my head."

"So we have any number of suspects," she said. "Including Mariel."

"I have nothing to do with it, Alyssa," he said. "Elizabeth was able to live in peace at Flying Clouds all these years, but times have changed.

This is a beautiful part of the world with easy access to one of the world's greatest natural wonders, the Great Barrier Reef. The tourist industry is thriving."

"So someone might be after the land?"

He sighed, leaning back in his chair. "Not me. And I can vouch for Dave. He does things by the book. I'm considering buying the Gambaro farm as a hideaway. Just an idea floating around in my head. I could work here."

"As a sculptor?"

"As a sculptor and architect both." Deliberately he changed the subject. "What about your parents? Will they come?"

She answered with forced calm. "Both of them were in court. I left messages for them to call me."

"Good, but I don't intend to leave you here on your own, Alyssa. I'll stay until your family arrives."

She looked away moodily. On the one hand, she was grateful for his support; on the other, she was shaken by suspicions. "There was no one on the widow's walk," she said. "Just my mind playing tricks."

"You don't believe that any more than I do. Even if you persist in mistrusting me, I'm still coming."

She offered him a sad smile.

"Don't look at me like that, Alyssa," he begged. "I would never hurt you. I would never allow anyone or anything to hurt you. You must know that."

"Oh, I do!" But she couldn't hide her frightened eyes. "I was afraid it could've been Brett stalking me," she confessed. "But he's in London. Mariel told me. He called her after we broke up. They always got on well. So, that takes care of Brett. It was awful of me to suspect him and that whole theory was just too neat. We'll have to leave it to McLean to find out who set fire to *Cherub.* It could've been vandals."

Adam seemed about to say something but apparently thought better of it. He stood up. "Ready to go?"

"Ready." She accepted his hand. "Make sure you lock up."

"Nothing here to take," he said. "I will lock the shed, however—though an intruder would be hard-pressed to walk off with huge blocks of marble."

THE *CHERUB,* AS IT TURNED OUT, wasn't the only destruction. What they saw inside the big agricultural shed sent a bolt of fear through Alyssa and a white-hot rage through Adam. This was one blow too many.

"How could anyone do this?" Alyssa gasped in horror. Adam's finished sculpture had been smashed with a hammer.

Adam's features seemed set in granite. Though his eyes blazed, his voice was icy cold. "Frightening you off Flying Clouds is one thing," he said. "We can see the sick reasoning behind it. But this is destruction for destruction's sake—or for revenge. Just because Mariel said Harris was off to London doesn't mean he actually boarded a plane. He could still be in the country. He could even be up here. He could be stalking not only you, but me. He could have seen us together. Since he was obsessively in love with you, that would set him on a rampage. Do you believe he'd do these things—start a fire, destroy a sculpture?"

Alyssa chose her words carefully. "Brett isn't unbalanced. I can't say that. All I can say is there's some spark of rage in him. He didn't handle the breakup well. Neither did I, for that matter. But I was glad to be free of him. Brett was *angry*." Her face told the story. "He made an appearance at Zizi's funeral. He said a few things that worried me."

"Like never letting you go? Then he's capable of anything. Is there anyone you could call to double-check his whereabouts? His family, for instance?"

Alyssa knelt to lay a despairing hand on a piece of the ruined sculpture. "Brett didn't see his family, but he has a friend, a fellow lawyer, who'd probably know where he is."

"Call him," Adam advised, his voice full of

anger. "We'll have to get in touch with McLean. These two acts of vandalism are connected. I'm sure of it."

"I'm so sorry, Adam." She reached her hand out toward him, but he looked so daunting, she dropped it. "I'm devastated on your behalf. Whoever did this is some kind of monster."

"Don't worry, I'll find him." Adam's tone was merciless. "Let's get away from all this." He pulled her to him, keeping his arm protectively around her trembling body. "No one's going to harm you, Alyssa. Not while I'm around."

THEY SPENT THE afternoon, nerves ragged, continuing their search for Zizi's private papers. Cleo did her bit, leading them from one place to another. Mariel knew her sister had kept journals, so that was a start. The big question was where. They found many things of interest but nothing from that crucial period in Zizi's life when, already involved with Julian Wainwright, she'd met and fallen madly in love with Richard Langford and had his baby. Alyssa couldn't help wondering if she'd planned the pregnancy as a way of binding him to her. Zizi wasn't there to answer that question. Maybe her journals would.

At one stage Alyssa went up to her room to check on a shutter. They could hear it banging from downstairs. Cleo, her constant companion, beat her up the stairs.

Adam followed more slowly. He stood in the open doorway, contemplating the beautiful room where they'd made love. He had visions of them together. Holding her, kissing her, sinking into her wonderfully receptive body. This journey that had begun as a debt of gratitude to the great-uncle who'd always been so loving and generous toward him had become *his* love story. He now knew the end of Julian's. But he wasn't about to repeat Julian's loss. He loved this woman. Given the way he felt, how could he possibly judge Langford?

"Would Elizabeth have hidden anything in here?" he asked, glancing around the spacious room with its beautiful furnishings. The room easily accommodated several large antique pieces, including a lovely nineteenth-century English bureau with many drawers.

"Nothing there," she said, following his glance. "I've already checked. There's a secret drawer in the bureau but only my things are in it."

"What about the armoire?" he persisted. "It's really magnificent." He moved into the room to study the towering, elaborately carved piece. "No secret compartments?"

She shook her head. "None that I could ever find. In any case, Zizi would've told me."

"You're sure of that?"

"No." She laughed jaggedly. "I'm not sure of anything about Zizi anymore."

"May I open it?" He looked back at her standing there so quietly.

"Of course." She picked Cleo up in her arms, then sat on the bed. "I don't keep much in there. I have the dressing room for my clothes. The armoire doesn't have drawers, just a single rail to hang clothes. Some really beautiful dress lengths are stored in the long boxes down there. Zizi gave them to me." Fiercely she blinked back tears.

"Try not to upset yourself. Your headache will come back again." Adam began to examine the interior carefully. An armoire like this with its carved pelmet and deep dimensions should have, at the very least one, two large drawers, yet the base beneath the boxes was firm and looked as if it had never been touched. There was no hollow sound when he tapped it. Still, trick compartments were often built into these things.

Adam closed the two doors, beginning his examination of the exterior. "*Why* doesn't it have drawers?" he asked of no one in particular. "That bothers me. Any craftsman designing a piece of furniture like this would include drawers."

Cleo took the opportunity to leap off Alyssa's lap and go to Adam, ears twitching. She wound herself around his ankles. "Maybe she knows something," Alyssa said, only half joking.

"Maybe she does," Adam murmured. "Now what do you make of this?" he gave a low whistle. Pressing hard against one of the lustrous stylized flower heads he heard not a click but a decided *pop*.

"What was that?" Alyssa laughed nervously. Over the years she'd pushed every knob, every wedge, every piece of carving on it. "Don't tell me you've found a secret compartment?"

"I think I have." Adam's trained fingers located a corresponding flower head on the opposite side of the decorative panel. He pushed the flower head that had popped flush with the panel and then pressed them together.

The doors flew open. "We had to find something sooner or later," he muttered with satisfaction.

By this time Alyssa was standing beside him. "You've found it." Her voice was trembling.

"You'll want to see this," he said. Cleo sprang into the depths of the armoire. She crouched over the boxes, gazing down at the drawer's contents as though rapt.

"I don't believe it." Alyssa shook her head. "I can't believe it. I've searched every inch of this armoire." She crouched down beside him, holding a hand to her mouth. "Adam!" she exclaimed. She was looking at one long drawer the length and depth of the carved panel.

He smoothed her shoulder, feeling a surge of triumph at the discovery. "We found what we were looking for."

"I would *never* have found it." Her laugh was more like a sob.

"Obviously you need me around." He brought her gently to her feet. "You'll want to go through this on your own."

It occurred to her, not for the first time, how sensitive he was. "Yes, but you were the one who discovered it."

"I'm glad." He kissed her mouth briefly. "But this is private business, intended only for you. I have a strong feeling Elizabeth was going to tell you about it one day, only she slipped away without warning. She didn't destroy her journals or her letters or whatever is in that jewel box. She kept them for you. I'll wait downstairs. Come, Cleo!"

The cat leaped into his arms.

CHAPTER EIGHT

THERE WAS A MOMENT Alyssa thought her heart would break. Here was what she'd been searching for and it'd been right under her nose all along. There were documents of all kinds, among them the title deeds to Flying Clouds. She withdrew the stack of letters tied with a red velvet ribbon. Love letters, almost certainly. She laid them unopened on the bed. Then she opened each of the three leather-bound journals. The binding still gave off a rich aroma.

She dived in headlong. Two of the journals covered a period from the great turning point in Zizi's life, a point from which there was no return, when she and Richard Langford first met, until just after he disappeared at sea. The third resumed several months later. Finally, Alyssa picked up a lovely inlaid walnut jewel box decorated with small gilded medallions.

She sat for some time holding the box close to her before she could open it. Secrets had been

Zizi's life, and now her secret history was about to be revealed. Alyssa breathed deeply, and then lifted the lid.

Inside was string upon string of lustrous pearls, white, gold and the Tahitian iridescent dark green, sometimes called black. There were baroque brooches and bracelets set with various precious stones and a number of stunning rings.

But one piece above all made Alyssa's eyelids flutter with awe. At first she couldn't touch it—she dared not—then with Zizi's name on her lips she withdrew the diamond-and-emerald necklace. It was exactly like the necklace the mermaid had worn in Zizi's paintings, paintings she was determined would one day go on show. She wouldn't rest until Zizi's great gift was publicly acknowledged.

Handmade notepaper bordered in gold confirmed the fact that Zizi had fully intended for her to have everything that was stored away in this drawer. The inscription read:

To my darling Alyssa, who has brought me great joy
All this, dearest girl, is now yours.

Zizi wrote:

These journals contain many shocking secrets. You will wonder, loving you as I did, how I could keep you in the dark so long. But as desperately as I wanted to confide in you once you became a woman, I had made the ultimate pact—to the death. That pact, so far as I am concerned, will come to an end with my passing. It will be your decision whether anyone else should see these journals. I pray daily that God will forgive me for the pain I have caused and grant you the courage and the wisdom to decide what is best.

Your loving grandmother.

Alyssa put the necklace back gently into the box, then closed her eyes on a warm, rising surge of tears. *What is best.* Wasn't that a towering responsibility? Yet she couldn't help believing the truth was the only way. The truth could be handled; lies were more difficult to come to terms with. At long last she had Zizi's confession. All that remained was to give her absolution. Indeed, she'd already given it.

Reading quickly, devouring the pages, Alyssa plunged into the journals, wanting desperately to know the full story. She fully intended to reread them thoroughly, but for now, she had to *know.* Locked inside these pages was Zizi without the mask, that impenetrable barrier of deception she'd worn for most of her life. As she read, Alyssa could feel the hard knot of emotion building in her chest. The tears that blurred her vision were impossible to hold back. Several times she had to dip into a box of tissues, wiping her streaming eyes and blowing her nose before she could continue reading.

The journals were written by a woman over-whelmingly and dangerously in love. Alyssa felt an enormous compassion, not only for Zizi but for the two men who'd loved her. As Julian Wain-wright claimed, Zizi had given him a commit-ment, happy about it, but that was before Richard Langford had sailed into her life to become the only man on earth for her.

It was on Zizi's favorite coral cay, where—wearing sneakers that didn't adequately protect her ankles—she'd trodden on a stonefish while reef walking at low tide. Alyssa experienced the fear, the sense of helplessness and hopelessness Zizi had felt, worrying that no one would find her in time. She was going to die. Then, drifting in and out of consciousness, she realized there was a man standing over her, handsome as a god, not gentle, but of high mettle, proud. He was staring down at her with eyes like diamonds. His skin, the part that wasn't hidden by a close beard, was darkly tanned. The wind was in his crow-black sweep of hair. He looked magnificent.

He had *saved* her. That meant her life belonged to him.

From out of the sea he had come to her aid. It was truly a miracle.

Hello, she said simply.

That was the beginning. *And the end of life as I had known it.*

Richard Langford had spirited Zizi away to Flying Clouds after her brief stay in hospital. Zizi was sick at heart for Julian, who loved her. Julian had come after her, *as fierce in his way as Richard.* Fighting with every weapon at his disposal, Julian had accused Langford of being an adulterer whose only decent course of action was to set Elizabeth free and return to his wife. Julian accused him of having no intention of breaking up his marriage, even if it meant an illicit love affair that could destroy them all. An unbreachable chasm had opened up between the two men, both of them wildly in love with the same woman.

Alyssa had to lower the journals many times to stare sightlessly at the swaying coconut palms. What a shocking waste. Zizi had a fine man who loved her, yet she'd chosen to give her heart to Richard, leaving Julian desolate. Richard Langford must have been quite a man, she thought, to inspire that kind of epic love. Instinct told her he was a man of strong passions, a caring man torn between duty and a love for the beautiful young Zizi that overwhelmed him. For that matter, neither Richard nor Julian could let her go. Such was obsessive love. It was obvious from Zizi's writings that she and Richard were tormented by their situation. Richard had already taken a vow to love and honor his wife.

Alyssa picked up where she'd left off, the journal shaking under her hand.

Julian returned to Flying Clouds again and again, hoping against hope that Zizi would come to her senses. Over time, the three lives became entwined, Julian bobbing up like a buoy whenever Langford sailed off. Richard hadn't seen his marriage as a prison—he loved his wife, adored his two children—but everything in him compelled him to keep his beautiful Zizi. He hadn't planned any of this. Fate had taken a hand, even switching his course so he could find her in danger of dying on an uninhabited coral island.

Alyssa felt deeply touched by Julian's persistence. No matter how much in love Zizi was with Langford, Julian continued to argue that she couldn't look to him for marriage. He *was* married. One of his children, the little girl, suffered from a rare disorder. The fact that Langford couldn't bring himself to desert them gained him no respect in Julian's eyes. Jealousy left him as cold as steel.

Zizi wrote movingly of the long separations and the loneliness she endured, but when Richard was at Flying Clouds or they were on their brief travels to exotic places, there was nothing but rapture. Intense, fierce, all-consuming. Rapture that shut out everyone else. Zizi asked for nothing from him but his love. Richard was forced to move between two worlds, but only with her did he reveal the full depth of his nature.

Alyssa had to pause in her reading, saturated by emotion. She was acutely aware that she now had a much greater understanding of the love between Zizi and her Richard, an understanding of the kind of man Richard was. He blazed like a meteor across the pages, as he must have done in life. It wasn't just an overwhelming physical attraction, although they possessed that in abundance. It was a meeting of minds and souls. No wonder Zizi had sunk into a profound emptiness with Richard gone.

Alyssa checked a date. In a mad rush to find out as much as she could, she had glossed over that piece of information. But it was important. Ah, there it was! Zizi wrote of missing two periods. Never regular in her cycles, she'd kept at bay the idea that she might be pregnant until the first symptoms appeared.

Morning sickness. All-day sickness. She knew she looked the same on the outside; inside she was growing a baby. She found it hard to think or even make a plan.

A baby, despite the protection they'd used.

Weeks before, in a fit of acute loneliness, near despair with Richard gone home, she'd given in to her need for comfort. Julian had in no way manipulated her, yet somehow she'd found herself sleeping with him that one time, so well did he comfort her. Julian, who never ceased to tell her she was wasting her life on an impossible *addiction.* That was how Julian saw Richard, as an addiction, not prepared to acknowledge Zizi's passionate feelings for the man. Richard was never going to give up his wife and family, his position in society. She was his *mistress.*

Now Zizi wrote she was pregnant. Her calculations reassured her that Richard, not Julian, was the father of her child. She spoke of her flash of fear at the thought of telling Richard.

Will he see it as a trap?

And what about Julian? His hope that they'd be together was impossible to extinguish. Julian would immediately leap to the conclusion that the baby was his. If Richard was *her* addiction, *she* was Julian's.

I love them both!

But each in a very different way. Zizi's love for Julian Wainwright was solid and sane, conventional even, a good basis for marriage. Her love for Richard was life-changing. It had made her a different person. Zizi relived the brief time—just under two years—of their intense affair to the end of her life. Relived and recorded it with extraordinary clarity and power. Richard Langford's marriage was an irreversible fact. He could've thrown that part of his life away, only he would've had to throw away his conscience as well. Duty kept him bound. But Zizi alone carried the joy and the burden of being his grand passion.

Alyssa frowned in confusion as she tried to make sense of the last journal. Zizi had written in such haste that her writing, stained with tears, was difficult to read. But the scrawled letters gradually resolved themselves into sense. There was so much passion in the recorded snatches of dialogue, often cruel, heralding a dramatic and disastrous denouement.

Richard had returned to Flying Clouds unexpectedly. Julian was at the house, although Zizi had begged him to stay away and go on with his life. The two men had fought. Both had sustained injuries. Richard had raged at her, literally half out of his mind at her perceived betrayal. She had destroyed his trust. He loved her above all else. Didn't she know that? Couldn't she accept that he simply couldn't turn his back on his wife and children?

It was his sworn duty, he told her, his face

ravaged with pain. Hadn't he given her Flying Clouds? Hadn't he made her financially secure? However much he wanted to be free, he couldn't be. His wife was a good woman, an admirable mother, his little girl needed constant treatment, his family needed his support.

"I do understand, believe me!"

Zizi had tried to take hold of him, but he held her off, ordering Julian out.

Julian had gone, but not without a promise that he would return.

Her betrayal, as Richard saw it, had him literally howling with grief. That was before he picked her up and carried her up the stairs….

It took him seconds to note the changes in my body.

Zizi had seen the terrible shock in his eyes. *"My God, you're carrying his child!"*

Alyssa pored over the wavery lines.

Zizi had tried desperately to convince him that what he feared wasn't true, but Richard was so locked into grief, everything she said was incomprehensible to him. She had betrayed him. She had betrayed their love.

"But Richard, it was only that one time. I was so unhappy and confused… I don't really know how it happened…every minute of every single day I've regretted it… You can't know!"

Zizi had opened appealing arms to him, begging him to forgive her for her moment of aberration. She had been feeling desperate. Julian who loved her was there. She had allowed him to make love to her. But if Richard loved her, he would *believe* her. She tried to talk dates, but he greeted her every word with stinging contempt. He could never forgive her for betraying their love and, most shockingly, carrying another man's child.

She tried every way she could think of to convince him. Nothing worked. The last Zizi saw of Richard was him storming through the front door of Flying Clouds, banging it so furiously, the hinges moved on the heavy timber frame.

Days later his yacht, the *Miranda,* was reported missing in heavy seas.

Zizi waited and waited for word he was safe, hoping against hope that he'd been washed ashore. She never stopped praying. Richard was so vivid, so vital, she told herself he'd be found. The baby she was carrying was *his.*

A committed father, Richard Langford would never have turned his back on his own child.

Increasingly desperate as the days went by without news of a sighting or a trace of the yacht, Zizi tried to strike a bargain with God.

Let Richard be safe and I solemnly promise I'll never see him again. I'll go out of his life.

The thought was destroying her.

As an interminable time wore on, Zizi was forced to accept that he was gone.

Lost to me. But not forever. Our love is everlasting.

He would come again, even if he was dead.

Richard will never leave me. Never leave Flying Clouds.

Richard, who would remain eternally young. A heart may be broken, but even then it is compelled to keep beating.

One can cry until there are no tears left, but grief is as deep as the ocean that took him.

IT WAS CLEAR that Zizi hated herself. Most of all, she wrote, she hated the terrible mess she'd made of three lives. She wasn't fit to be a mother. She had to turn to her sister, Mariel, far away. Mariel needed a child. Mariel would make a good mother.

She couldn't sleep. She couldn't eat. She was in some dark place of the soul. It was hideous, her grief. She'd sent for Mariel. Mariel was the strong one. She would stay with her. Mariel would know what to do. She couldn't face anyone but her sister. She couldn't face the world. She was all mixed up. She'd been a wonderful painter, but she didn't know if she could ever paint again.

That was when Zizi had gone into hiding.

Mariel had appeared to offer Zizi a ladder out of her pit of despair, only Mariel was following her own agenda. That was when the whole idea took root. Mariel hadn't sought professional help for Zizi, who'd slipped into a deeper and deeper depression. Nothing but intense misery, when counseling and the proper regimen of medication might have stabilized her. Zizi essentially had fought her breakdown on her own.

Of course, Mariel would've seen to it that she ate properly, as befitting an expectant mother. At the same time Mariel, a resourceful woman, had managed to convince her husband that she was pregnant herself. Having had no success in conceiving, it was understood Mariel had to look after herself very, very carefully. Her husband, Lewis, turned to business while Mariel left him for long periods to stay in beautiful North Queensland with Elizabeth. Mariel, the good and devoted sister.

Stephanie, Richard Langford's child, had been born at Flying Clouds with only the highly organized Mariel in attendance....

ALYSSA SAT BACK, staring into space. It seemed incredible to her now that Mariel had carried it off but she'd returned home with a lovely new baby. The longed-for baby—a beautiful child who resembled her aunt Zizi.

As for Zizi? Emotionally fragile, immensely vulnerable, Zizi had taken it very, very hard. Once she had her baby in her arms she'd started saying she wanted to keep her.

That upset Mariel terribly. She screamed at me day in and day out. I'd promised! In the end I couldn't withstand her. I hadn't the strength. All I had left was Flying Clouds. And Richard. All I have to do is wait for him to come back.

By the time she'd finished, Alyssa's head was spinning and her chest was so tight she could hardly breathe. She rose from the armchair where she'd been sitting to walk onto the veranda. There didn't seem to be any air out on the veranda, either, although the fronds of the palm trees were waving. A pair of rainbow lorikeets, all the colors of the spectrum in their plumage, took up a position on the railing, untroubled by her presence. Directly beneath her, a section of grass was thick with chattering galahs, their white heads and rose-pink breasts glowing in the sunlight. Everything seemed normal. But it was not.

As she stood there caught in the grip of the past, a car drove out of the long corridor of trees. It swept halfway around the graveled drive before coming to a halt. Alyssa moved closer to the wrought-iron railing to look over, causing the lorikeets to fly off.

Gina Rossi. She recognized the car. The sun gleamed on Gina's glossy hair with its dark-wine sheen.

The very last thing Alyssa wanted to do was go downstairs with Gina casting her speculative looks. She was certain her face and manner would reveal how deeply distressed she was. Then again, wouldn't Gina expect her to be upset, given the recent incidents? Zizi's journals had all but driven them from her mind.

Alyssa moved quickly to the bathroom, where she splashed her face with cold water, then patted it dry. She looked decidedly pale but normal enough. In any event, Gina hadn't come to see *her*.

Adam hadn't invited Gina in. The two of them were standing on the front veranda deep in conversation. About what? Adam seemed calm and collected, Gina flushed and excited.

"Oh, hello there, Alyssa." Gina turned to face Alyssa as she walked out to join them. "I've been trying to track down Adam for Dave Belasco. Dave urgently wants to make contact with Adam, but couldn't raise him at the farm. Neither could I, so I took a chance on coming here." She stared at Alyssa intently, taking in her pallor. "You're quite pale. Aren't you well?"

"Just a headache." Alyssa shrugged it off.

"Come in and have a cup of coffee." She found it difficult to treat anyone rudely, even someone as nosy as Gina.

"I'd love that!" Gina responded with enthusiasm. "Wow, this is really *something!*" Her voice echoed down the hallway. "At least Ms. Calvert lived in comfort!"

At least? Alyssa felt a wave of resentment. It stopped her from taking Gina on a tour. "Come through to the garden room," she said, leading the way.

"No wonder *you're* interested in the place, Adam," Gina said in a teasing voice.

Adam greeted this suavely. "I am an architect, after all. Let me do the honors, Alyssa."

"Would you?" Her eyes barely flicked his face. How much credence could she put in Gina's teasing?

"You know you can rely on me to make a good cup of coffee," Adam said over his shoulder.

Seated in the garden room, Gina gazed around with relish. "I'm impressed," she announced, glancing back at Alyssa. "Coming here is like visiting that place in the movie *Brigadoon*. It's like you've stepped into another world."

"It does have a kind of magic," Alyssa agreed.

"Yeah, but I don't think I'd want to live here." Gina pulled a face. "Too isolated, too big and the grounds! You ought to sell. You'd do really well. How are you coping, by the way?"

How was she coping? She was living on an emotional seesaw. But Gina, it seemed, didn't require an answer. Without missing a beat she went on. "You know, my old gran used to talk about this place. She used to tell me it was haunted." Her dark eyes glistened so much Alyssa was further unnerved.

"It is," she told her soberly.

"I wouldn't be a bit surprised!" Gina looked expectant, as though Alyssa was about to add to the folklore. "I hear there were quite a few tales in the village about Flying Clouds in the old days. These days you can't get the old-timers to talk much about it except to say the ghosts have the run of the place. Some reckon they've seen the old captain. Gran used to say Ms. Calvert was very beautiful. She had a man friend, a fellow artist who used to visit her, but she never married. How odd was that?"

Alyssa would have found it difficult to talk about Zizi to anyone. She certainly couldn't to someone as insensitive as Gina. "Falling in love doesn't guarantee that a woman's going to find happiness, Gina, let alone marriage. Perhaps my great-aunt loved the wrong man."

Gina considered that, wriggling to make herself more comfortable. "But why would she hide herself away in an old plantation house?" she persisted. "I mean, a girl doesn't have to marry the love of her life. Most of the time she doesn't. But when it comes to marriage, there are more considerations than romantic love, don't you think? People have to settle for the best deal they can get. Have you ever been in love?"

Alyssa smiled, to take the edge off her answer. "I'm not going to tell you that, Gina."

"Okay, but you like Adam, don't you?" The big dark eyes were as probing as a laser. "I can see why he likes you. You're beautiful and classy but your trump card is you *own* this house. Why can't *I* have a house like this? Adam has pretty much told me he'd love to buy the place, lock, stock and barrel."

For a moment Alyssa felt the world had tilted off its axis. Was Gina making it up? But what reason would she have to say such a thing? "Why don't we ask him?" she suggested. "I can hear the trolley"

Gina inched forward quickly. "Oh, don't do that," she begged. "It might wreck a possible sale. And my commission, let's not forget! What I said was in confidence. I have a feeling Adam wouldn't want me to say anything about it."

"Then why did you?"

"Oh, it just slipped out." Gina had the grace to blush.

"I think you've got it all wrong, Gina," Alyssa said, so upset the air around her seemed blurred.

Gina gave a philosophic shrug. "Could be. He could've changed his mind."

"THERE, THAT WASN'T long, was it?" Adam asked good-naturedly, wheeling in the trolley set with coffeepot, cream, sugar and a small plate of cookies. He looked at Alyssa, noting the distress written all over her. He shouldn't have left her with Gina chattering away, apparently artlessly, but in his experience, to some purpose. Gina had a bad habit of confiding things he was certain she'd sworn to keep private.

Now she accepted cream and sugar, refused a cookie, claiming she had to watch her figure. "Aren't you going to ask me what Dave wants?" She offered Adam a sunny smile.

"I'll wait for him to tell me." Adam moved slightly to take one of the cookies.

"You're not even a little curious?" She laughed. "I'll give you a clue. Lucinda Point."

Adam's dark brows came together rather ominously. "You've discussed this with Dave, have you?"

Gina laughed again, though a tide of red swept into her cheeks. "This coffee is great, smooth and rich! Dave talks to me quite a bit, Adam. I thought you knew that. He's lonely now he's on his own again, but we're strictly friends."

"It looked to me like you were hoping for rather more than that the other night," he returned crisply.

She sputtered, then shot him a challenging smile. "Sure you're not jealous?"

"I'm trying not to be," he answered with a sardonic glint.

"I'll take you over Dave any day!" She laid her hand on top of his, then withdrew it slowly. "That was a real nightmare, Ms. Calvert's yacht getting torched. Everyone's shocked. Nothing like that's ever happened around here before. An arsonist on the loose! Aren't you worried?" She turned her head to address Alyssa directly.

"Of course." Alyssa nodded. "That's why I have Adam *staying* with me."

Gina's coffee nearly sprayed out of her mouth. "Adam's staying here?" Whatever she'd been thinking, it wasn't that.

"Would you really want me to leave Alyssa here on her own?" Adam asked, looking totally at ease with Gina's knowing.

"Well…surely, you have friends to call on, Alyssa?" Gina leaned forward. "There must be someone who could stay with you."

Alyssa shook her head. "I can't come up with a single name. All my friends work."

"While you paint?" Gina's fingers hovered over

the plate of cookies. Finally she selected one, then lost no time polishing it off.

"I wanted to be a painter far more than I wanted to be a lawyer," Alyssa said.

"My, aren't you clever!" Gina allowed a touch of malice to escape her.

"Not clever enough to solve who set fire to *Cherub*."

"I'd leave that to Chief McLean if I were you," Gina advised. "Now, this has been nice, but I really must be going." She spoke determinedly as though Alyssa or Adam or both were about to restrain her. "Do give Dave a call, Adam," she said, catapulting out of her chair.

"Goodbye, Alyssa."

"Nice to see you, Gina." Alyssa forced a smile. "I'll walk you to the door."

Gina all but bounded ahead like a woman who couldn't wait to get out of the place—only she was brought up short by the sight of a long, lethal-looking snake sliding sinuously along the top rail of the balustrade.

"Oh, my God!" she cried as though Cairo was ready to strike.

"It's okay. It's okay!" Adam got between her and the railing. "It's a pet."

"What? Can't you afford a bloody cat?" Gina put a hand to her thumping heart.

"I have a cat, Gina," Alyssa said. "Cairo, that's the snake, is quite terrified of her. I'm sorry he frightened you like that, but Cairo's harmless."

"So *you* say!" Gina wasn't having any of it. "How could you be stupid enough to encourage a snake? I'd have it killed."

"Whatever for? Cairo *is* harmless, though I'm sorry he chose right now to sun himself. He only does that while Cleo's taking a nap."

"Yeah?" Gina let out a strangled breath. "You're more like your aunt than I thought."

"Thank you, Gina," Alyssa said smoothly. "I love it when people say that."

Gina lurched down the steps on her high heels, still shaken by Cairo's untimely appearance. Alyssa went back into the house and Adam accompanied Gina to her car. Gina was scowling darkly, either at the very idea of keeping a snake for a pet or, more likely, Adam's staying over at Flying Clouds. No question about it, that piece of information had really affected her. Was it possible Gina had been telling the truth about her blossoming relationship with Adam, even though he denied it? Did they swim in the sea, make love on the sand, have long leisurely lunches? She wouldn't be the first woman who'd been lied to.

ADAM FOUND HER in the garden room, sitting on the yellow couch with its colorful piled-up cushions. "Everything okay?" Silly question, she thought. The tension crackled and burned.

She turned her head, wondering how she could be head over heels in love with someone without quite trusting him. "I might ask you the same thing? From what I could see, Gina was quite agitated."

He shrugged, moving toward her. "Cairo scared the hell out of her."

"Yes, I'm sorry." She bit her lip. "But honestly, I don't know why. She was born and bred up in the tropics. I've been used to the sight of snakes since I was a child."

Grinning, he shook his head. "Then you wouldn't know what a city guy like me thinks of them. When I first saw Cairo sliding along the veranda railing, I had to seize Elizabeth to protect me."

"I bet." Somehow she managed a smile.

"She told me it was a pet. In fact, she laughed out loud. Listen, you seemed upset when you came downstairs. It's a pity Gina had to call, especially then."

Alyssa looked back at him with a solemn expression. "Did you ever sleep with her?" She realized she couldn't bear it if he answered *yes,* although she had no real claim on him.

He gritted his teeth. "Of course I did," he said

crisply. "The very first night. It was marvelous, the sex of a lifetime!"

"She's a very attractive woman," she said, knowing she'd seriously angered him.

"Yes," he exclaimed, "Gina *is* very attractive. She's also a bit on the nasty side, very indiscreet. She's not averse to telling the odd lie, either. I'm even starting to wonder how she holds down her job." He leaned forward to take her hand. "I know you want to find something to pin on me, since your trust has taken a beating lately, but I *didn't* sleep with Gina. Okay? And she's a very smooth operator. It may be ungentlemanly to mention it, but I couldn't relax my guard around her for a single minute. Most guys would probably describe her as *hot,* but she's definitely not my type. I like to fall in love with my *head* as well as my hormones. I'd say it was blindingly apparent I've lost my head over *you.*"

She looked down at their joined hands. His long, tanned fingers were curled tightly around hers. She loved the feel of his skin against hers, the pads of his fingers callused from working with marble, but strong and warm. "I don't understand why she wants me to think you had something going."

"Some women are troublemakers." He sighed. "Have you forgotten jealousy is one of the deadly sins?"

"I considered it," she admitted, "but I don't understand her reasons for telling me that before you even met me, you were dead keen on buying Flying Clouds."

He stood up abruptly, moving to the French doors and looking out onto the jungle that was the rear garden. His voice, when it came, sounded terse. "You'll have to decide whom you trust, Alyssa. Is it Gina, or is it me? There can be no real intimacy without trust. I think Flying Clouds is a wonderful house, but I can't see myself living in it." *Unless I had you*—but he didn't say it. "Still, it's very much part of the past. I've never thought much about ghosts, but I can *feel* them walking around. They're probably hanging around now, always in the background, and they're not very peaceful. I admit to telling Gina how fascinating I found the place, but she was really jumping to conclusions if she thought that implied I'd like to buy it."

She abandoned herself to her heart. "Okay, I accept that. But it would be easy enough to tear the house down."

Silence.

Alyssa bit down on her lower lip. "It's the *land* that's become extremely valuable. You pointed that out yourself."

"I'm not a developer, Alyssa," he said in a hard voice. "I'm an architect."

"Who works with developers."

"Say what you want to say." His gaze was unflinching.

"I'm only offering reasons, explanations."

"I'd rather you weren't looking at me with such suspicion."

"Is that really how it seems? I suppose I am a suspicious woman now, Adam."

Empathy was in his eyes. "I can understand that, Alyssa," he said in a gentler voice.

She smiled shakily. " I know you're angry with me."

"But I'm not angry enough to leave," he told her. "I'll do that when reinforcements arrive."

"Probably this weekend. Are we fighting, Adam?"

He wanted to go to her, cover her in kisses. He wanted to chase away that haunted look in her eyes, yet he had to hold back enough of himself to think clearly. He was losing more and more of himself to her. As her lover, he was drowning in a sensual sea, a mere mortal lured into unfathomable depths by a beautiful mermaid.

Could history be repeating itself? Nothing was impossible at Flying Clouds.

"We're not fighting, or anything like it," he said soothingly, "so don't go retreating to the safety of your shell."

"You've noticed I've got one?" She lifted shimmering eyes to him.

"We've all got one, but you're quicker than most to go there."

"Maybe that's because I've never been really in love before, Adam. It's the most wonderful feeling in the world. At the same time, the loss of self can be very… threatening."

"I agree." He drew in a harsh breath. "It's not safe exposing one's heart. In a way it's an annihilation of self, just as you've said. That's why Elizabeth disappeared into her fortress. Don't do that to me." He returned to the chair opposite her. "Did you find out everything you wanted to know? I can't wait to hear. Damn Gina and her malicious little tricks!"

She wanted to give thanks for that. "I rushed through the journals when I wanted to take my time, but I had to *know*. I couldn't bear to read the love letters. They weren't written to me."

"Yet I think Elizabeth wanted you to read them."

"I've never had a love letter myself," she confessed.

The intensity of his expression lightened. "There's still plenty of opportunity. I haven't, either, but I don't see why that state of affairs should go on much longer. I'll write you one tonight when you're asleep. I'll leave the little desk light on so I can keep looking at your sleeping face."

Suddenly her whole body glowed. How perfect everything was when they were locked safely in each other's arms. Two against the world. Only it wasn't possible to shut out the world. In bed she abandoned all her doubts. Out of bed, she set up her defenses again. Defenses were important at this dangerous time.

"What do you want of me, Adam?" she asked, staring intently into his eyes. They were so crystal clear she ought to be able to read his soul.

He didn't answer, but swooped down, using his superior strength to pull her to her feet. "You really want to know?" He encircled her with strong arms.

"Yes." She sighed deeply, nestling her head against his chest.

"Okay, I'll tell you but you have to look at me." He raised her chin, staring down into her eyes. "I want *everything,* Alyssa. I want your beauty, your intelligence, the whole *substance* of you. I want the lot. I'm that greedy."

"But haven't I given you everything already?" she protested. "I kept nothing back when we made love. What we share is like a miracle to me."

"It is, but I want more. I want you to trust me with your life."

Her voice shook with emotion. "But I've never given up so much of myself to anyone else, Adam."

"There's no place for distrust," he said quietly.

"Do you think what we have could last a lifetime?" she asked, taking a deep breath to steady herself.

Adam answered very seriously. "Alyssa, I thank God you've come into my life. I want to keep my arms wrapped around you and never let you go." He bent his head to kiss her mouth with passionate intensity. "Everlasting love is not impossible. It does happen. Take Elizabeth and Richard. Only our story isn't going to end in tragedy like theirs. Nor like Julian's," he added, a little roughly.

"I want to give you Zizi's journals to read," she said.

His eyes held steadfast to hers. "Are you absolutely sure?"

"Yes. It's what I want."

"Then you have to read them to me. I want to hear them in *your* voice."

A breeze from nowhere sprang up, making the curtains dance. One fanned out, settling on Alyssa's blond head like a veil. "I'll read them to you tonight," she promised.

"It sounds as if I'll find them heartbreaking."

"You will." She nodded sadly.

He raised a hand to push the filmy fabric from

her head. "You'll make the most beautiful bride," he declared.

"Do you see yourself standing beside me?"

"As if I'd let anyone else take my place!"

"No one could."

The intimacy of the moment was broken by the sound of a ride-on lawn mower kicking powerfully to life. An explosion of parrots burst out of the mango trees, screeching their protests. The noise got louder....

Alyssa drew back, trying to keep the panic out of her voice. "Who's that?"

"Sorry, I should've told you," Adam quickly apologized, "but what with everything else, it slipped my mind." He walked out onto the terrace. "That's Billy Byrd, Byrd's Ground Force Garden Care. The truth is, unless something's done soon, the grounds are going to revert to jungle. Billy does slashing, clearing, lopping, taking away all garden waste. I'll go down and have a word with him. He's a nice bloke. I've had him do some work for me in the past."

"So what are you going to do about Dave Belasco?" she asked before he strode away. "Do you have any idea what he wants? Gina mentioned Lucinda Point." The well-known beauty spot was less than a mile away.

He turned back to her. "It's not the site for

Dave's dream home, I'm sure, although he does intend to build one of these days. It's more likely another luxury resort."

"And he wants *you*." If that was true, it meant a huge commission.

"I'll have to wait and see." He answered casually, as though missing out on that contract wouldn't make much difference.

"Should you waste time? Why don't you go see him now?" she urged.

"I prefer to stay here."

"Nonsense! I'm fine. I've got Billy Byrd. How long do you think he'll be here?"

Adam glanced at his watch. "I'll have him stick around until I get back. He's got plenty of ground to cover. He's a great big guy, built like a water tank. But…I'm not sure I *should* go."

She went to him, shook his arm. "Let's not argue about this. I told you I'm fine. Just go!"

Adam nodded reluctantly. "I'll tell Billy to keep his eye on the place while I'm gone. He's a reliable guy. Anyway, come down and say hello. If you're not happy, I don't go. It's as simple as that. Dave can wait."

Billy Byrd, a gently spoken giant who looked like he could lift trees, passed muster.

CHAPTER NINE

THE PATCH OF rain forest was the perfect cover. At first it had terrified him. The jungle wasn't a benevolent world. It was full of snakes, including the great amethyst python. So far he hadn't encountered one, or a perentie, the giant goanna in its yellow spotted armor, ready to attack anything that got in its path. But there were minor hazards that, city-born, he had to contend with—rain-forest wallabies, bandicoots, legions upon legions of possums, the cuscus, the giant tree rats, the godawful bats, all of them weaving and dodging and flying across the forest floor, the lizards and geckos, the spiders, the beetles, all foraging for food and themselves providing food for the hosts of birds. Dead trees and branches were always collapsing and crashing to the ground, frightening the living daylights out of him Even along the edge of the rain forest, there were stinging trees, the fruit and leaves covered in furry toxic hairs. He was still feeling the effects of the stings he'd suffered more than a month before.

She was at the house. Mariel had told him she was dead set on coming. There was some other reason for Mariel's strong objection, he thought, but she hadn't been willing to tell him. Still, Mariel was an ally.

He had made the rounds of Flying Clouds before Alyssa arrived. Nothing had changed.

Except he'd killed a woman there. Her beloved Zizi. Even thinking about it brought on such nausea he spewed his guts out. He'd killed her but he was no murderer. It had been an accident. He had been pleading with her, reduced to near weeping, desperate to stop her from interfering between Alyssa and him. His obsession with Alyssa grew more powerful the longer she was out of his sight. He'd set up the whole scenario for coming here. After he'd resigned from the firm, he'd fostered the story that he was going overseas for a couple of years. Trust Mariel to spread it! Even Alyssa's father had accepted it. He'd taken to going out to the airport, hanging around the overseas terminal in the hope that someone he knew or knew him would see him there and jump to the conclusion that he was leaving the country for a while.

It had all worked so perfectly, he occasionally allowed himself a moment of triumph. Except that woman, Elizabeth Calvert, had turned on him with such…contempt. Where he'd hoped for sympathy, a bit of cooperation, she'd given him a hearing so cold that—in a fit of frustration—he'd pushed her. That was all he did. He pushed her. His temper had betrayed him as it so often did. But it was scary when she'd stopped moving. She had fallen, hitting her head on the marble surround of the fireplace. How strangely her head had lolled.

The horror he'd felt when he realized she was dead! The back of her short white hair was clotted with blood. Her face wore the unmistakable pallor of death, the peculiar draining. God knows how long it had been before a plan forced its way into his petrified mind.

But the most amazing thing! His plan had worked. He'd wrapped her head, then carried her upstairs to her bathroom, removing her clothes—it seemed impossible that the body of a woman her age could look so youthful—lowering her into a tub he had filled with hot water. Then he'd sat on the side of the bath, giving way to great tearing sobs that threatened to split him apart.

He'd toughened up a lot since then. He wasn't about to let a dead woman disrupt his ambitions. After this was all over, he would get back on track. From the very day Alyssa had arrived, he had started to stalk her, always using the wild bush for a cover. He'd even begun to roam freely around *the rain forest that bordered Flying Clouds. He had spent a few nights in the studio where the old bitch had painted, wondering if he was going to die of starvation, he was getting so little to eat. He'd always hated fruit, but fruit and nuts were keeping him alive. Once or twice he'd even prowled the house, finding food in the pantry, or the odd thing in the fridge she wouldn't miss, before making his way out onto the widow's walk, eyes tightly closed, arms spread, wondering if he should jump. He imagined himself splayed on the grass, Alyssa crying her heart out over him. Since that damn woman's accident, he'd turned into a different person. An outcast!*

That was when they'd seen him. When he was up on the widow's walk. For a moment he'd been afraid because the big guy looked more than capable of protecting her, but he had his escape route prepared. Fury squeezed his heart. Another man had come into her life. How was that possible when they'd barely split up? This man he actually did want to kill. It had taken all his energy to disfigure the sculpture. Another bloody artist! God damn them all! Anger still fermenting, he'd set fire to the little yacht. People and boats everywhere, but no one had seen him slip aboard or slip away in the stolen tender. He'd become very good at fading into the woodwork. All they heard was the roar of the flames. Tramp that he'd become, he had kept his ear to the ground. The police had no idea who'd done it. Nothing happened in places like this. He made sure he had left no evidence anywhere. He'd thought it all through. He wasn't a monster. He wouldn't be portrayed as a monster. He was a man whose mission in life was to win back Alyssa, his Alyssa, the woman who belonged to him.

A few minutes ago, he saw the man leave in his Range Rover. He could hear the distant din of a powerful mower. Someone was on the property, looking out for her. He glanced around one final time, and then stumbled back into the wide green mouth of the rain forest. He could bide his time....

As soon as Adam reached the temporary office Dave Belasco had set up in the village, he put through a call to the house. Alyssa answered, telling him Billy was still hard at work. She was fine, nothing to worry about. How glad he was to hear her voice! Nevertheless he explained to Dave that he had to keep this meeting short. Dave, being Dave, got down to business after first expressing concern about the arson at the marina.

"There's a helluva lot of money tied up there, you know, Adam."

"I do know." Dave's super-yacht alone would be

worth a cool fifteen million and more super-yachts were coming in.

"Who could possibly have had a grudge against Miss Calvert or her great-niece?" Dave asked with disgust in his eyes.

Adam looked back at him grimly. "Let's hope the police find out pretty soon." He didn't mention the destruction at the farm. He couldn't bear to talk about it anyway, and McLean had asked him to keep the incident quiet.

"I've put on extra security," Dave said with a tightening of the mouth. "It was probably kids. Young vandals."

"I think it was more personal than that, Dave," Adam said quietly and left it at that.

DAVE WAS PLANNING to build another luxury hotel, this time on the coast. His last venture had been the Angel Island resort off the Reef. "I'm anxious to get you on board, Adam," he said in his gravely baritone. "Understand me, I have the greatest respect and admiration for your dad, but I want this new place to be entirely different. I was really drawn to that beach house you did for Tom and Amy Thurman, the one that won the award. It worked with the environment. You're great at that. This isn't going to be a big hotel, more like a boutique model. I've found the right spot, I think.

Bishop's Bay. It's just up from Lucinda Point, but I want you to take a look. I want it to have artwork and sculptures around the place. I want it classy, but balanced with the environment. There are hundreds of the usual beach resorts. We're going for something different. The objective is to draw in the rich tourist who expects nothing less than the best. You're the man to take on the challenge."

"Well, I'm glad you have confidence in me, Dave," Adam said, his manner easy and relaxed. "But I need a little time to think about it."

"Sure! How little is a *little?*" Dave narrowed his eyes.

"I need to see the site first. If I'm as enthusiastic about it as you are, say forty-eight hours?"

"That's fine!" Dave seemed relieved. "I suppose there's no possibility Flying Clouds will come on the market?"

Adam was so surprised, he just stopped himself from snapping. "How would *I* know, Dave?"

"You're very friendly with the new owner, aren't you?" Dave asked, a wide grin splitting his face. "Lucky man, she's one of the most beautiful girls I've ever seen."

"She is beautiful," Adam agreed. "And very gifted. She has a law degree. She practiced for a few years but gave it up to dedicate herself to her art. She paints like her great-aunt, Elizabeth Calvert."

"What was the big mystery with that woman?" Dave's voice sounded wondering. "She was beautiful, too, and gifted, but she became a recluse. I know the house and all the surrounding land once belonged to Richard Langford, the yachtsman who disappeared at sea."

"He left it to Elizabeth, yes." No point in denying it. Dave had probably checked out the title deeds.

Dave looked back in benevolent curiosity. "So they *did* have an affair. Can't get much out of the old-timers around here. They're still very protective of Elizabeth."

"Why the interest?" Adam asked.

Dave spread his hands. "It's a great love story, don't you reckon? That house has quite a history."

"Gina didn't happen to show you the grounds?" Adam asked, seeing her hand in this.

Dave's florid skin reddened a notch. "Just a quick peek. We didn't go near the house. It's a fantastic-looking place but it's the land I'm interested in. Gina's a smart woman. Stands to reason Alyssa will be going back to Brisbane."

"It's not coming on the market, Dave. Alyssa doesn't want to sell. She's like her great-aunt. She's rooted to the place."

"Pity!" Dave shrugged. "The old house would have to be torn down, of course, but we could really do something there. A tropical hideaway with splendid views of the Coral Sea and the offshore islands."

Adam shook his head. "It's not going to happen, Dave, so don't get your hopes up," he warned.

But he knew Dave Belasco had heard such things before. "Circumstances change," he said, mildly amused. "You can always put in a good word for me if the time ever comes. But for now, we've got plenty on our plate. What about taking a run out to Bishop's Bay Monday afternoon?"

"Sure!" Adam glanced discreetly at his watch. "Monday afternoon is fine. I'll meet you there if you like. Okay if I bring Alyssa?"

Dave's face broke into a big grin. "Great! Make it two p.m. I might bring Gina. We can make it a foursome."

Adam paused, looking at the developer with calm, direct eyes. "I'd rather you didn't, Dave," he said.

"Hey, what are we talking about here?" Dave's brow furrowed. "You and Gina weren't getting close, were you?"

"Lord, no." Adam didn't want to offend Dave, but by the same token he didn't like to see Dave mixed up with Gina. Still, Dave was an experienced man who made his own choices. "It's just that Gina's in the business and I'd like to keep the situation private for the time being," he offered by way of explanation. "Alyssa isn't going to say anything to anyone. Gina, on the other hand, managed to give Alyssa the idea that I was after the plantation."

"O-kay," Dave said slowly. "You're not?"

Adam controlled his flash of anger. "Listen, Dave, I'd tell you if I were. You're the developer, not me. We can't work together if things aren't straight between us. As an architect I find Flying Clouds absolutely fascinating, so the idea of knocking the house down has no appeal."

"It could be repositioned," Dave suggested carefully, still sizing up Adam's reaction.

Adam shook his head. "No way! The house belongs in that spot. Anyway, Alyssa really loves it. She's been visiting Flying Clouds since she was a little girl. I don't lie, Dave," he added.

"Come to that, neither do I," said Dave. "Well…not to my friends. If it makes you happier, we'll keep Gina out of this for as long as it takes to stitch up a deal."

"See you Monday. I'm looking forward to it." Adam stood up. It wasn't polite to inquire too closely, but he found himself asking, "Interested in Gina, are you?"

Dave gave him a fleeting smile. "She's a very sexy lady but that's as far as it goes. I'm like you. I believe you need trust to make it work."

There was certainly wisdom in that statement. But didn't it imply Dave was none too sure of Gina Rossi?

AT LOOSE ENDS, Alyssa made her way to the attic, where she began to open the trunks Zizi had used to store the beautiful things she'd worn on her travels with Richard Langford.

My grandfather! For proof positive, the Langfords would have to be persuaded to give DNA samples. But first, they'd have to be told the whole story. That was the stumbling block. It was one thing for her to want to put all the pieces together, but the Langfords might have vastly different views. Hadn't anxiety arisen within her, all related to the true identity of her mother and, therefore, herself? She suddenly felt like a stranger in her own family. Loving her mother so much, she couldn't bear to upset her, even though she knew her mother was exceptionally well-balanced, a coolheaded professional woman. Stephanie had a wholeness about her. Could that be destroyed? With Mariel's threat still echoing in her head, mightn't the wisest course be to let the whole thing rest? People took drastic measures to protect themselves. It happened every day. Had any member of the Langford family been aware of Richard's ongoing affair with Zizi? If not his wife, then someone else? Someone he might have confided in? Brother, sister, cousin? She had to ask herself if she could keep such a secret. The answer was probably no. The irony was, in a similar position she would've confided in Zizi.

Richard Langford had perished at sea. He knew and loved the sea, felt at home in it, but the sea was a turbulent place. In the end, it had taken him down to its watery realms. Even with someone of Richard's great skills the sea set traps. Alyssa had a primal feeling that he'd had no intention of killing himself. But he'd died despite that.

Thereafter, Zizi had lived out a fantasy.

If I'm related to the Langford family, Mom's connection is even closer. Could they really turn their backs on such relationships? Richard Langford's children were her mother's half siblings. She felt frantic to lay the whole story at her mother's feet, but such a move could lead to upheaval. Strong emotions were involved. And she could never forget she had Mariel to contend with. She was a little afraid of Mariel. Though she'd tried and tried, she had never been able to cast Mariel as her loving grandmother. Mariel's love was all for Stephanie. Mariel, who had masterminded a massive deception.

No wonder Mariel wanted the past sealed shut. Alyssa didn't have the slightest doubt that if exposed, Mariel would find a way to put the best possible interpretation on her own actions. Within her framework of morality, she'd done nothing wrong. Alyssa could only sit and ponder how her mother would react. Her father, initially shocked, would rally behind his wife.

But perhaps the story shouldn't be told until after Mariel's death. Even with that reassurance, the autocratic Mariel wouldn't welcome it. Her reputation would be besmirched. Unthinkable! And what about Zizi's exhibition? Alyssa was determined it would go ahead. One phone call to Leonard Vaughn, and a showing could be arranged. The "mermaid" paintings couldn't go on show, given the presence of Richard's sunken yacht, the *Miranda,* in every painting. That would be too provocative, causing a great deal of gossip and speculation, not to mention pain.

Was it possible that Richard's wife had never suspected her husband had fallen in love with another woman? She didn't even know if his widow was still alive or had died years ago. She could easily find out. And what about his handicapped child? So many true identities were hidden….

SINCE CHILDHOOD she'd been fascinated by the contents of the trunks. Almost reverently she drew out the emerald-green silk. How beautiful it was, how delicate the perfume that still clung to it. The hem was heavy with glittering decoration, the same decoration that gave weight to the tiny bodice. The years seemed to have had no effect on the condition of the fabric. A pair of satin shoes matched the gown. They fit as though made for her.

She was smiling and crying at the same time. Wearing only her briefs, she put on the beautiful dress, marveling at how smoothly it slid over her body. Impossible to wear a bra with it, but the bodice had been so constructed that her breasts were gently lifted and molded. She loved the effect. It was a wonderfully romantic dress and Zizi had worn it. She must've looked beautiful in it. But happy? It seemed unlikely that she ever knew true happiness. Rapture was something else again. Having to hide one's love, to endure the long separations, must often have filled Zizi with bleak despair.

And yet, she could've had a good life with Julian....

WITH HER LONG HAIR LOOSE, she walked through the empty house, enjoying the tap of her high heels on the polished floors. Cleo was asleep on the couch in her bedroom, but as soon as Alyssa entered the room, she was instantly alert, ears pricked, basilisk gaze fixed on her. Next she rose, back arched high, rigid tail swishing whiplike.

"Hey, don't be alarmed. It's *me!*" Alyssa hastened to reassure her. "I'm wearing Zizi's dress, that's all."

Cleo didn't relax. Her sleek body was full of tension.

"I know. I know. I gave you a fright. But it's just me."

Cleo leaped off the bed and began sniffing around Alyssa's ankles.

"It's me, for goodness' sake!" Alyssa repeated. "I should've warned you. Anyway, I thought I'd wear it tonight for Adam. A romantic dinner. What do you think?"

Cleo's answer, half meow, half yowl, might have been unintelligible to anyone else, but to Alyssa it said: *Go on then. Go right ahead.*

SHE WALKED TO the French doors, looking out on the front of the house. Not exactly a garden, it was more an incredibly exotic flowering wilderness, with everything growing in abundance. She saw that Billy was making inroads in the long grass, and the crescent had been pushed back a considerable distance.

"What am I going to do with this place, Cleo, this marvelous place of secrets?"

Like Zizi, she'd fallen into the habit of talking to the cat. "I love it so much I don't think I could bear to sell it, but how can I keep it when my life is elsewhere? Or is it?" She sighed deeply. How was she going to find a safe path through the labyrinth of dilemmas? If it weren't for Adam, she would feel utterly lost.

Adam! The very thought of him had her dizzy, hot with longing. She was beginning to understand extreme love. How it broke down all the normal defenses. She'd known him such a short time, yet she felt as if she'd known him forever. How did one handle feelings like that? Adultery was wrong, taboo, yet Zizi, a woman of integrity, had surrendered to an illicit passion. Who was *she* to judge? Her feelings for Adam were growing day by day. She hadn't expected any grand passion in life, but now she had it and it hadn't come on her gradually. It had simply arrived to fill up her world.

Loving wasn't an act of will any more than was the ability to forget.

Zizi without her lover had been a lost soul. Alyssa told herself she'd better begin praying that wouldn't happen to her. She was taking her relationship with Adam very, very seriously. Adam now had the power to change her life.

She turned her mind deliberately to the destruction of Adam's sculptures. That sick episode was linked to the burning of *Cherub*. Instinct made her sure of it. And both incidents were linked to *her*. As so frequently happened when she was struggling with her fears, she thought of Brett. She remembered the last time she'd seen him, how he'd sworn he would never give her up. What she had to do was check on his whereabouts without delay.

As she reached for the phone, it rang, startling her so much she gave a choked gasp. Cleo lifted her head, scratching an ear vigorously.

"Hello?" She spoke into the receiver, hoping it was her mother.

It was. "Alyssa, darling. I got your message." Her mother's voice was so similar to Zizi's, she had to swallow on a thickening throat. Stephanie was telling her she and "Gran" would be coming up that weekend.

"Lord knows why Mother wants to come." Stephanie sounded surprised. "She's never wanted to before. I thought she loathed the place. Always going on about the ghosts. You've inherited a haunted house, darling." She paused. "Shocking news about *Cherub*. Probably some vagrant sleeping on the boat. Could've started out as an accident. It was an old rust bucket, though, wasn't it?"

"No, Mom, it wasn't." Alyssa knew her mother cared little about boats or sailing. *She* was the sailor.

"Sorry, darling. I know you and Zizi loved it,"

Stephanie said. "Daddy and I are terribly worried about you being up there on your own. You really will have to think of selling. Mother is absolutely adamant it's the only way to go."

Alyssa was well aware of that. "We'll see." Her tone was noncommittal. She sank down on the bed while her mother told her what flight they were catching and when they'd arrive. "You'll meet us, darling?"

"Of course! I'm thrilled you're coming, Mom. I love you so much."

"I love you too, darling. Your father and I couldn't have asked for a more wonderful daughter. He sends his love. He was going to cancel an important meeting and come with us, but I persuaded him not to. We girls can sort things out on our own."

That was something Alyssa very much doubted.

SOON AFTER, she put through a call to Nigel Morton, probably Brett's closest friend and a fellow lawyer. Nigel became genuinely pleased to hear from her, asking about her family, what she was doing with herself; a whole string of questions. She answered without rushing him, then asked if he knew whether Brett had left for London yet.

"Heavens, he left weeks ago," Nigel confirmed.

"Not having second thoughts, Lyss? He really does love you."

"You're sure, Nigel? Brett's in London?"

"I haven't spoken to him as yet," Nigel told her. "He has to get settled. But yes, we all know poor old Brett wanted a bolt-hole. Not that you could call London a bolt-hole. But he needed a break."

She murmured some appropriate remark, distracting him by asking after a mutual friend, also a lawyer. She ended the call a few moments later.

Brett was in London. That should've made her feel easier.

"WHERE WILL WE have dinner tonight?" she asked Adam when he got back to the house.

"The garden room suits me." It was the ideal place to retreat to, filled with colorful abstract paintings, tubs of flowering orchids and bromeliads, giant hanging ferns and tropical philodendrons.

"The garden room it is." She smiled, perfectly in accord. "How did your meeting go?"

He went to her and put his arms around her, feeling her melt into him. He studied her face for signs of strain. "How beautiful you are!" He bent to kiss her cheek, inhaling her fragrance. "Be patient. I'm going to tell you all about it over dinner. Anything I can do to help?"

She shook her head. "I've got it all worked

out. Mom called, by the way. She and Mariel are coming this weekend. I'm picking them up at the airport."

"Good. At least Mariel has seen the wisdom of coming," he said, hoping it didn't all turn into a nightmare rather than clear the murky air.

"She *has* to come. The journals let me see into Zizi's heart. Mariel's actions were the very essence of ruthlessness and self-interest."

"Then you'd better think twice about who you're dealing with," Adam reminded her, with no intention of allowing her to face things alone. He released her with a light kiss. "I'll go back and have a word with Billy. He's done a good job but there's plenty more ground to be covered."

"Oh, another thing!" she called, watching him pause at the door. "I rang one of Brett's friends, the one I like the best, anyway. He said Brett was in London."

"He's spoken to him there?" Adam frowned.

She answered with a confidence she didn't feel. "Well, not as yet. But everyone knew he was going. Nigel called it a bolt-hole. Brett told him he wanted to put a lot of distance between us."

"That's good to hear." Adam's reply was brisk. "I was afraid he felt more like getting closer." He had no wish to add to her anxieties, but they couldn't afford to think her ex-lover was out of the country until they actually *knew*. There was real hatred behind the destruction of his sculptures; much more concentrated than the burning of the little yacht. From all accounts, Brett was an obsessive, and his obsession was Alyssa.

"Brett did tell Mariel he was going." Alyssa felt his uncertainty.

It hurt him to see the brightness draining out of her. "Then he's gone and good riddance. Stop worrying, Alyssa. The police will get to the bottom of it."

She smiled. "We hope!"

Adam dealt with necessary phone calls, then went downstairs to make a pitcher of dry martinis they could enjoy before dinner.

Alyssa had left the front door open. He hastened to shut it; he not only shut it, he turned the lock. He wanted no intruder creeping up on them. He supposed that Alyssa and Elizabeth had always left the door open. But then, for many years Elizabeth had kept dogs. Dogs barking would herald the arrival of anyone at the house.

"Hi, where are you?" he called, making his way toward the huge kitchen that could do with some modernizing.

"Here."

Her voice didn't come from the kitchen. "Do you want me to go looking for you?" he called with a laugh in his voice. "This is the ideal house for hide-and-seek."

"I'm right here behind you," she said, having moved up on him as soft as a shadow.

Adam turned, his expression amused. Only what he saw wiped all trace of amusement from his face. His heart began kicking against his ribs. Here was the full power of a beautiful woman. Though *beautiful* didn't adequately describe her. *Magical?* That might do. Magical in every sense. He felt the hot rush of desire, mixed with a kind of awe.

"Wherever did you get that dress?" he murmured, his eyes sliding over her with fascination. "You look exquisite! And my God, the necklace!" A fabulous glitter of emeralds and diamonds encircled her white throat.

She floated toward him, like some marvelous apparition. "It was Zizi's."

Wordlessly, he held out his arms to gather her in, his expression that of a man totally ensnared.

Passion rushed like a fire out of control. He could almost hear the roar and the crackle. Adam lowered his head, kissing first her arched throat, then the upward swell of her breasts above the bodice so daringly cut. He kissed the point of her chin, her cheeks, her temples, her mouth. All the while his hands smoothed, caressed, shaped. There was a bonfire all around them, blazing away as their kisses became more needy and passionate. They were standing in perfect safety within a ring of fire.

OUTSIDE THE WINDOWS, a sinister dark figure, thin as a scarecrow, witnessed the whole tumultuous episode. Little chatterings, curses, issued from his mouth. He felt the sickest he'd ever felt in his whole life. Sicker than when he realized the old witch, Zizi, was dead. But…how could she be *dead* when he often sighted her just ahead of him in the rain forest, wearing a billowing, diaphanous dress? Or maybe it was just mist descending from the forest canopy?

His beautiful Alyssa was betraying him, offering up those small perfect breasts to another man's mouth. How he hated that man for being there, taking his rightful place. He was kissing her as though he *owned* her, as though he knew every inch of her body. Not gentle kisses, either, but wildly passionate, proof of their intimacy. She was responding in a way *he* didn't recognize. He could see her face, illuminated from above and beneath. She looked fragile against the man's big, powerful frame, his wide shoulders crouched over her.

The bastard!

Hatred broke over him. He wanted to scream out at them. Hurl abuse. He wanted to smash the man to a pulp but knew he wasn't capable of it. He had gone a little way toward relieving his hatred by smashing the man's sculptures and burning the old witch's boat. How easy it was to get away with things under the cover of darkness.

He had never seen the emerald gown she wore. Had she bought it for *him?* And the necklace! Where had that come from? The straps of the dress had slipped from her shoulders now, exposing more of her near-naked breasts.

Grim tears sprang to his eyes. It looked like she wore nothing under that dress. His modest, luminous, delicate Alyssa was no more than a common slut in this man's arms. Even then, he'd never desired her so much.

The man was picking her up in his arms, burying his face between her breasts. There was only one way this could end!

Ahhhh. Inside he was howling. They were moving away, out into the entrance hall on their way up the staircase, where his usurper would push her down onto a bed, looming over her while she abandoned herself to him…

He couldn't believe it, only he'd seen it with his own eyes.

It was like having the heart ripped out of his body. As they moved farther away, completely out of his sight, he sucked in huge, heavy gulps of air. Mosquitoes, big as aircraft carriers, were making a feast of him. His dirty skin was on fire. He hated the way he couldn't go for a swim anymore. But he dared not venture into the water in case people now on the alert would start to ask who he was. He couldn't go back to the old farmhouse, either. Not for a while. He'd seen the two police cars cruising the district, stopping to ask the locals questions, searching all the abandoned buildings. At least he'd packed up his things and stashed them safely. For the time being, anyway.

You won't get away with this, he sobbed through claimed teeth. *I'll kill you, do you understand? I'm going to end this somehow.*

Something soft and heavy crashed against the side of his face, causing a split second of pure terror. A claw ripped his hood back, clamped into the skin of his black-bearded cheek.

You stinking wretch!

It was that bloody, eerie cat.

He screamed abuse at it silently, but the vicious animal, having made its attack, streaked off into the trees. Was it a *real* cat or had the old witch transformed herself?

He'd take care of the cat, too. Now he was shivering, shaking, bleeding. He rose like an old man, wincing as his leg muscles went into an agonizing cramp. He'd been crouched for too long.

Stumbling one-legged, unable to put the other leg down, he backed into the inky darkness, wailing softly to himself. Finally the cramp eased. He wasn't as fit as he used to be, but he'd never lived like this. This life wasn't just purgatory, it was *hell*.

He stopped to look back up at her bedroom. The main lights were off, and there was only a rose-gold glow. Nothing to see. But he knew what they were doing inside. His whole body shook with jealous rage. Wild-eyed, he walked straight into the branch of a tree, skinning his forehead and nose. He leaned against the tree, hanging on to the trunk, so weakened the tears poured down his face.

What am I going to do? What's happening to me?

Was he going crazy? He hardly knew anymore. He certainly wasn't himself, Brett Harris, up-and-coming lawyer, man about town, in the full bloom of his youth. That man had been destroyed. The death of Zizi the witch had let loose a monster. She was always there. Just ahead of him or moving stealthily at his back. The place swarmed with ghosts. He'd never believed in them until now, but that was before he'd been incarcerated in this green prison. He wasn't ashamed of his fear. He now knew the ghosts really existed.

He remembered once when Alyssa had started to tell him and he'd laughed scornfully, marveling that such an intelligent women could be so foolish. How those same ghosts were gloating now. It was all Alyssa's fault. It was his love for her that had driven him, making him so reckless. He'd never wanted to kill her precious Zizi. He'd been there to remonstrate with her. If only he could go back in time, live it through again!

If only…if only…

All right, he'd hit her, but it had been an *accident,* over in seconds.

Watch out for your temper, Brett!

His grandma had always said that.

One day it will be your undoing.

She wasn't wrong.

Maybe when he'd done what he had to do he'd hand himself over to the police.

CHAPTER TEN

ALYSSA HAD TRIED to persuade Adam to come to the airport with her, but he'd said it would be best if she greeted her family alone. Maybe Sunday, when they'd settled in, he would drop over. He very much wanted to meet them, he told her, and Alyssa could see that he meant it.

They'd read Zizi's journals in bed together, each taking turns.

Adam's verdict had come in without hesitation. "It's like a Greek tragedy!"

Both of them, deeply emotional after their love-making, could understand how blindly Zizi had fallen in love with Richard Langford and never fallen out again. Wasn't that what eternal love was all about? From their own experience they could see all too clearly how it had happened. And afterward, it wouldn't have taken Mariel much time to realize how she could get her pregnant grieving sister to play into her hands. Mariel, not unable to conceive a child of her own—now had a baby. Her own flesh and blood. Niece into daughter.

"Mariel has a lot to answer for," Adam muttered, quietly wondering if Mariel had ever had moments of remorse. And yet…Mariel obviously enjoyed being in command.

ALYSSA ARRIVED at the airport ten minutes before the plane carrying her mother and Mariel landed. Stephanie greeted her with kisses and hugs, naturally demonstrative. "Darling, we're here at last!"

"Dreadful trip!" Mariel, who always had a grievance, stood with a dour face. A tall, substantial woman, Mariel's snow-white hair was piled high. She looked both stately and smart in her dark blue linen tunic over matching linen trousers, the outfit enlivened with lashings of expensive beads and chains. Even silent, she managed to convey impatience at the display of affection between mother and daughter. Alyssa thought she'd finally discovered a reason for Mariel's attitude. Mariel was jealous when even the tiniest bit of Stephanie's love was deflected from her. However, she did condescend to favor Alyssa with an air kiss.

"All ready?" Alyssa asked brightly, looking around for a luggage trolley.

"We'll never be readier," Mariel, who had

brought two large Louis Vuitton suitcases with her, responded acidly.

"Mother's not a good traveler," Stephanie whispered, wrapping her arm around Alyssa's waist. Mariel had become a perpetual grouch, and increasingly imperious into the bargain. "You look wonderful, darling. I was afraid you might be feeling a bit depressed with everything that's been happening."

"Flying Clouds suits me," Alyssa said. She couldn't confide right off that she'd fallen passionately in love. It had happened so swiftly that even her mother might question it. Besides, she'd rather wait for a more private moment....

Stephanie chatted all the way home. There was so much to catch up on. She carried loving messages from Alyssa's father, briefly outlined the two big law cases they were working on, brought news of friends, the latest gossip. The miles flew.

In contrast, Mariel, her expression suggesting she'd been forced into the back of a police car, maintained a heavy silence. She gave no murmur of assent when Stephanie exclaimed over the glorious display of poincianas. The great trees were everywhere, standing in fields and lining both sides of the winding coast road. But then Mariel had never warmed to the beauties of North of Capricorn. She confined her comments to repeating that it had been a *horrendous* trip, followed by the expected news that she already had a splitting headache from the heat.

"Frankly, I find this part of the world vastly overrated!"

Stephanie rolled her eyes in her daughter's direction. In reality, the trip couldn't have been smoother, Mariel had actually dozed off. But Mariel had a point to make. She was anything but delighted to visit. She was here under duress.

"WELL, WELL, a lot's been done around here!" Stephanie remarked in surprise as they cruised up the old plantation's tree-canopied driveway. "Did you hire someone?"

"Yes, I did, a mowing-and-slashing service," she answered. "The operator's name is Billy Byrd. That's his real name."

"And it's splendid! I won't ask you if he whistles."

'Actually, he does. He also acts as a part-time bodyguard."

"You're joking."

"Why would you need a bodyguard?" Mariel boomed from the backseat.

"We won't go into detail now," Alyssa said. "But as I told you, the police are treating *Cherub* as arson. There's been another incident, as well."

"But darling, you never said." Stephanie shot her daughter a worried look.

"It has to do with Adam Hunt."

"That's the young man who found Zizi?"

Alyssa nodded in confirmation. "You'll be meeting him, possibly tomorrow. I told you his father is Philip Hunt of Hunt-Hebron?"

"Yes," Stephanie said. "And I know he's an architect, too. We'll be happy to meet him."

"*I* won't be," Mariel announced abruptly. "I don't want to talk about how he found Elizabeth."

"I'm sure he doesn't want to talk about it, either," Stephanie said.

"So what is this other incident?" Mariel demanded. "I hope we're not getting ourselves into a crisis here. With my high blood pressure, I have to avoid stress."

"Now, now, Mother, Dr. Edwards told me your blood pressure's stabilized with the new medication. There's nothing to worry about."

"A lot *he'd* know!" Mariel retorted. "He's only a G.P." Mariel always trotted out her high blood pressure whenever she was cross or being crossed.

"Adam is a sculptor in his spare time." Alyssa picked up the conversation again. "He studied with Mario La Spina."

"Really!" Stephanie glanced at Alyssa, obviously impressed. "He must show a lot of promise."

"Better than that," Alyssa said. "But someone—a vandal—attacked one of his marble sculptures with a hammer."

There was a shocked, "Good Grief!" from Stephanie.

"Maybe they didn't like it," Mariel said, sounding bored.

"Mother, you *are* in a bad mood." Stephanie looked over her shoulder. "We're here now. I'll make you a cup of tea and something to eat." She turned back quickly to Alyssa. "What does it mean, darling? Who would do such a thing? You've informed the police?"

"They're working on it," Alyssa said.

ALYSSA SETTLED Stephanie in her room first, then Mariel. The bedrooms adjoined, both of them light and airy, with a beautiful view of the Coral Sea. Afterward she'd prepare lunch. She had all the fresh ingredients to hand. Nothing like food to soothe the savage breast, and Mariel's mood could only be described as savage. At least she'd agreed to come.

"Let your mother make the tea," Mariel instructed. "She makes a much better cup than you do," she commented irritably, flinging her beads and chains on the bed, as if they'd been choking her.

Alyssa didn't bother with a reply, groaning as

she lifted one of Mariel's heavy suitcases onto the bed. What exactly was in there, rocks? "Would you like me to put your things away?" she offered, wanting to be helpful.

"I think I can do that." Mariel's reply was stern. She stalked to the door, then closed it. "Anything we discuss must *not* be in front of my daughter," she said, her voice dripping menace.

"Your *niece,* Mariel," Alyssa corrected quietly.

"Don't you start with me, my girl!" Anger flared in Mariel's eyes.

Alyssa shook her head. "I'm not starting anything. More like trying to finish it. I don't want to upset you, but I don't have any option. We need to talk. It doesn't have to be right now. We'll have lunch first. Give you time to settle. We can talk later."

Mariel walked to the French doors, fanning herself violently. The magnificent view apparently didn't soothe her. She turned back to drill Alyssa with a stare. "That's very obliging of you, my dear, but there's nothing to talk about. You really don't think I'm going to allow you to destroy the life I've had all these years?"

"A life of lies, Mariel," Alyssa pointed out. "One gigantic hoax. Did Grandad *know?*"

"For heaven's sake!" Contempt gripped her now. "That man thought I was a saint!" She advanced on Alyssa, taller and more than twice Alyssa's bulk. Her jaw was resolute; there was heat in her greenish-brown gaze. She thrust her face forward. "How *dare* you speak to me about hoaxes! You know nothing about respect."

Alyssa didn't back off. She'd backed off for years and years with "Gran." She wasn't about to now. "I've shown you respect all my life, and a lot of good it did me. Now I know you didn't deserve it! And don't please attempt to strike me," she said as Mariel's hand flailed. "We might have to explain the red mark on my cheek. Mom wouldn't like that. She wouldn't understand. She's never lifted a hand to me in my entire life."

"Well, I'd *love* to!" Mariel said grimly, looking anything but the enfeebled old lady she sometimes elected to play.

"That's pretty obvious," Alyssa remarked. "I don't want any acrimony between us, Mariel. I just want us to get this dilemma sorted out."

"What *you* want sorted and what *I* want sorted are two entirely different things," Mariel snapped.

"Why did you come, then?"

Mariel snorted. "I came because I don't trust you, Alyssa. You've made *a lot* of mistakes."

"Like what?" When all was said and done, Brett was her only *big* mistake.

Mariel's look was contemptuous. "You can't deny

you gave up a promising career. You can't deny you rejected a fine young man like Brett Harris. You sabotaged your chance at happiness. You caused Brett great pain. Maybe you can't control your need to destroy. Maybe you want revenge."

There was such a maddened edge to Mariel's voice, Alyssa stepped back. "Revenge has an ugly habit of recoiling. I don't want revenge, Mariel. That's ridiculous. What I *want* is to give Zizi back her child." Alyssa had to struggle to hold back a flood of emotion. "I'm still mourning her even if *you* aren't. I want my mother to know who her *real* mother is. I want to acknowledge my *real* grandmother. I want to know what we're going to do about the Langfords. They're my mother's relatives, *my* relatives. Or do we just keep quiet and perpetuate the myth?"

Mariel lunged at Alyssa, pushed her hard in the shoulders. "You've just answered your own questions, you little fool!"

Alyssa righted herself, feeling a resurgence of spirit. "Might I respectfully suggest you're the fool, Mariel? I did tell you to keep your hands off me. I'm prepared to wait until after—"

"I'm *dead?*" Mariel gave such a strange laugh Alyssa's heart skipped several beats. "At the end of the day we all finish up dead. Even the young."

" I'm not planning to die for a very long time,"

Alyssa said immediately. She'd been astounded by the strength in Mariel's hands.

Mariel stood looking at her with something like hatred. "The young don't believe in death, do they? It can't happen to them…but it does. If I were you I'd heed this warning. Blacken me in my daughter's eyes and I'll haunt you for the rest of your life."

"If you do, it won't be around here," Alyssa said wryly. "Flying Clouds doesn't want you, Mariel. It *remembers*. You know a lot about being haunted, don't you?"

"Figured that out, have you?" Mariel swung away with a harsh laugh. "I've had my bad times."

"And I'm sorry," Alyssa said. "I pity you. But how could you *do* it? It was so cruel, so ruthless. You could've helped Zizi through her crisis. Instead you turned her agony into your gain. You couldn't control your overwhelming desire for a child."

"And it was worth it." Mariel threw up her head with pride, although her expression was drawn and hard. "Don't think it was easy. It took an enormous amount of planning. Even I doubted I could pull it off. But I did."

Alyssa nodded dully. "There can be no more lies, Mariel."

"Elizabeth and I made a pact to the death." She said it as though that settled everything.

"Zizi *is* dead," Alyssa pointed out, trusting her

voice not to break. "The pact has been broken. Zizi left it to me to decide what has to be done."

"*You?*" Mariel's eyes appeared to glow. "Which just goes to prove what a fool she was. Who'd trust *you* with such a decision? You think you could go to Stephanie and tell her I'm no longer her mother?" She gave Alyssa such a bitter stare, Alyssa winced.

"I know it's a very big thing I'm asking. I've agonized over this."

"Rubbish!" Mariel's voice shook with wrath. She picked up a cushion and sent it flying across the room.

Alyssa was caught up in her anger. "I'm sorry. I'm sorry. But this is for Zizi, Mariel. Zizi and my mother. It's not for me. I'm ready to step aside and allow you to tell Mom the whole story in your own way and your own time. I'll even let you gloss over the part where you raged at Zizi for days when she changed her mind and wanted to keep her child."

Mariel sank onto the bed."I did *not!*"

"You did. It's all in the journals. Mom will want to see those journals. She'll go through them with a fine-tooth comb."

Mariel knew her "daughter" well enough to heave a great noisy sigh. "It's all there, is it?" she asked coldly.

"It's a wonder you never managed to persuade

Zizi to hand them over," Alyssa said. "You could've destroyed them."

"It wasn't for lack of trying." Now there was black humor in Mariel's voice. "Tell me this. Where were they?"

Alyssa felt a jolt of distaste surge through her. "So you searched for them?"

"Just like *you*," Mariel thundered, giving Alyssa another murderous glance.

"But you weren't here. So you had someone else search?" Alyssa tried to see Mariel's hand in the destruction of the boat and Adam's sculpture. Mariel had shown herself to be a merciless woman, loath to let anyone stand in her way.

Mariel ignored the question. "Where were they?" she repeated, a faint sheen of sweat on her brow.

"Where they're going to stay," Alyssa said firmly, walking to the door.

"I shouldn't speak ill of the dead," Mariel said from behind her. "But…"

Alyssa spun around. "Don't let *that* stop you!"

"Elizabeth was mildly deranged."

"And you're not?" Alyssa retorted.

Mariel's smile was icy. "I could do without your smart tongue. You know as well as I do, that I can't possibly tell Stephanie. It would kill me. I could have a heart attack or a stroke. Would that satisfy you?" she asked bitterly.

Alyssa spared her a compassionate glance. "You did this, Mariel. Now you have to undo it. I don't want anything bad to happen to you, believe me. But Zizi deserves justice. It's been a long time coming and you've had half a lifetime of being able to play the doting mother. Not grandmother, though. You've never shown me much in the way of affection. All your love's been for Mom. I've always accepted that. But then you're not my grandmother, are you? You're my great-aunt."

"And you're *Richard Langford*'s granddaughter," Mariel retorted viciously. "Adulterer that he was." Mariel's demeanor held real menace. "Do you really think the Langford family would thank you for causing a scandal?" She glared at Alyssa.

"I guess not," Alyssa admitted with a sigh. "But we should consider this. It might have been a great scandal *then,* but times have changed. There are so many scandals now I wouldn't lay money on this even making the news. The fact that Elizabeth Jane Calvert and Richard Langford had an affair fifty years ago that produced a child, probably wouldn't cause a ripple outside the respective families. Maybe a spate of gossip for a couple of weeks. But that's it."

"You seem to have no regard for me at all. Don't you see that it would *kill* me?"

Alyssa gave a slow shake of her head. "Mariel,

you're as tough as nails. You always trot out the ailments, but that's your way of trying to bind my mother to you. Your ailments, at this point at least, are imaginary. But I do understand your position. It's not a good one to be in. Rest assured that the story need not be told until after you…pass on."

"Pass on? Pass on!" Mariel spluttered. "Why can't you say *dead?*"

Alyssa ignored that. "My loyalty is to my mother and Zizi. I believe Mom has the right to know the truth. She's a strong woman and she has my father's unstinting support. I'm happy to let Mom take over and decide how much further the story goes."

Mariel rose to her feet, looking as indestructible as a granite Easter Island statue. "Don't even try it," she announced, her voice full of warning.

Alyssa tried not to feel alarm. She was a grown woman, not a child. "That sounds like a threat. God knows your suitcase was heavy enough. You don't have any weapons, do you?" Mariel's expression suggested it was something she might have contemplated.

"No, but I daresay I could find someone who does," she said facetiously, then sobered. "Do you really want to cause your mother pain?" She made a final appeal. "Can't you see she's better off not knowing?"

The question stung, but Alyssa had to answer it. "I'm sorry, Mariel, but I can't agree. I know Mom. She could handle it better than both of us." She turned away again. "I'll go and prepare lunch. I won't do anything without telling you first."

"That's a promise?" Mariel surged up from the bed, then forward, getting an iron clamp on Alyssa's arm.

"You have my word." Alyssa looked down. There would be bruises on her arm tomorrow. "Let go, please!"

"You've never crossed me, Alyssa," Mariel said, releasing her. "Don't start now."

THE FOLLOWING EVENING Adam was invited to dinner and naturally accepted. He arrived looking handsome and full of vigor, wearing a summer-weight beige suit with an open-necked striped shirt beneath. The blue stripe picked up the color of his eyes. Alyssa felt very proud of him. He'd brought a couple of bottles of fine wine and a basket of freshly roasted macadamia nuts coated in rich dark chocolate from the village. It was one of the area's specialties.

Stephanie greeted him warmly, expressing her gratitude for what he'd done for the family, while Alyssa smiled with pleasure. Her mother was looking her best, a dozen years younger than her age, charming Adam effortlessly with her beauty and joie de vivre.

Now he's met all three of us. Zizi, her daughter and me.

Their attention was so focused on one another, it took a few minutes for them to realize Mariel was standing stiffly on the stairs.

"Mother, are you all right?" Stephanie broke the tableau, her voice holding a note of concern. Mariel looked so *odd,* one might have thought she'd encountered a ghost on the way down.

Mariel, for once, didn't say a word.

"Mother?" Stephanie repeated, starting toward the stairs.

"I'm perfectly all right," Mariel said, having found her voice at last.

"That's good!" Stephanie murmured, in relief. "You looked so strange for a minute."

Mariel ignored that. "And this has to be Julian Wainwright's great-nephew?" she asked, the words brittle on her lips.

"Good evening, Mrs. Banville." Adam's response was smooth. He gave a respectful inclination of his head. "I've been looking forward to meeting you."

Mariel didn't seem particularly gratified. She waited until she reached the floor before answering. There, she drew herself to her full height, a regal figure in imperial purple, her large hands covered in an eye-popping array of diamonds. "Alyssa failed to mention you're the living image of your great-uncle."

Stephanie frowned. "How could Alyssa know that, Mother?"

A taut smile played on Mariel's lips. "Oh, Alyssa knows lots of things. I'm sure she's seen photographs of Julian in his heyday."

"Then she's one up on me." Stephanie glanced from Mariel to her daughter.

Alyssa shook her head. "Gran's mistaken." The *Gran* stuck in her throat. "I've never seen a photograph of Julian, although Adam did tell me he's thought to resemble his great-uncle as a young man."

"Resemble? He looks exactly like him," Mariel snorted.

Stephanie smiled in an effort to lighten the thunderous atmosphere her mother had brought with her. "Then he must have been a very handsome man."

"He's still alive, Stephanie." Adam smiled into Stephanie's eyes. "Although he's very ill."

"I'm sorry to hear that!" Stephanie touched his arm. "But this is all news to me. I've never heard you mention Julian Wainwright, Mother. Of course I'm aware that Zizi owned several of his paintings. They're here in the house."

"Julian gave them to her, Stephanie. At one stage they were very good friends," Adam said.

"Really?" Stephanie was looking slightly bewildered. "I would've expected Zizi to mention that. To the best of my knowledge, she never did. Did she say anything to you, darling?" Her green eyes, so much like Zizi's, sought her daughter's.

Alyssa shook her head again.

"Elizabeth was a great one for secrets." Mariel gave a wolfish smile that had nothing of humor in it.

"Well, let's not stand about in the hall," Stephanie said, pressing on. "Come in, Adam. Alyssa tells us you're a sculptor as well as an architect. How exciting!"

Alyssa and Mariel followed, warning bells ringing in Alyssa's head. Bells she knew she'd do well to heed.

"The new boyfriend, eh?" Mariel murmured in a mocking undertone.

Alyssa didn't answer.

The time of reckoning had arrived.

SHE WAS HAPPY to let her mother play hostess. Stephanie was not a woman to take a backseat in any case. She had a great capacity for enjoying herself, as Zizi had once appeared to. But Stephanie had allowed Alyssa, the superior cook, to handle dinner.

For starters Alyssa had decided on scallops wrapped with bacon, put under the grill and served with a red wine sauce, crab lasagna for the main course and peppered pineapple and vanilla ice cream to finish.

"This is something new, isn't it?" Mariel asked, dubiously pushing a spoon around her dessert bowl.

"I daresay Trudie has never tried it." Stephanie's tone was lightly amused. Trudie was her mother's long-suffering cook.

"Sugar, lemon juice, orange juice, a sprinkle of black pepper, unsalted butter, crème de cacao to flame it." Alyssa listed the ingredients. "Try it… Gran."

"No, thank you." Mariel pushed the dish away.

DESPITE MARIEL'S best efforts to put a damper on the proceedings, the evening went well. Stephanie, full of enthusiasm as she always was in congenial company, had obviously taken a great liking to Adam. Her mother shone at any gathering, Alyssa thought affectionately, having witnessed it dozens of times over the years. She was pleased to let her mother direct the conversation. It covered a wide range of subjects, down to their favorite films and Broadway musicals. They all joined in with the exception of Mariel, who sat there as if only familial duty kept her in her chair.

Adam, like Stephanie, was very much a social animal; he told a number of stories about the demands of rich clients that had everyone laughing helplessly. Everyone except Mariel.

Though she'd eaten well—settling for a dish of *plain* ice cream—Mariel kept determinedly to raised eyebrows and one or two diluted smiles she couldn't prevent. Once she tut-tutted disapprovingly at one of Stephanie's slightly risqué stories, causing Stephanie to turn to her.

"You *are* serious tonight, Mother. The last time I told that story you laughed."

True.

"Perhaps I'm tired," Mariel said, folding her napkin as a signal to them all. "Would you mind if I excused myself now? You'll come upstairs with me, Stephanie?"

"Of course," Stephanie agreed.

Adam rose to hold their chairs. "Good night, Mrs. Banville."

Mariel waved a lethargic hand.

Stephanie, effervescent as ever, led Mariel off, giving a little backward wiggle of her fingers. "Back soon."

ALYSSA BEGAN clearing the table. Adam pushed the trolley laden with used china, cutlery and crystal, back into the kitchen.

"I don't think Mariel likes me," he said dryly.
He could scarcely label her an appallingly rude old
bitch, which was what he thought. Swiftly he took
the opportunity to put his arms around Alyssa,
trailing kisses along her neck into the curve of her
shoulder. "I'd love to ask her straight out about
Julian. How well did she know him?"

"But you could ask Julian yourself." Alyssa
relaxed her body against him.

Adam nodded. "I'll call him first thing in the
morning."

Alyssa nodded, then turned away to set the
dinner trolley with the coffee things.

"Julian still wants to meet you."

Alyssa paused. "There's really no point."

"I think there is," Adam insisted. "Julian would
love to meet your mother, too. She's a real
charmer—beautiful, witty, clever. You and your
father must be very proud of her."

"We are. Dad worships her." Alyssa smiled.
"I was waiting for that famous line, *you could
be sisters!*"

Adam laughed and reached for her again,
holding her close. "She's certainly very youthful.
But you are *you*. By the way, you're right about
your mother looking more like Elizabeth than you
do. She has her green eyes and the voices are eerily
similar, although when I think about it, all three

of you sound—sounded—very much alike. Did you manage to have that talk with Mariel yet?"

Alyssa sighed forlornly. "She wants no part of it."

"I suspect she's had her own way for most of her life." Adam took over from her to make the coffee.

"Well, she's not getting it now." Alyssa's voice was determined. "Nothing is going to keep us from having that talk."

IT WAS WELL AFTER midnight before the evening broke up. Adam had deliberately parked the Range Rover a short distance from the house so when they were saying good-night he could take her in his arms, knowing they were screened by the overhanging branches of the trees.

It was a kiss to be savored, a yearning kiss they held for as long as possible, wanting so much more, but constrained to wait.

"Marry me," Adam said in a low voice.

"Adam?" Her heart shook.

He lowered his head to kiss her again, taking her upturned face between his hands. "I said, marry me, Alyssa. I'm not expecting you to set the date. Not right here and now, anyway."

"You're serious?" She grabbed hold of his lapels.

"Surely you're not surprised?" His voice was ineffably tender.

"I'm excited! I'm *ecstatic!*"

"That's my girl!" He felt alight with exultation, the most fortunate of men. "I hadn't intended to say it tonight. I wanted everything to be perfect for us. All our problems resolved. But the way I feel, it just popped out. God knows I've thought of little else. You make me happier than I ever dreamed I'd be, Alyssa. I need you. I want you. I love you. I think your parents will approve. Although Mariel will probably object."

"Well, that would be normal," she teased. She didn't bother telling him Mariel had considered Brett an "excellent catch." She didn't want to mention Brett ever again.

"You haven't said *yes*," he prompted.

"*Yes, yes, yes!*" She threw her arms wide to encircle his lean powerful frame, then rested her head against his chest. "I choose you above every other man in the world."

"And I choose *you*. I want to take you home with me so badly," he groaned.

Her mouth curved in a satisfied smile. "That's the way a man in love should feel. When do we announce this to the world?"

"Whenever you want is fine by me. I've already told Julian I've fallen madly, deeply, passionately in love."

"And?" she asked, a shade anxiously.

"He's very happy about it. In fact he positively applauded."

"Then he must stay alive for the wedding."

"Exactly my thoughts, which means we have to set a date as soon as possible."

Alyssa felt swept away on a magic carpet. "All I have to do is strike a bargain with Mariel. I want this business of Zizi out of the way first. Do you mind?"

"Of course I don't," he said gently. "I understand perfectly. We'll keep it our secret for the moment." Adam moved to kiss her one more time, covering her mouth ardently with his.

WATCHING THEM FROM the shadows was a white featureless face.

IT WAS HARDLY necessary to say a word to her mother.

As soon as Alyssa walked back inside, carrying Cleo, who'd bounded to her from out of the darkness, Stephanie appeared in the entrance hall, her face full of questions. "Have you met the man of your dreams, or haven't you?"

"What do you think?" Alyssa laughed, lowering Cleo to the floor. Since Mariel arrived, Cleo had stayed far away, taking up residence in the great outdoors.

Stephanie went to her daughter and gave her a

delighted hug. "It's hard to imagine a more captivating young man. He has so much to offer, and he's such a good match for you, both of you creative artists. I suspect it won't be long before his sculpting takes over from the architecture."

"He intends to try for both," Alyssa said, turning to lock the front door. "At least for some time. He told you about the Belasco project. He's fairly certain to get it."

Stephanie's eyes were shining. She wound her arm around her daughter's waist as they walked into the living room, with Cleo leading the way. Apparently Cleo had discerned that Mariel was already in bed. "I'm just so happy for you both, darling. You deserve the best. Wait until your father hears!"

"Just give us a little time, Mom," Alyssa begged, happiness and excitement almost reducing her to tears.

They sat opposite each other, all tremulous smiles. Cleo turned a full circle in Alyssa's lap before settling herself comfortably. After that she stared across at Stephanie sphinxlike, with unwinking golden-green eyes.

"Are you sure Cleo isn't human?" Stephanie asked.

"I think she was at one time," Alyssa said. "Either that or she's a shape-shifter."

Stephanie laughed, looking so relaxed Alyssa wondered if she should abandon her plans to reveal the past. Dared she risk bringing pain into her mother's ordered life? She'd believed things were becoming clearer. Suddenly everything appeared even more complicated.

"She's really taken to you," Stephanie remarked. "She's generally very standoffish."

"She's my best friend now," Alyssa said, stroking Cleo's fur, which glowed like polished amber. "Aren't you?"

Cleo meowed a smug *yes*.

"Poor darling is keeping her distance from Mother," Stephanie said with a rueful smile. "Mother isn't a cat-lover, or a dog-lover for that matter. I don't understand it. I stopped begging for a pet at around age ten. Mother always said animal hair made her ill."

"I've never actually seen her ill," Alyssa muttered.

"Well, you know, most of Mother's problems are imaginary. The truth is, she has a cast-iron constitution."

"Why do you allow her to get away with it?"

Stephanie shrugged. "I'm rather ashamed of myself, really, but it's a case of peace at any price. I had to battle for independence when I was growing up. It was a battle to hold to my convictions, too. Anyway, I made it with your father's help. But let's get back to you. To think you had to come up to Flying Clouds to find the love of your life! Zizi would be very happy about that. She loved you so much."

"She loved you, too, Mom," Alyssa said gently. How could she go about telling her mother the truth? Should she even tell her? Impossible to blurt it out. But then Stephanie was a woman who handled problems, she reminded herself. Her mother was the epitome of grace under pressure. She also had, as she was always quick to point out, a devoted husband.

"It can't have been easy for Zizi up here on her own," Stephanie said with a musing expression. "I always thought she had a great love affair that went disastrously wrong. Zizi was the sort of woman who only gave her heart once, the sort of woman who mated for life. Rather like me, actually, and I would think you. I love your father today even more than I loved him when we were young and crazy." She grew quiet for a moment. "I've never spoken about it, but tonight I'll tell you that Mother gave your father a hard time. There were others she preferred among my admirers. The sort of young men she thought she could manipulate and control. Your father would have none of that. There *is* such a thing as everlasting love, Alyssa, my darling. Somehow I think you've found it. I certainly have."

Alyssa felt emboldened to speak. "Would you really want to know if Zizi had a secret life? One she may have kept from us?"

Stephanie's response was swift. "I'd *love* to know. Zizi was a mystery woman. She wanted it that way. She kept so much from us, her early history, her *secret* history. She was a good person, but nothing about Zizi would surprise me. She was haunted by something. Someone. We both know that. Mother claimed Zizi had a serious breakdown in her twenties and never fully recovered. She's convinced Zizi would have been dead except for her, that she saved Zizi's sanity. In those days Mother visited her a lot." Stephanie broke off. "You haven't found anything, have you, like love letters tied with a ribbon?" Stephanie tried for humor, but the green eyes searching Alyssa's face were dead serious. "It's only to be expected that Zizi had a lover. Then there's this business with Julian Wainwright. Didn't our Zizi keep quiet about *that!*"

"What if Zizi's love letters would only make you unhappy?" Once started, Alyssa realized she didn't have complete control over the flow of questions. She had to sound out her mother, Mariel or no Mariel.

"Sad, you mean," Stephanie corrected. "Zizi is at peace now. Maybe at peace with a secret lover. You've found the letters, haven't you?"

"You're convinced she had a lover?"

"Of course!" Stephanie's tone was matter-of-fact. "I'll tell you a really strange thing now that Zizi's gone and we're talking quietly together. I always had a weird feeling *Zizi* was my mother."

For a moment Alyssa's heart stopped, then went rockily on. "Why would you think that?" Her eyes focused on Stephanie in absolute amazement.

"It was an intuitive thing. I didn't *know* it, of course. I *felt* it. I don't expect you to understand." She sounded defensive. "I also felt Zizi was lost to me, somehow. She could have *you,* but not me."

Wasn't that the deal that had been struck? Alyssa didn't need to affect shock. She was overwhelmed by it. Her mother had felt this for much of her life, yet had never mentioned it. Had she confided in her father? Her parents couldn't have been closer; and as far as she knew, they had no secrets from each other.

"It's all right, darling. I'll stop now," Stephanie said, turning remorseful eyes on her daughter's stricken face. "I didn't mean to upset you, but it seems to be a night for confidences. This house always did have a profound effect on me. When I was young, the notions in my head·upset me so much I used to stay away from Flying Clouds. Mother did her level best to alienate me from Zizi, anyway. There was such conflict between those two, although they did their level best to hide it. Mother was tremendously jealous of Zizi, you know. They were such a stunning contrast, weren't they, in looks, in manner? Zizi seemed to have got it all. Then, as it turned out, I took after Zizi, not Mother."

"This is incredible!" Alyssa gasped. "You've never breathed a word of this, not even about their conflicts." She desperately wanted to continue the conversation, bring it all out into the open, but she remembered her promise to Mariel. Not that either of them owed her anything.

"Because it was all so…strange."

"Are our primal instincts *strange?*" Alyssa asked. "I don't think so. Surely some part of us is forever attached to our mothers. Perhaps if we're separated from them, we're separated from part of ourselves."

Tears filled Stephanie's eyes. "You've hit the nail on the head, my darling. I've always felt this *separation*. But if what I thought was true, that meant Zizi had rejected me. I couldn't have coped. With time, of course, thanks to your father and you, my own beautiful child, there's real contentment in my life. As a woman I could handle such a revelation. I couldn't as a child. We *are* speaking hypothetically, aren't we?" She looked at Alyssa with a pained expression.

"God knows!" Alyssa felt her heart flutter in agitation.

"I think you *do* know, darling," Stephanie said. "I can see it in your eyes. The greatest worry of all for your father and me was the thought of hurting *you*."

"You wouldn't have!" Alyssa instantly dismissed that. She'd been worrying herself sick about how to approach her mother, when it seemed her mother had spent years agonizing on her own.

"Goodness, me, what are we talking about anyway?" Stephanie visibly shook herself, trying for a smile. "The wine has loosened my tongue. Lovely, wasn't it? Adam has excellent taste." She was silent for a moment, then asked, "So what *did* you find?"

"Does Gran know or guess how you feel?" Alyssa asked quietly.

"God, no!" Stephanie recoiled. "I think we both know how Mother would react if I suddenly asked her if Zizi was my real mother. She would fly into a passion. Mother's world isn't the way things *are,* it's the way she wants them to be."

"Surely she could endure a few questions?"

Stephanie gave a brittle laugh. "All right then. Could *I* endure it? That's the thing!"

Alyssa tried a different tack. "It sounds like you've talked to Dad about this?"

Stephanie's expression softened. "Of course I have, darling."

"So what does *Dad* say?" Alyssa felt desperate to know.

Stephanie stared at her daughter intently. " I told you. Our main concern has always been you, my darling."

Alyssa found herself trembling. "You really believe Zizi was your mother, don't you?" She felt their talk had progressed to a level beyond pretense.

Stephanie gazed down at her locked hands. Just as Alyssa thought she wasn't going to answer, she inhaled deeply. "I could never shake that feeling. It's haunted me all my life. I truly believe it's worse *not* to know than to be left perpetually wandering in the dark. When I was a girl I used to feel a little crazy with everything that was going on in my head. I never had the courage to tackle Mother about it, though. What if I was dreadfully wrong? She would never have forgiven me. Dad and I—" Stephanie's mouth twisted "—used to tiptoe around her. If you think she's formidable now, you should've seen her around the time your father and I became involved. But no one's ever defeated your father. For that matter, no one was going to stop me from marrying *him!*"

"You were made for each other," Alyssa said in simple explanation.

Stephanie smiled her agreement. "Your father was the great turning point in my life. From him I derived a great part of my strength. But you, how would *you* feel if history were to be rewritten?" Stephanie's tone showed deep concern. "The very last thing I want to do is bring pain and disruption into your life."

"Now, isn't this *touching!*" said a voice like a blunt knife from the doorway.

CHAPTER ELEVEN

DESPITE HIS EUPHORIA, or perhaps because of it, Adam drove back to the farm at a sedate eighty kilometers, listening to a CD of Tom Waits he particularly liked and singing along with it. There were no other vehicles on the country road—traffic was sparse at any time, and it was after midnight—so he had his headlights on high beam. That way he'd have early warning of a roo, a wallaby or some small nocturnal creature on the road. He had no wish to injure or kill some poor wild creature and he didn't fancy damaging his brand-new Range Rover. He hated bull bars but he might have to get one. As a seventeen-year-old with his first car, he had narrowly avoided crashing into a tree to avoid hitting a golden retriever on the loose.

He was halfway between the plantation and the Gambaro farm when a wallaby bounded out onto the road in front of him and, in its completely silly, no-road-sense fashion, stood transfixed by the sight of his approaching vehicle.

"Damn!" Adam touched the brakes to ease up, hoping the wallaby would bound off into the bush, but instantaneously, within a heartbeat, he realized something was terribly wrong. The improbability of it shocked him.

His brakes weren't working.

Next thing he knew, he had plowed into the unfortunate wallaby, leaving it dead on the road with him struggling mightily to bring the 4WD under control. Adrenaline flowed through him until he was nearly drunk on it. He had little option but to steer off the road and plunge into whatever would stop the vehicle without killing him. Vine-laden old fences came up in the headlights. There was a big stand of sugarcane that grew right up to the roadside just ahead.

If he could make it round this blasted sharp bend…. The tires were spraying up dust and debris. He'd spotted the abandoned old farmhouse on previous drives, its timbers bleached and baked dry by the sun. There were quite a few derelict farmhouses in the district. It was the land that was now valuable, not the rich cane that had once brought in a fortune.

Thank God, there it was! Its hulk stood in silhouette against the diamond-studded sky. Towering coconut palms surrounded it, the great fronds waving in the strong sea breeze. The dense wall of sugarcane that came right down to the road was a good twenty feet high. The copper moon was very much on his side; it came out from under a cloud and shone on the corrugated iron roof of the farmhouse, turning it into a beacon. The abandoned cane fields lay spread out before it.

Don't think. Do it! This is the place.

Twenty yards on he picked his point of entry. He thanked the Lord he had superb night vision. The Range Rover careered off the road with a screech of tires, heading like a rocket for the dense forest of cane.

Someone out there doesn't like you, Adam.

FOR A SPLIT SECOND her beautiful, brilliant mother looked like a frightened child who didn't know how to protect herself. Alyssa jumped up quickly, dislodging Cleo, who yelped more than yowled, then tore into the entrance hall, obviously making for the safety of Alyssa's bedroom. Alyssa took her mother's hand in hers, squeezing her fingers reassuringly.

"It's true what they say. Eavesdroppers never hear well of themselves." Alyssa addressed Mariel's daunting figure.

"You distrustful little bitch!" Mariel hissed back. "You *told* her."

"Told me what?" Stephanie spoke forcefully, herself again, the color returning to her face.

"How despicable you are, Alyssa!" Mariel's eyes seemed to have sunk back in her head. She had braided her copious white hair for the night. It hung over the shoulder of the elaborate kimono-style robe she wore.

"Why don't you sit down and join us," Stephanie said, her tone quiet, but in firm control. "We obviously need to talk."

Mariel flinched as though from a blow. "There's nothing to talk about, dear girl."

"Then why did you come downstairs?" Stephanie queried, calm as a judge. "You must sit down and help us find the truth."

"With some things it's better *not* to know, Stephanie," Mariel retorted harshly, holding her body ramrod straight.

"How long have you been standing there listening to us?" Alyssa continued to hold her mother's trembling hand.

Mariel turned on her with near-manic fury "I don't want to talk to *you* ever again, Alyssa."

"Talk to *me* then," Stephanie invited in that same level tone.

Mariel shook her head violently. "You're my daughter, Stephanie. I demand respect."

Stephanie shook her head. "I think there may

be proof that I'm Zizi's daughter," she said simply.

The silence seemed to grind on forever, then Mariel snapped, "Where is it then, this proof?" Her eyes flicked venomously to Alyssa. "Go on, show me. If you're talking about those journals, let me tell you that when she wrote them, Zizi was off her rocker."

Stephanie's gaze didn't waver. "She *was* my mother, wasn't she?"

Alyssa tried to regain control, but the tears were streaming down her cheeks.

Stephanie, on the other hand, looked calmer and more judicial than ever. "*Wasn't* she, Mariel?" she repeated.

Before Mariel could answer, or demand to know if Stephanie had taken leave of her senses, the phone on the console in the entrance hall began to shrill loudly.

"Who could that be?" Stephanie turned to Alyssa her forehead pleating.

"I'll get it." Alyssa flicked away tears with the tips of her fingers.

"Sit down, Mariel, before you fall down," Stephanie suggested. "No matter what you're telling yourself at the moment, no matter how hard you try to destroy Zizi's memory, the long pretense is over. I need—Alyssa needs—the kind of resolution we've been looking for."

THE AIR BAG RELEASED on impact with the cane. He leaned back, feeling like he'd been hit by a hammer. The thing was bloody near smothering him, though it had done its job, preventing him from being pitched into the windshield. For a few wild minutes he thought he might suffocate. Just when his world had come miraculously right, he was going to be crushed by an air bag.

No!

His heart was throbbing in his chest, the air was unbreathable, he was covered in sweat but he had to get out.

At least he was alive and in one piece.

He estimated the vehicle was some twenty-five to thirty meters into the cane, which would be full of vermin—rodents, spiders, giant cane toads, vicious *snakes.* God, how he hated them! His hand moved to the door, pushing hard, trying to open it sufficiently to get out. A rain of debris and dried blades of cane came down onto the roof of the vehicle and blew into the interior, making him cough violently. What he needed was a big machete to hack his way out. Why didn't someone just burn the abandoned fields off and let them lie fallow? Or plant something, for God's sake. He wasn't even wearing boots, but loafers. He pulled a handkerchief out of his pocket and wrapped it around his right hand. He'd rather not get cut by the cane.

Gingerly he made his way around to the passenger side, reaching in for his heavy-duty torch. He straightened, shining it about. Its white beam immediately picked out the hideous giant cane toads that mercifully were leaping *away* from him, back into the cane. Thirty seconds later, the beam raked over rats on the move. He sucked in a lungful of surprisingly sweet air. A snake was right in front of him, whipping its head from side to side like a cobra.

Bloody hell!

He stood perfectly still. A moment later, the snake flattened itself out, then slithered away. That made him feel better. What he had to do was get to the top of the rise for the best reception. He could call Alyssa on his cell phone. They couldn't be in bed yet; he'd been traveling less than fifteen minutes. After that, he'd call the police. Someone out there was playing deadly games and had to be stopped.

"I'LL COME WITH YOU," Stephanie said, after Alyssa returned with the news of Adam's lucky escape. "Thank God it's nothing more serious. He could've been killed!"

"Don't even say it, Mom!" Alyssa had found

the car keys and was moving purposefully to the front door, totally focused on getting to Adam.

"What exactly am *I* supposed to do?" Mariel demanded in an aggrieved voice.

"Lock the door after us," Stephanie said. "We'll be as quick as we can."

"I'm sure Alyssa doesn't need you," Mariel thundered.

"Oh yes, she does!" Stephanie was already out the door on her way to the garage.

MARIEL DIDN'T LOCK the front door. She was past caring what happened to her. She slumped into an armchair feeling incredibly heavy in body and mind. The whole deadly business would come out and there wasn't a thing she could do about it.

"Are you happy now, Elizabeth?" she addressed the empty room. Not so empty, she decided. She could see Elizabeth's shadowy figure over in that corner. "You got the last laugh."

Some people could never escape a guilty conscience. Mariel had no such difficulty. She blamed her sister for everything and would continue to do so until the day she died.

HE SAW THEM LEAVE in the car Alyssa had rented. What did it mean? He'd heard the phone in the still night air. Surely he hadn't bored a hole in the

reservoir, allowing the brake fluid to escape, for
nothing! Perhaps not. The bastard could be badly
injured. They must be racing to his side. He'd
seen Mariel go up to her room an hour and a half
ago. What an ally she'd been! He didn't like her—
she was dreadfully dictatorial—but she'd always
been on his side. He meant Mariel no harm. Nor
Stephanie, although he knew Alyssa's parents had
never really taken to him. His charm hadn't
worked on them the way it had worked on Mariel.

He moved stealthily toward the house, pausing
every so often to check for movement inside. But
Mariel was an old woman. She'd be fast asleep,
dead to the world. He'd had a key to the front
door for some time now. He could slip inside and
grab some food. He was starving, sick to death
of nuts and fruit. He craved bread and something
to put on it, ham, chicken, anything, even jam. He
was starting to wonder if he should seize the
initiative and hide in Alyssa's room. He was desperate to speak to her, *touch* her, explain the
whole terrible business. What troubled him was
the condition his body was in; he who had once
been so fastidious. How low he'd sunk—it didn't
bear thinking about. Could he risk a shower or
would the sound of running water wake Mariel?
He lifted his hands to his bearded face, revolted
by the thick tangle of hair. A few weeks back

he'd tried to get a part-time job with Byrd's Grounds Service, reasoning it could get him access to Flying Clouds during the day. He knew Byrd was working there. He'd tried to clean himself up before he applied, but he'd come away from the place shaking with anger.

"Sorry, mate! I'm not putting anyone on at the moment."

Lies, all lies! He hadn't trusted himself to respond. He'd wanted to throw a punch, but the guy was built like a tank and was looking at him very closely. By now he reckoned Byrd would've rung the cops, saying he had a suspect for the arson at the marina. Everybody knew everybody else in these bloody one-horse towns.

He felt scared, no question. Scared to the point of doing something crazy.

And all this horror had started because of Zizi.

THE DOOR wasn't locked. The great bronze knob turned easily. Fools! Didn't they know there was a madman at large? He nearly laughed aloud at that description of himself. His only sin was he had loved a woman too much. A woman who'd abused his trust. Women were the root of all evil, he mused. Take that bitch Zizi, for example. Her controlling role in Alyssa's life had been instrumental in their breakup. Somehow she'd persuaded Alyssa to get rid of him. She had deserved to die, but her death had created even greater problems.

He was inside the house. Although it was ablaze with lights, he was instantly aware of the ghosts. The whole house was *listening* for him, knowing what had happened here. What he needed to do first was get some food inside him. He was almost fainting from hunger. There was only so much fruit a man could eat and the nuts stuck in his dry throat.

He started to move, but the sound of a woman's voice had him freezing in his tracks. God Almighty, it was Mariel.

"Who's there? Stephanie, Alyssa?"

Even now she had that authoritative bark. He put up his hands, covering his ears as she continued to call.

Silly old fool! He muttered under his breath.

"Brett? Is that *you?*"

She was standing a few feet from him, a witch-like figure in a magnificent dressing gown, strands of her long white hair hanging about her face. She was staring at him with such disbelief.

"Brett?" She took a step closer, her face as white as her hair but her voice perfectly controlled. "Whatever has happened to you, poor boy?"

Too much shock cut his vocal chords. He held up a hand to ward her off. The Brett she knew had disappeared long ago.

"Speak to me, my boy!" Mariel commanded, her stare intense. "Where have you been hiding? Tell me. I want to help you."

Help? She had to be as mad as he was. He was beyond help.

To keep her away from him, he backed onto the veranda, his heart thumping so hard he thought he might suffer cardiac arrest.

"Brett!" She came after him, that bloody *theatrical* voice taking on soothing tones. What was she trying to do, calm him? "You need my help. Don't go!"

For an instant he listened, hope flaring, but then in the next breath something fell from the awning above him and landed heavily on his shoulder. It wrapped itself around his neck.

He screamed. He couldn't stop screaming. It was the vilest of vile *snakes!*

He was in the middle of a nightmare. He couldn't go on. He staggered backward in absolute terror, lost his footing, tumbled down the short flight of stone steps. He was lying on the graveled drive, but now the snake was nowhere in sight. Had he imagined it? The old woman was leaning over him. She was saying something to him. "Be calm, be calm, dear boy. The snake is harmless. It's Cairo."

That made no sense. He felt exhausted, dazed....

"Listen, Brett. You have to get up," she said urgently. "They could be back anytime. You'll be interviewed by the police. Was it you who set fire to the boat? I understand how betrayed you've felt. But you must get up. You *have* to! I don't want to see you arrested. Alyssa's not worth it. I could help you get away."

"But I don't need help," he sobbed, very close to cracking. "I need to be locked up. I need to be certified." At that he started to laugh. It was a compulsive reaction that had nothing to do with amusement. It was hysteria pure and simple.

THAT WAS HOW they came on them. Mariel crouched over a long dark shape lying on the ground.

Alyssa cried out, shock in her voice. "It's a man!" She brought the car to an abrupt halt, her instincts working overtime. "And what's Mariel doing?"

Adam was already out of the car. "Stay there, both of you," he said. "Do you hear me, Alyssa? Do it this time."

"Take the torch with you," she said, not at all sure she'd obey him.

"Got it!" Adam slammed the door shut.

"Who's this person lying on the ground?" Stephanie asked worriedly. "And what exactly is Mariel doing? This doesn't make any sense."

But it did. Alyssa already knew who it was.

"It's Brett, Mom," she said, feeling sick to her stomach. "I'm sure of it."

"Brett?" Stephanie was shocked and enraged. "My God!" she breathed. "So much for his being in London."

"Just a red herring he planted."

They saw Adam standing over the prone man, dressed from head to toe in black.

"Who is he, do you know?" Adam demanded of Mariel, stunned by her presence. She *had* to know him, he reasoned. She wasn't exhibiting fear but an oddly protective attitude.

Mariel shrugged. "It's the man Alyssa betrayed. Brett Harris."

Adam felt his body go rigid. He was so angry he thought he might explode. What a fearful woman Mariel was! "Give me the sash on your robe," he ordered, putting out an impatient hand. At the sight of him, Brett had begun to lash out with his feet, kicking upward in an effort to do Adam damage.

"I will not!" Mariel was protesting in her most affronted voice. "You're not going to tie this poor boy up."

Adam didn't ask a second time, but pulled the sash loose.

"How dare you!" Mariel pressed a hand to her chest as though she feared an imminent heart attack.

"We have a possible killer here, Mrs. Banville," Adam grunted, only just managing to subdue the frenzied Brett and tie his hands securely behind his back. "Your trying to help him doesn't look good. *Why* are you trying to help him, by the way? That's what you were planning, wasn't it? I hope you aren't involved in any of this."

"In any of what?" Mariel asked with the greatest scorn.

"I'll leave that to the police to find out. They'll be bringing charges against your friend. I expect Jack McLean will be here shortly."

"I resent your interference," Mariel retorted, trying to adjust her robe and rise at the same time.

"That's an appallingly stupid thing to say, Mrs. Banville." Adam's voice was thick with disgust. Nevertheless he assisted Mariel to her feet. She flung off his hand disdainfully. She couldn't have been more different from the Elizabeth he'd briefly known, let alone Alyssa and Stephanie. "I think the police will find that your friend here tampered with my vehicle with intent to cause injury, or worse. We also believe he set fire to *Cherub* and did his best to destroy a fairly major sculpture of mine. Who knows what else he had in mind for tonight? Burn down Flying Clouds, attack Alyssa?"

Mariel's response was extraordinary. "I don't

believe a word of it!" she cried, giving Adam a withering look. "The crimes don't fit the man. Brett's behavior has always been exemplary."

Brett, trussed up on the ground, saw Mariel's spirited defense as downright funny. He began to laugh hysterically. It was a far from pleasant sound.

Alyssa and Stephanie were out of the car, rushing toward them. They stood gaping down at Brett, their faces revealing their intense dismay and shock.

"Damn you, Alyssa!" Brett began to yell passionately. "Damn you, damn you, damn you…"

"I'd stand back if I were you," Adam warned Brett's self-appointed guardian, Mariel, as Brett resumed kicking. As far as Adam could see, he'd gone into meltdown.

"There's some rope in the garage," Alyssa said, already turning away. "I'll get it."

By the time she returned, a police car was sweeping up the drive, the headlights lighting up the dark tunnel beneath the canopy of trees.

Brett released a veritable storm of abuse, punctuated by ferocious, incoherent babble.

"Dear God!" Mariel gasped with horror. "He sounds quite *mad!*"

"Why don't all three of you go inside." Adam spoke with some urgency. "You don't want to witness this."

"Wicked, wicked, woman, but I paid her back!"

Brett shrieked, continuing to strike at the gravel with his feet, causing pebbles to fly up like bullets.

"Yes, come in, come in," Stephanie got an arm around Mariel, compelling her up the short flight of steps and into the house.

"I'm staying with you," Alyssa declared, slipping her hand into Adam's. "This is all my fault," she said, her voice shaky. "I should've known Brett would want to pay me back." She had assumed Brett was railing at *her,* never guessing Zizi was the wicked woman in Brett's mind. " In paying me back he had to attack you," she said, feeling a heavy burden of guilt.

"Well, he failed!" Adam gave her a comforting hug. "There's nothing you can do out here except upset yourself. McLean will be coming into the house to ask his questions, anyway."

"No, I'll stay," Alyssa said, watching the two policemen get out of the car, then walk toward them. "Brett, oh, Brett!" She sighed deeply. "Did you want to hurt me?"

Brett turned his bearded face to give her his full glaring attention. "Yes! You betrayed me. You…you—"

"Shut up!" Adam dropped to his haunches and applied a little pressure somewhere around Brett's neck that made Brett wince.

"Careful, Adam," Alyssa said.

"He's all right, don't worry," he assured her. "A little the worse for wear, but we don't need any more of his outpourings."

"So, we've got ourselves a suspect, have we?" Chief McLean called in time-honored fashion as he and his deputy joined them. "Do you know him?"

Alyssa simply nodded when she wanted to hang her head in shame. She wondered if Brett had come here tonight with the intention of killing her. That thought was enough to shake anyone up.

BRETT WAS HANDCUFFED and put into the back of the police car. He stared vacantly out the window, all the while rocking back and forth.

"He has to be the guy Bill Byrd rang me about," McLean told them. "He tried to get a job with Bill's outfit, presumably to get on to the property, but Bill smelled a rat. Looks like he's in a real mess. Our forensic psychiatrist will give us an evaluation in due course. He'll need a lawyer—I imagine he'll have one flown up from Brisbane. I think, somehow, we've got our man. Lord knows what else he had in mind, eh? That was very brave of Mrs. Banville, confronting him the way she did." Mariel, brave lady that she was, had gone straight to her room, a point-blank refusal to be questioned writ large on her brow. "A *remarkable* lady if I may say so."

"Remarkable!" Adam agreed sardonically while Alyssa and Stephanie case a sidelong glance at each other. They would decide on a better word for Mariel after the police drove off.

THERE WAS NO QUESTION of Adam's leaving. He had brushed aside his hair-raising plunge into the field of sugarcane but the shock of the evening hadn't worn off. He was covered in little gashes from the cane and there was a pallor beneath his deep tan. None of them wanted to go to bed. There were too many long-kept secrets to be revealed.

At one point Stephanie asked if she could look at Zizi's journals, as Alyssa knew she would. Stephanie had every right to. Alyssa told her mother she and Adam had read them together, Stephanie didn't appear to mind.

They discussed the fact that Brett's all-consuming jealousy had caused him to try to eliminate his perceived rival by sabotaging his vehicle. They could only speculate on what else Brett might have planned.

"He's as good as destroyed the rest of his life," Stephanie said. "Jealousy and rejection make people do desperate things. Brett's only hope is to plead unsound mind. His solicitor is bound to use it as a defense."

DESPITE HIS HEAVY workload, Ian Sutherland flew up the following day to be with his wife and daughter. At the airport he folded them in his arms. "Someone up there's been looking after you," he said with enormous gratitude. "How did Brett go from being a high-functioning young man, with the world at his feet, to a potential killer?"

Alyssa found a quiet reply. "His capacity for hatred and aggression was central to it all. Brett has a violent temper. He was able, for the most part, to keep it under wraps. I blame myself for a lot of this. Because of me, Brett projected his anger onto the people I love. My poor Zizi!"

"*Don't,* darling!" Stephanie cautioned, compassion in her eyes. "That serves no purpose."

For now they knew the stark truth. In custody, Brett had experienced a near-total breakdown. Though appropriately cautioned, he had blurted out a confession, telling his whole shameful story—not only setting *Cherub* alight, sabotaging Adam's 4WD and taking to Adam's marble sculptures with a hammer, but also the details of Zizi's death. It had been abundantly clear to McLean that Brett was trying to rid himself of the entire terrible episode.

"I'm so ashamed, ashamed, ashamed…"

Brett had become a stranger to himself. The whole structure of his life had collapsed.

Worst of all was the admission, *"I'm haunted!"*

As well he might be. They were all stunned by the revelations. Elizabeth Calvert's death might have been an accident, as Brett claimed, but it was his subsequent behavior that was the most reprehensible. He was very lucky his other victim, Adam, had survived the accident so clearly intended for him. But then, they all knew men did terrible things when fuelled by the witches' brew of love and hatred, jealousy and revenge.

IN THE END IT WAS Stephanie who decided how to deal with the truth. It was her own identity, after all, and that of her daughter. Just as Alyssa and Adam had read the journals together, so too did Stephanie and Ian, with Stephanie in floods of tears. As far as they were concerned, the family truth was established. Stephanie was left to make the decision. It would remain in the family and not go beyond it, she said. To do otherwise might present extreme difficulties for the Langford family. Richard Langford's widow was still very much alive, as was her eldest son. The younger, the handicapped child, had died before reaching her teens. There were also grandchildren involved.

"We've considered this from all angles, Alyssa," Ian Sutherland explained to his daughter. "The most important thing is for you and your mother to have closure. You know the truth.

Mariel's part in this is anything but admirable but in her own way she's tried to be a good mother to Stephanie. As a grandmother, however, she fell short. Nevertheless, it would be too cruel to expose her to the world. Appearances mean everything to Mariel as we're well aware. The only exceptions to all this are you, Adam, and your great-uncle, Julian." Ian looked questioningly at him as he spoke.

Holding Alyssa's hand, Adam answered very seriously. "I've kept Julian informed. He's said nothing all these years and he doesn't intend to now. So far as he's concerned, the decision lay with Elizabeth's family. He has, however, expressed his fervent wish to meet you all, if you could find it in your hearts to meet him. Richard Langford wasn't the only one to love Elizabeth passionately. He's been faithful to her memory."

"Poor man!" Stephanie answered quietly. "Of course we'll meet him, Adam, and we'll make it very soon. How does that sit with you, Alyssa?"

Alyssa felt Adam increase the gentle pressure on her hand. "I agree with you, Mom," she said simply. "Zizi wanted us to know the truth. Now we do."

"Not only Zizi, I suspect." Ian Sutherland sat back, stroking his chin. "Richard Langford has been a presence in Zizi's life all this time. You can't separate those two. After reading the journals and seeing that magnificent portrait, you can't think of one without the other. There was tragedy in their love, but it lasted right up to their deaths and who knows? Maybe beyond... No one, for instance, is ever going to separate me from your mother." He leaned sideways to kiss his wife's cheek while she leaned into him. "In this life or the next."

EPILOGUE

One year later

THE OPENING NIGHT of the Elizabeth Jane Calvert retrospective was destined to be a brilliant success. It was held in Sydney at the Leonard Vaughn Gallery, one of the most prestigious in the country, and attended by everyone who was anyone in the art world, as well as the socialites and celebrities who liked to be seen at major events and get their photographs in the glossy magazines.

Alyssa had been staying in Sydney for a week prior to the gala opening. Now she stood with Leonard, greeting various VIPs and Leonard's most valued clients, all the while keeping an eye on the entryway waiting for her husband and parents to arrive. They'd flown in from Brisbane in the late afternoon, but she'd come early to make a final check. She and Leonard had chosen forty of Zizi's paintings for the opening. They bloomed on the walls of the four large interconnecting rooms of the gallery, with magnificent antique consoles placed strategically here and there, bearing exquisite arrangements of tropical flowers that complemented the paintings of tropical Queensland.

Her parents arrived first, immediately greeted by longtime friends and colleagues.

"We're going to do extremely well out of this," the silver-haired Leonard murmured delightedly to Alyssa. "I say, my dear, your husband's just come in. Look at the women's heads swivel!"

"But he's all mine!" Alyssa rushing to greet the tall, smiling figure of her husband and lover. "You're here at last!"

He bent to kiss her cheek. "It wasn't easy getting away from Dave. Work on the hotel is moving a lot faster than we anticipated. Dave's so thrilled about everything he doesn't want to risk letting me out of his sight. By the way, it looks like Gina's finally landed him."

Alyssa raised her eyebrows. "Well, well, persistence has won the day."

"And there's always the divorce settlement when love runs out," Adam added dryly.

"Not our problem. Dave's a grown man." Very happily Alyssa took her husband's arm, drawing him into the packed gallery.

It took Leonard only a moment to break away

from a group and come toward them. "Come along, you two lovebirds," he said. "I'd like you to meet the Davenports. You remember Rosemary, don't you, Alyssa?"

"Of course!" Alyssa answered, smiling. "I read her biography of Geraldine Moreton, the opera star. It was excellent."

"Don't be surprised if she wants to do one on Elizabeth. And *you* in due time, I shouldn't wonder!" he chortled.

They moved off, the champagne-sipping crowd parting courteously to allow them to make their way through. Adam kept his hand tucked beneath his wife's elbow. He was so proud of her. She'd worked very hard on this exhibition, a tribute to Zizi, her grandmother, and she had an exhibition of her own scheduled for early in the new year, also with Leonard. Adam didn't notice the admiring glances he was receiving; he was too busy taking note of the many eyes glued to Alyssa. She wore a lovely white dress decorated with silver, fashionably short. It showed off her beautiful skin and her long slender legs. Around her neck she wore Elizabeth's diamond-and-emerald necklace. As a wedding present he'd given her the diamond-and-emerald drop earrings she was wearing tonight. They matched beautifully, as was his intention.

She was his *wife!* They'd decided to spend six months of the year at Flying Clouds. They both loved it and it was the ideal place for their creative work. The other six months they were based in Sydney. Caretakers, husband and wife, were already in place at the plantation house. He was managing to combine his architectural commissions with his passion for sculpting. In fact Leonard had been so impressed with his work he was talking about a possible showing at some future date.

Life with Alyssa was a miracle, a miracle that never stopped. Far from dying, as the family had conditioned themselves to accepting, Julian had rallied after meeting his beloved Elizabeth's daughter and granddaughter. He'd attended their wedding and thoroughly enjoyed himself.

I have so much to be grateful for, Adam thought. The gentle ghosts that had inhabited Flying Clouds were gone. Alyssa swore to him she'd seen Zizi and her Richard leaving hand in hand.

"Even our dead have tasks to fulfill," she'd said. "Now the truth is finally known, their souls have been set free. They're not here anymore, Adam. They've moved on."

He believed her. And Flying Clouds welcomed them with a graciousness that reminded him of Zizi herself.

An hour later, when Alyssa was looking at all the red dots stuck to the gold frames, signifying the paintings had been sold, a woman's voice, soft and quavery with age, spoke from directly behind her. *"You have his eyes!"*

Shock stole her breath. Alyssa turned quickly, even fearfully, as though to confront yet another ghost from the past.

Before her stood a tiny lady. Alyssa hadn't been introduced to her; neither had she seen her anywhere all evening. She had to be a late arrival. In her late seventies, the lady was very frail in appearance but beautifully groomed, with magnificent pearls sitting perfectly around the high neckline of her blue-and-white silk dress.

"Constance Langford, my dear," the lady said, giving Alyssa a delicate hand. "You see, I always *knew* the identity of Richard's grand passion."

ALYSSA NEITHER SAW nor heard from Constance Langford again.

* * * * *

THOROUGHBRED LEGACY
*The stakes are high when it comes to love,
horse racing, family secrets
and broken promises.*

*A new exciting Harlequin
continuity series coming soon!*
Led by New York Times *bestselling author
Elizabeth Bevarly*
FLIRTING WITH TROUBLE

Here's a preview!

THE DOOR CLOSED behind them, throwing them into darkness and leaving them utterly alone. And the next thing Daniel knew, he heard himself saying, "Marnie, I'm sorry about the way things turned out in Del Mar."

She said nothing at first, only strode across the room and stared out the window beside him. Although he couldn't see her well in the darkness—he still hadn't switched on a light…but then, neither had she—he imagined her expression was a little preoccupied, a little anxious, a little confused.

Finally, very softly, she said, "Are you?"

He nodded, then, worried she wouldn't be able to see the gesture, added, "Yeah. I am. I should have said goodbye to you."

"Yes, you should have."

Actually, he thought, there were a lot of things he should have done in Del Mar. He'd had *a lot* riding on the Pacific Classic, and even more on his entry, Little Joe, but after meeting Marnie, the

Pacific Classic had been the last thing on Daniel's
mind. His loss at Del Mar had pretty much ended
his career before it had even begun, and he'd had
to start all over again, rebuilding from nothing.

He simply had not then and did not now have
room in his life for a woman as potent as Marnie
Roberts. He was a horseman first and foremost.
From the time he was a schoolboy, he'd known
what he wanted to do with his life—be the best
possible trainer he could be.

He had to make sure Marnie understood—and
he understood, too—why things had ended the
way they had eight years ago. He just wished he
could find the words to do that. Hell, he wished
he could find the *thoughts* to do that.

"You made me forget things, Marnie, things
that I really needed to remember. And that scared
the hell out of me. Little Joe should have won the
Classic. He was by far the best horse entered in
that race. But I didn't give him the attention he
needed and deserved that week, because all I
could think about was you. Hell, when I woke up
that morning all I wanted to do was lie there and
look at you, and then wake you up and make love
to you again. If I hadn't left when I did—the way
I did—I might still be lying there in that bed with
you, thinking about nothing else."

"And would that be so terrible?" she asked.

"Of course not," he told her. "But that wasn't why I was in Del Mar," he repeated. "I was in Del Mar to win a race. That was my job. And my work was the most important thing to me."

She said nothing for a moment, only studied his face in the darkness as if looking for the answer to a very important question. Finally she asked, "And what's the most important thing to you now, Daniel?"

Wasn't the answer to that obvious? "My work," he answered automatically.

She nodded slowly. "Of course," she said softly. "That is, after all, what you do best."

Her comment, too, puzzled him. She made it sound as if being good at what he did was a bad thing.

She bit her lip thoughtfully, her eyes fixed on his, glimmering in the scant moonlight that was filtering through the window. And damned if Daniel didn't find himself wanting to pull her into his arms and kiss her. But as much as it might have felt as if no time had passed since Del Mar, there were eight years between now and then. And eight years was a long time in the best of circumstances. For Daniel and Marnie, it was virtually a lifetime.

So Daniel turned and started for the door, then halted. He couldn't just walk away and leave things as they were, unsettled. He'd done that eight years ago and regretted it.

"It *was* good to see you again, Marnie," he said softly. And since he was being honest, he added, "I hope we see each other again."

She didn't say anything in response, only stood silhouetted against the window with her arms wrapped around her in a way that made him wonder whether she was doing it because she was cold, or if she just needed something—someone— to hold on to. In either case, Daniel understood. There was an emptiness clinging to him that he suspected would be there for a long time.

* * * * *

THOROUGHBRED LEGACY
coming soon wherever books are sold!

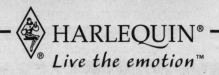

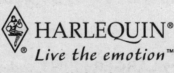

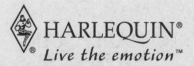

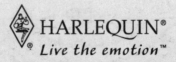

Harlequin® Historical
Historical Romantic Adventure!

Imagine a time of chivalrous knights and unconventional ladies, roguish rakes and impetuous heiresses, rugged cowboys and spirited frontierswomen——these rich and vivid tales will capture your imagination!

Harlequin Historical . . . they're too good to miss!

HARLEQUIN®
Presents

**The world's bestselling romance series...
The series that brings you your favorite authors,
month after month:**

Helen Bianchin...Emma Darcy
Lynne Graham...Penny Jordan
Miranda Lee...Sandra Marton
Anne Mather...Carole Mortimer
Susan Napier...Michelle Reid

and many more uniquely talented authors!

Wealthy, powerful, gorgeous men...
Women who have feelings just like your own...
The stories you love, set in exotic, glamorous locations...

HARLEQUIN®
Presents

Seduction and Passion Guaranteed!

HPDIR104

Dear Reader,

Most families, even dysfunctional ones who carry the baggage of old conflicts, have within their annals a story of enduring love, a love that triumphed over every obstacle thrown in its way.

It might be a great-aunt's story, or that of a grandparent, an uncle, a sister. Or maybe it's the story of a veteran of war who finally got to marry his foreign-born sweetheart and bring her home.

True love dreams, even when that love seems impossible. Is it any wonder, then, that families still get caught up in the passion and excitement of a love affair that played out long ago, whether it ended happily or not? The grand passion was there, and therefore miraculous. Miracles pass many of us by, so when it happens it must be celebrated.

The story you are about to read, *Hidden Legacy*, is just such a tale. It begins with our present-day heroine trying to unravel a mystery; during this exploration she has to reinvent a beloved great-aunt and in the process learn that time has no place in affairs of the heart. True love has the power to outlast it.

Now welcome to Australia's beautiful north Queensland....

Margaret Way

"Zizi never had a child!"

Alyssa said the words angrily. She gave a slightly hysterical laugh, afraid of Adam's effect on her, afraid of the sensation, the *intimacy*, of his touch.

His eyes held compassion. "If Elizabeth told you so little—after all, you were a child when she was already a middle-aged woman—surely someone in your family knows. Her sister, Mariel, perhaps?"

"My *grandmother*? And she kept it from us? No way! Zizi never married. She never had a child. Do you seriously believe we wouldn't know?" Why were clouds of confusion blanketing her mind?

He sat back, staring at her. "It's happened before," he said. "The thing is, secrets don't always remain buried. My aim isn't to shock you, Alyssa, but you must trust me on this. Elizabeth *did* have a child. And for reasons of her own, she appears to have led a life of deception."

"Why should I sit here and listen to you destroying all my illusions about the Zizi I loved?"

"The closer the link, the more intense the pain," he said. "Elizabeth Calvert was a riddle. Secrets were her way of life."